HE:

SHORTER WRITINGS OF FRANZ KAFKA

Selected and with an Introduction by
Joshua Cohen

Franz Kafka was born in 1883 in Prague, where he lived most of his life. During his lifetime, he published only a few short stories, including "The Metamorphosis," "The Judgment," and "The Stoker." He died in 1924, before completing any of his full-length novels. At the end of his life, Kafka asked his lifelong friend and literary executor Max Brod to burn all his unpublished work. Brod overrode those wishes.

Joshua Cohen was born in 1980 in Atlantic City. His books include the novels *The Netanyahus*, *Moving Kings*, *Book of Numbers*, *Witz*, *A Heaven of Others*, and *Cadenza for the Schneidermann Violin Concerto*; the short-fiction collection *Four New Messages*; and the nonfiction collection *Attention: Dispatches from a Land of Distraction*. Called "a major American writer" by *The New York Times* and "an extraordinary prose stylist, surely one of the most prodigious at work in American fiction today" by *The New Yorker*, Cohen was awarded Israel's 2013 Matanel Prize, and in 2017 was named one of *Granta*'s Best of Young American Novelists.

HE:

SHORTER WRITINGS
OF FRANZ KAFKA

HE:
SHORTER WRITINGS
OF FRANZ KAFKA

Franz Kafka

Translated from the German by
Willa Muir and Edwin Muir, Eithne Wilkins and
Ernst Kaiser, Joseph Kresh, Tania Stern and
James Stern, and Clement Greenberg

Selected and with an Introduction by
Joshua Cohen

PICADOR

New York

Picador
120 Broadway, New York 10271

Selection and introduction copyright © 2020 by Joshua Cohen
All rights reserved
Printed in the United States of America
This edition first published in 2020 by Riverrun, an imprint of Quercus Editions Ltd.,
Great Britain
Published in the United States by Picador
First American edition, 2022

The texts in this selection were drawn from *The Diaries of Franz Kafka* (Secker/Schocken 1948),
Description of a Struggle and *The Great Wall of China* (Schocken 1958, Secker 1960), and
Parables and Paradoxes (Schocken 1961).

Owing to limitations of space, all acknowledgments for permission to reprint previously
published material can be found on pages 293–294.

Library of Congress Cataloging-in-Publication Data
Names: Kafka, Franz, 1883–1924, author. | Muir, Willa, 1890–1970, translator. |
Muir, Edwin, 1887–1959, translator. | Wilkins, Eithne, translator. | Kaiser,
Ernst, translator. | Kresh, Joseph, translator. | Stern, Tania, translator. | Stern,
James, 1904–1993, translator. | Greenberg, Clement, 1909–1994, translator. |
Cohen, Joshua, 1980– editor, writer of introduction.
Title: He : shorter writings of Franz Kafka / translated from the German by Willa
Muir and Edwin Muir, Eithne Wilkins and Ernst Kaiser, Joseph Kresh, Tania
Stern and James Stern, and Clement Greenberg ; selected and with an
introduction by Joshua Cohen.
Description: First American edition. | New York : Picador, 2022.
Identifiers: LCCN 2021048191 | ISBN 9780374538941 (paperback)
Subjects: LCGFT: Short stories. | Diaries. | Personal correspondence.
Classification: LCC PT2621.A26 H4 2022 | DDC 838/.91209 [B]—dc23/
eng/20211008
LC record available at https://lccn.loc.gov/2021048191

D   10   9   8   7   6   5   4   3

Contents

III

IV

Introduction

I

Reading the work of Franz Kafka is a pleasure, whose punishment is this: writing about it too.

In Kafka, no honour comes without suffering, and no suffering goes unhonoured.

Being asked to write about Kafka is like being asked to describe the Great Wall of China by someone who's standing just next to it. The only honest thing to do is point.

Once, a student approached Rabbi Shalom of Belz and asked, 'What is required in order to live a decent life? How do I know what charity is? What lovingkindness is? How can I tell if I've ever been in the presence of God's mercy?' And so on. The Rabbi stood and was silent and let the student talk until the student was all talked out. And even then the Rabbi kept standing in silence, which was – abracadabra – the answer.

Having to explain the meaning of something that to you is utterly plain and obvious is like having to explain *the meaning of someone*. Providing such an explanation is impossible and so, a variety of torture. One of the lighter varieties, to be sure, but torture nonetheless. It is a job not for a fan, or even for a critic, but for a self-hating crazy-person.

Kafka's work should be standard reading for a time that cannot define its standards: a time that treats all identities as spectrums but all judgment as binary ('like' or 'dislike'); a time that insists on appropriate behaviour but forbids appropriation (people should read more books from other cultures, but must never write a book set in a culture not their own); a time that has replaced literacy with numeracy, but then laments that its only common culture is political ('Remember 2017?' 'Whose 2017?').

Kafka: 'What have I in common with Jews? I have hardly anything in common with myself, and should stand very quietly in a corner, content that I can breathe.'

2

I've been asked to write about Kafka six times in my life. The first five times I said no. Because I was too busy, too depressed, too busy, too busy, too depressed.

None of Kafka's novels were finished, or published, during

Kafka's lifetime. Only nine of the fictions included in this volume were published during his lifetime. It's not clear how many of them were finished. *Are* finished.

The aspect of essay-writing that I loathe the most: giving a biographical account of the author. It's ridiculous to give an account that I've inevitably sourced, at least in part, from the very same online omniscience that's equally available to the reader. I've resolved, then, not to consult the Internet for this – not to consult anyone, or anything. If the world burned now, and all of the Internet with it, and then all of the libraries, and then all of the books, this is what I would know and must be judged by: Kafka was born in Prague, the third city of the Austro-Hungarian Empire, in 1880-something, and, due to complications from tuberculosis, basically starved to death in a sanitorium located in a town that starts with a *K*, in post-Empire, independent Austria, in 1920-something. He was trained in law at Charles University and practised as a lawyer in the insurance industry. He was engaged to be married three times, twice to the same woman, whose name was Felice Bauer. He left instructions for all of his work to be burned after his death, which his friend Max Brod disobeyed. In 1918, which year I remember because it's the last year of the First World War, Kafka wrote in the notebook that he otherwise used for his Hebrew lessons, 'Work as joy, inaccessible to the psychologists.' I think I recall a few other Kafka quotations, but this is the one I repeat to myself aloud like a prayer, dragging home after my expensive, every-Wednesday-at-4-p.m.

appointment describing my childhood to a stranger: 'Work as joy, inaccessible to the psychologists.'

3

Kafka's characters have no choice but to suffer Kafka. We readers, however, have chosen to submit to his machinery of our own free will, and we have done so in every generation since Kafka's own, in the process producing thousands of essays and academic papers, over a hundred biographies, over a dozen films and TV shows, not to mention the Kafka-branding industry, which includes a computer-font that reproduces the author's handwriting (and features, alongside the author's signature Capital-*K*, a whimsically anachronistic € sign), t-shirts, hats, keychains, and smartphone-covers emblazoned with his face, *und so weiter*. From a psychoanalytic perspective, our Kafka-cathexis can be read as a product of the subject's rejection of us – a reaction to the fact that every time a new merchandiser of scholarly Kafkaiana claims to have finally gotten a grasp on a certain aspect of the author's life – on his identity as a Germanophone Czech, or Jew, or Zionist, or Anti-Zionist, or Marxist, or Feminist, or Americophile, or vegetarian, or hypochondriac, or lawyer, or brother, or son – Kafka, whoever Kafka was or is, floats away even further. It's my conviction that we keep abasing ourselves in this unrequited pursuit because Kafka was the last truly great writer that any of us have had, and by *us*, I mean Germanophone Czechs, Jews, Zionists, Anti-Zionists, Marxists, Feminists, Americophiles, vegetarians, hypochondriacs, lawyers, brothers, and sons.

What's most notably missing from even the major studies of Kafka is a technical consideration of the writing itself – of the style of a Kafka sentence – which typically opens with a perfectly lucid idea and then proceeds to get mired in a murkiness of commas, as it strives to contain all of the ideas that might conceivably be derived from that idea, often including even the counter-idea, before the final period. This attempt to present the complete consequences of a single thought within the span of a single sentence – which torrent of thinking would almost always be more comfortably accommodated in two sentences, or even in an amply bourgeois warm-hearthed paragraph – imparts to the prose an accruing intensity that's constantly being undercut by grammatical delay, which is less evident in English than it is in the original German, with its 'inverted' word-order. English's SVO (subject-verb-object) order results in sentences about *who is doing what to whom*, while German's SOV order is more concerned with *who to whom is doing what*. This syntactical difference is one reason, but only one reason, why English-language natives tend to expect a sentence to express itself immediately – to state from the start what it's all about – whereas German-language natives are more conditioned to uncertainty, given that their full comprehension of a sentence must be suspended until its end. Because an English-language sentence usually announces its basic purpose at the top, it almost always can only amplify or modify that purpose, and never, or rarely, upend it. A German-language sentence, however, can expand a reader's understanding as it itself expands, becoming less provisional as it heads past the object toward the concluding verb of each subordinate clause, as the sentence itself heads toward its ultimate semantic consummation.

Here is a quintessential Kafka sentence, on the building of the Great Wall of China, translated by Willa and Edwin Muir:

> *In fact it is said that there are gaps which have never been filled in at all – according to some they are far larger than the completed sections – though this assertion is merely one of the many legends to which the building of the wall gave rise, and which cannot be verified, at least by any single man with his own eyes and judgment, on account of the extent of the structure.*

And here is the same sentence translated by Stanley Corngold:

> *Indeed, it said that there are gaps that have not been filled in at all; according to some people these are much larger than the completed sections, although this assertion may be only one of the many legends that have grown up around the Wall*

and which, given the length of the Wall, is not something one person can verify, at least with his own eyes, and by his own standards.

The Muirs' version strains for such torque that it risks becoming not merely unfaithful, but incomplete, while Corngold's version is so intent on attempting both accuracy and explanation that it risks achieving neither. I'm not saying that I could do any better – I couldn't. I'm just saying that neither version captures the anxiety of the German:

Ja, es soll Lücken geben, die überhaupt nicht verbaut worden sind, eine Behauptung allerdings, die möglicherweise nur zu den vielen Legenden gehört, die um den Bau entstanden sind, und die, für den einzelnen Menschen wenigstens, mit eigenen Augen und eigenem Maßstab infolge der Ausdehnung des Baues unnachprüfbar sind.

If I have to make a fool of myself, I'll do so not by translating, but by making a rough English approximation of the German syntax, preserving a mix of the Muirs' and Corngold's word-choices:

Indeed, it is said that gaps there are, that filled in have never been at all, an assertion, however, that probably only to the many legends belongs, that around the Wall have arisen,

*and that, at least by any single person with their own eyes
and standards, on account of the extent of the Wall, cannot
be verified.*

When verbs come at the close of a clause, the clause's sense
is adjourned until that closure arrives, and so the arrival is read
as a verdict.

Try it this way:

Indeed, it is said that gaps there are,
    that filled in have never been at all,
an assertion, however, that probably only to the many legends
    belongs,
that around the Wall have arisen,
*and that, at least by any single person with their own eyes
    and standards, on account of*
the extent of the Wall, cannot be verified.

The manipulation of this nested 'inversion' for purposes of
variation, rhythmic drive, cliché-lampooning, and subversive
humour is a significant feature not merely of Kafka's style, but
of Kafka's mind, and is at least as important for English-language
readers to countenance as the author's religiosity, eschatology,
libido, and insomnia.

4

The sentence – the *Satz* – is what writers are judged by. 'Sentence' is more than a bad pun on Kafka's vocation. His prose – especially the fictional prose that he wrote at night and during his sick-leaves and sanitoria-vacations – imitates the aspiration of the law: both are attempts to engineer through sections, subsections, and subordinate clauses a stately structure of utterly coherent logic within an utterly incoherent illogical world. It's that coherent logic that is the principal fiction, of course: because the world cannot be made to unfold as orderly as prose, with the same balanced elegance of form. Kafka's fiction only diagnosed, and refused to ameliorate, the crises experienced by his characters, as if to mimic the limits of the law, which can only compensate for damages, but remains powerless to prevent them. Where Kafka's writing and legal writing share the greatest similarity, however, is in their ambiguity – in their precise relationship to ambiguity. Both are made out of the author's efforts to perpetually measure and define exactly what leeway is being left for interpretation and application. In his fiction, Kafka leaves certain elements undescribed (character's faces), and under-described (settings), in order to allow the reader to impose descriptions of their own that personalize the universality. He furthers this permissiveness by rarely writing surface metaphors, preferring instead to inculcate structural metaphors (or allegories, or parables) by defining his subjects negatively: 'Our little town does not lie on the frontier, nowhere near; it is so far from the frontier, in fact, that perhaps no one from our town has ever been there' (*The Refusal*). In general, Kafka prefers not to associate things or people inside his fiction with things or people outside it. Self-reference is his primary mode: His fiction is full of formulations like 'as I used to do', and 'as I had often thought', which, by comparison and contrast, establish precedent. Kafka's most profound ambiguity, though, inheres in his use of the subjunctive – his moments of 'as if' and 'as though' (in German, *als*): 'If I merely walk in the direction of the entrance, even though I may be separated from it by several passages and rooms, I find myself sensing an atmosphere of great danger, actually as if my hair were growing thin and in a moment might fly off and leave me bare and shivering, exposed to the howls of my enemies' (*The Burrow*). Here, and elsewhere, Kafka harnesses the humblest grammar to metamorphic power, until the predominant effect ceases to be the presence of an unreliable narrator, but the absence of the universe's only reliable narrator. Who is God.

The ambiguity of the law is more infamous, and more materially consequential. In brief, the most heinous law is written by those most hoping to evade it. Legislators are systemically incentivized to omit or obscure all provisions of the law that check their power. To be clear, the law I am referring to here does not include that overtly oppressive legislation that makes no attempt to obfuscate its discriminatory intent (such as the Nazis'

Nuremberg Laws, which ensnared Kafka's three sisters, or my own country's slavery legislation, Black Codes, and Jim Crow). Instead, I am referring to the law of wilful inadequacy, which employs loopholes to enable policy circumventions, and cloaks corruption in beneficent rhetoric before burying it deep beneath superficial reforms. More ambiguous still, at least in terms of its authority, and certainly more pernicious, is a country's body of classified or secret law, which contravenes the law as it is publicly known. One example, again from my own country, is the officially secret law that, in violation of the US Constitution, lets the US government surveil all of its citizens' communications, including what I am now writing on my computer.

As the law becomes ever-more ambiguous, literature becomes ever-less, and we humans become mainly legible as data – as points of habit, preference, and demographic information used to generate algorithms, which are the strictures, the sentences, that bind us. Algorithms are sentences that calculate outcomes based on inputs (I almost wrote *incomes*). They are constructed out of a series of binary choices – *If* this happens, *Then* that should happen; *If* this doesn't happen, *Then* that shouldn't happen – in a constant calibration of inclusion and exclusion. The earliest algorithms were written by humans, as a way of instructing computers to perform calculations that humans were incapable of performing on their own. Today, these algorithms are written by computers "themselves," as a way of instructing other computers to perform increasingly convoluted, world-controlling tasks.

This automation is the ultimate sign of the decline of the law's authority – an authority that once came from churches and monarchies that claimed the sanction of God, and then came from governments that claimed the sanction of election, and now comes from our machines, which generate for each of us an individual law based on our every click and keystroke, our every weak decision. These automated laws now define our lives. They are responsible for nearly everything that we see and hear. They tell us where to eat, when to exercise, and even whom to have sex with. They tell us what to read and so, they tell us who we are. There is no way to calculate what effect this automation is having on our souls, because our souls do not exist in the domain of calculation. Any attempt to enumerate that harm just strengthens the enumeration-harm of the technocracy.

5

Once, in Jerusalem, I was sitting at a café reading Kafka (in English). At some point the café had become a bar – meaning that the coffee-and-tea-drinking had given way to alcohol – and when I took a break from the pages and looked around, I realized, a lot of people were drunk. One man came over to my table, turned an empty chair around, sat down straddling its back, grabbed the book out of my hands, and examined it. 'What's it about?' he asked. He was in his early twenties, twitchy, aggressive, entirely serious. 'It's about impossible situations,' I said in Hebrew, and the moment that the phrase was out of my mouth, I regretted the fact that, especially given my foreign accent, it sounded like I was quoting some journalistic euphemism for the conflict between Israel and Palestine. The guy leaned in close and said, with boozy breath, 'Impossible situations like what?' Realizing that I'd have to defuse *this impossible situation*, I told him that one of Kafka's books was about a man who is accused of a crime, but no one will tell him what that crime is, and so he is unable to defend himself. I told him that another of the books was about a man who incompetently surveys land – I didn't know the Hebrew for 'land-surveyor', so I said something like 'map-maker' – who comes to a strange town in the course of his duties and must receive permission to practise his trade there, and even just to stay there, from the authorities who rule the town from its castle, but the castle-authorities refuse to grant him a labour or even a residency permit and defer any decision about his legal status indefinitely. Meanwhile, the face of the man in front of me had turned siren red and the vessels in his neck swelled and throbbed. Not knowing what I had said to enrage him, or what else I could do that might calm him, I just continued with my explanation, by saying that this book – the one that he was still holding, and gripping so tightly that I thought he'd tear it in half – was called *Amerika*, and that it was about America, and, because it was the author's first novel, it wasn't quite typical of—

The man jumped out of the chair and banged the book on the table, yelling (in my loose translation), 'So the people in the books are fucking idiots? Is it supposed to be funny that they're so stupid? When I had to get a new passport on short notice, because my old one expired and I had to go to London for business, at the passport office they told me no, it's not possible. And I could have just left it at that and given up, but I didn't. It was too much money to lose. So I just phoned my cousin, whose wife's brother works for the Ministry of Interior, and I got my new passport within a week. That's how you have to be. I mean, you have a job to do, you do it. Don't let anything get in your way.' He flung the book to the floor, and now all the café-bar's patrons were paying attention to what was happening, but also moving away, giving him some room to have his tantrum. 'And if someone accused me of some crime that I didn't do,' he continued, 'I'd get this friend of mine from the army who's a lawyer to sue them for all their money and take their apartment and car. And if they kept on accusing me after that, I'd beat the shit out of them. I'd find out where their offices were and wait outside until they came out and I'd jump them from behind and go like this and like that –' he was air-punching and air-kicking some imaginary nemesis, putting phantom opponents in headlocks and choking them out.

I ran away down the block and turned around only at the corner: the man was being restrained by waiters. *Amerika* was lost – it is the only book by Kafka that I have never finished. But to this day, the man's words, and his air-fighting, remain with me, and I'm still not sure how to take them – as anything other than an indication of the differences between the *Mitteleuropean* will to ambiguity and the near-universal impatience of the present.

Kafka is buried in the New Jewish cemetery in the crumbling suburbs of Prague. The original gravestone was stolen (some say by a literary-minded Nazi, others say by the Czechoslovak Communist government). Then the replacement gravestone was stolen (some say by a Czechoslovak anti-Communist underground youth movement, others say by a private collector from the West). Today the stone under which the author reposes is a replacement's replacement – an ugly hexagonal monolith. The last time I visited the cemetery, for the funeral of a man, a Holocaust survivor whose memoir I ghostwrote, workers were installing CCTV cameras.

JOSHUA COHEN

HE:

SHORTER WRITINGS
OF FRANZ KAFKA

I

Paradise

We were created in order to live in Paradise, and Paradise was ordained to serve us. What was ordained for us has been changed; it is not said that this has also happened with what was ordained for Paradise.

We were expelled from Paradise, but it was not destroyed. The expulsion from Paradise was in one sense a piece of good fortune, for if we had not been expelled, Paradise would have had to be destroyed.

Expulsion from Paradise is in its main aspect eternal: that is to say, although expulsion from Paradise is final, and life in the world unavoidable, the eternity of the process or, expressed in temporal terms, the eternal repetition of the process nevertheless makes it possible not only that we might remain in Paradise permanently, but that we may in fact be there permanently, no matter whether we know it here or not.

The Tower of Babel

If it had been possible to build the Tower of Babel without ascending it, the work would have been permitted.

The Pit of Babel

What are you building? – I want to dig a subterranean passage.
Some progress must be made. My station up there is much too
high. – *We are digging the pit of Babel.*

The Bush

Many people prowl round Mount Sinai. Their speech is blurred, either they are garrulous or they shout or they are taciturn. But none of them comes down a broad, newly made, smooth road that does its own part in making one's strides longer and swifter.

The thornbush is the old obstacle in the road. It must catch fire if you want to go further.

The Building of the Temple

Everything fell in with his intention and contributed to the building. Foreign workers brought the blocks of marble, already hewn and ready to be fitted together. In accordance with the indications given by his moving fingers, the blocks rose up and shifted into place. No building ever rose into being as easily as this temple did, or rather, this temple came into being in the true manner of temples. Only on every block – from what quarry did they come? – there were clumsy scribblings by senseless childish hands, or rather, entries made by barbaric mountain-dwellers in order to annoy or to deface or to destroy completely, scratched into the stone with instruments that were obviously magnificently sharp, intended to endure for an eternity that would outlast the temple.

The Holy of Holies

Before setting foot in the Holy of Holies you must take off your shoes, yet not only your shoes, but everything; you must take off your travelling garment and lay down your luggage; and under that you must shed your nakedness and everything that is under the nakedness and everything that hides beneath that, and then the core and the core of the core, then the remainder and then the residue and then even the glimmer of the undying fire. Only the fire itself is absorbed by the Holy of Holies and lets itself be absorbed by it; neither can resist the other.

The Coming of the Messiah

The Messiah will come only when he is no longer necessary, he will come only one day after his arrival, he will not come on the last day, but on the last day of all.

II

The Great Wall of China

The Great Wall of China was finished off at its northernmost corner. From the southeast and the southwest it came up in two sections that finally converged there. This principle of piece-meal construction was also applied on a smaller scale by both of the two great armies of labour, the eastern and the western. It was done in this way: gangs of some twenty workers were formed who had to accomplish a length, say, of five hundred yards of wall, while a similar gang built another stretch of the same length to meet the first. But after the junction had been made the construction of the wall was not carried on from the point, let us say, where this thousand yards ended; instead the two groups of workers were transferred to begin building again in quite different neighbourhoods. Naturally in this way many great gaps were left, which were only filled in gradually and bit by bit, some, indeed, not till after the official announcement that the wall was finished. In fact it is said that there are gaps which have never been filled in at all – according to some they are far larger than the completed sections – though this assertion is probably merely one of the many legends to which the building of the wall gave rise, and which cannot be verified, at least by any single man with his own eyes and judgment, on account of the extent of the structure.

Now on first thoughts one might conceive that it would have been more advantageous in every way to build the wall continuously, or at least continuously within the two main divisions. After all, the wall was intended, as was universally proclaimed and known, to be a protection against the peoples of the north. But how can a wall protect if it is not a continuous structure? Not only can such a wall not protect, but what there is of it is in perpetual danger. These blocks of wall left standing in deserted regions could be easily pulled down again and again by the nomads, especially as these tribes, rendered apprehensive by the building operations, kept changing their encampments with incredible rapidity, like locusts, and so perhaps had a better general view of the progress of the wall than we, the builders. Nevertheless the task of construction probably could not have been carried out in any other way. To understand this we must take into account the following: the wall was to be a protection for centuries; accordingly, the most scrupulous care in the building, the application of the architectural wisdom of all known ages and peoples, an unremitting sense of personal responsibility in the builders, were indispensable prerequisites for the work. True, for the more purely manual tasks ignorant day labourers from the populace, men, women, and children who offered their services for good money, could be employed; but for the supervision even of four day labourers an expert versed in the art of building was required, a man who was capable of entering into and feeling with all his heart what was involved. And of course the higher the task, the greater the responsibility. And such men were actually to be had, if not indeed so abundantly as the work of construction could have absorbed, yet in great numbers.

For the work had not been undertaken without thought. Fifty years before the first stone was laid, the art of architecture, and especially that of masonry, had been proclaimed as the most important branch of knowledge throughout the whole area of a China that was to be walled around, and all other arts gained recognition only insofar as they had reference to it. I can still remember quite well us standing as small children, scarcely sure on our feet, in our teacher's garden, and being ordered to build a sort of wall out of pebbles; and then the teacher, girding up his robe, ran full tilt against the wall, of course knocking it down, and scolded us so terribly for the shoddiness of our work that we ran weeping in all directions to our parents. A trivial incident, but significant of the spirit of the time.

I was lucky inasmuch as the building of the wall was just beginning when, at twenty, I had passed the last examination of the lowest-grade school. I say lucky, for many who before my time had achieved the highest degree of culture available to them could find nothing year after year to do with their knowledge, and drifted uselessly about with the most splendid architectural plans in their heads, and sank by thousands into hopelessness. But those who finally came to be employed in the work as supervisors, even though it might be of the lowest rank, were truly worthy of their task. They were men who had reflected much, and did not cease to reflect, on the building of the wall, men who with the first stone they sank in the ground felt themselves to some extent a part of the wall. Such men, of course, had not only a desire to perform their work in the most thorough manner, but were also impatient to see the wall finished in its complete perfection. Day labourers have not this impatience, for they look only to their wages, and the higher supervisors, indeed even the supervisors of middle rank, could see enough of the manifold growth of the construction to keep their spirits confident and high. But to encourage the subordinate supervisors, intellectually so vastly superior to their apparently petty tasks, other measures must be taken. One could not, for instance, expect them to lay one stone on another for months or even years on end, in an uninhabited mountainous region, hundreds of miles from their homes; the hopelessness of such hard toil, which yet could not reach completion even in the longest lifetime, would have cast them into despair and above all made them less capable for the work. It was for this reason that the system of piecemeal building was decided on. Five hundred yards could be accomplished in about five years; by that time, indeed, the supervisors were as a rule quite exhausted and had lost all faith in themselves, in the wall, in the world, but while they were still exalted by the jubilant celebrations marking the completion of the thousand yards of wall, they were sent far, far away, saw on their journey finished sections of the wall rising here and there, came past the quarters of the high command and were presented with badges of honour, heard the rejoicings of new armies of labour streaming past from the depths of the land, saw forests being cut down to become supports for the wall, saw mountains being hewn into stones for the wall, heard at the holy shrines hymns rising in which the pious prayed for the completion of the wall. All this assuaged their impatience. The quiet life of their homes, where they rested some time, strengthened them; the humble credulity with which their reports were listened to, the confidence with which the simple and peaceful burgher believed in the eventual completion of the wall, all this filled their hearts with a new buoyancy. Like eternally hopeful children they then said farewell to their homes; the desire once more to labour on the wall of the nation became irresistible. They set off earlier than they needed; half the village accompanied them for long distances. On every road they met with greetings, flags, banners; never before had they seen how great and rich and beautiful and worthy of love their country was. Every fellow countryman was a brother for whom one was building a wall of protection, and who would return lifelong thanks for it with all he had and did. Unity! Unity! Shoulder to shoulder, a ring of brothers, a current of blood no longer confined within the narrow circulation of one body, but sweetly rolling and yet ever returning throughout the endless leagues of China.

Thus, then, the system of piecemeal construction becomes comprehensible; but there were still other reasons for it as well. Nor is there anything odd in my pausing over this question for so long; it is one of the crucial problems in the whole building of the wall, unimportant as it may appear at first glance. If I am to convey and make understandable the ideas and feelings of that time I cannot go deeply enough into this very question.

First, then, it must be said that in those days things were achieved scarcely inferior to the construction of the Tower of Babel, although as regards divine approval, at least according to human reckoning, strongly at variance with that work. I say this because during the early days of building a scholar wrote a book in which he drew the comparison in the most exhaustive way. In it he tried to prove that the Tower of Babel failed to reach its goal, not because of the reasons universally advanced, or at least that among those recognized reasons the most important of all was not to be found. His proofs were drawn not merely from written documents and reports; he also claimed to have made inquiries on the spot, and to have discovered that the tower failed and was bound to fail because of the weakness of the foundation. In this respect at any rate our age was vastly superior to that ancient one. Almost every educated man of our time was a mason by profession and infallible in the matter of laying foundations. That, however, was not what our scholar was concerned to prove; for he maintained that the Great Wall alone would provide for the first time in the history of mankind a secure foundation for a new Tower of Babel. First the wall, therefore, and then the tower. His book was in everybody's hands at that time, but I admit that even today I cannot quite make out how he conceived this tower. How could the wall, which did not form even a circle, but only a sort of quarter- or half-circle, provide the foundation for a tower? That could obviously be meant only in a spiritual sense. But in that case why build the actual wall, which after all was something concrete, the result of the lifelong labour of multitudes of people? And why were there in the book plans, somewhat nebulous plans, it must be admitted, of the tower, and proposals worked out in detail for mobilizing the people's energies for this new project?

There were many wild ideas in people's heads at that time – this scholar's book is only one example – perhaps simply because so many were trying to join forces as far as they could for the achievement of a single aim. Human nature, essentially changeable, unstable as the dust, can endure no restraint; if it binds itself it soon begins to tear madly at its bonds, until it rends everything asunder, the wall, the bonds, and its very self.

It is possible that these very considerations, which militated against the building of the wall at all, were not left out of account by the high command when the system of piecemeal construction was decided on. We – and here I can probably speak for many – did not really know ourselves until we had carefully scrutinized the decrees of the high command, when we discovered that without the high command neither our book learning nor our human understanding would have sufficed even for the humble tasks which we performed in the great whole. In the office of the command – where it was and who sat there no one whom I have asked knew then or knows now – in that office one may be certain that all human thoughts and desires revolved in a circle, and all human aims and fulfilments in a countercircle. And through the window the reflected splendours of divine worlds fell on the hands of the leaders as they traced their plans.

And for that reason the incorruptible observer must hold that the command, if it had seriously desired it, could also have overcome those difficulties that prevented a system of continuous construction. There remains, therefore, nothing but the conclusion that the command deliberately chose the system of piecemeal construction. But the piecemeal construction was only a makeshift and therefore inexpedient. Remains the conclusion that the command willed something inexpedient. Strange conclusion indeed. And yet in one respect it has much to be said for it. One can perhaps safely discuss it now. In those days many people, and among them the best, had a secret maxim which ran: Try with all your might to comprehend the decrees of the high command, but only up to a certain point; then avoid further meditation. A very wise maxim, which moreover was elaborated in a parable that was later often quoted: Avoid further meditation, but not because it might be harmful; it is not at all certain that it would be harmful. What is harmful or not harmful has nothing to do with the question. Consider rather the river in spring. It rises until it grows mightier and nourishes more richly the soil on the long stretch of its banks, still maintaining its own course until it reaches the sea, where it is all the more welcome because it is a worthier ally. Thus far may you meditate on the decrees of the high command. But after that the river overflows its banks, loses outline and shape, slows down the speed of its current, tries to ignore its destiny by forming little seas in the interior of the land, damages the fields, and yet cannot maintain itself for long in its new expanse, but must run back between its banks again, must even dry up wretchedly in the hot season that presently follows. Thus far should you not meditate on the decrees of the high command.

Now though this parable may have had extraordinary point and force during the building of the wall, it has at most only a restricted relevance for my present essay. My inquiry is purely historical; no lightning flashes any longer from the long since vanished thunderclouds, and so I may venture to seek for an explanation of the system of piecemeal construction which goes farther than the one that contented people then. The limits that my capacity for thought imposes upon me are narrow enough, but the province to be traversed here is infinite.

Against whom was the Great Wall to serve as a protection? Against the people of the north. Now, I come from the southeast of China. No northern people can menace us there. We read of them in the books of the ancients; the cruelties they commit in accordance with their nature make us sigh in our peaceful arbours. The faithful representations of the artist show us these faces of the damned, their gaping mouths, their jaws furnished with great pointed teeth, their half-shut eyes that already seem to be seeking out the victim which their jaws will rend and devour. When our children are unruly we show them these pictures, and at once they fly weeping into our arms. But nothing more than that do we know about these northerners. We have not seen them, and if we remain in our villages we shall never see them, even if on their wild horses they should ride as hard as they can straight toward us – the land is too vast and would not let them reach us, they would end their course in the empty air.

Why, then, since that is so, do we leave our homes, the stream with its bridges, our mothers and fathers, our weeping wives, our children who need our care, and depart for the distant city to be trained there, while our thoughts journey still farther away to the wall in the north? Why? A question for the high command. Our leaders know us. They, absorbed in gigantic anxieties, know of us, know our petty pursuits, see us sitting together in our humble huts, and approve or disapprove the evening prayer which the father of the house recites in the midst of his family. And if I may be allowed to express such ideas about the high command, then I must say that in my opinion the high command has existed from old time, and did not come together, say, after the fashions of high mandarins, who at the prompting of a fine morning dream hastily summon a meeting, hastily decide things, and drum the people out of their beds the same evening to carry out their decisions – even if it should be merely to stage an illumination in honour of a god who has shown favour to their masters the day before, only to belabour them in a dark corner on the morrow, almost before the lanterns are extinguished. Far rather do I believe that the high command has existed from all eternity, and the decision to build the wall likewise.

Already to some extent during the building of the wall, and almost exclusively thereafter, I have occupied myself with the comparative history of races – there are certain questions that one can probe to the marrow, as it were, only by this method – and I have discovered that we Chinese possess certain folk and political institutions that are unique in their clarity, others again unique in their obscurity. The desire to trace the cause of these phenomena, especially the latter, has always intrigued me and intrigues me still, and the building of the wall is itself essentially involved with these problems.

Now one of our most obscure institutions of all is unquestionably that of the empire itself. In Peking, of course, especially in court circles, there does exist some clarity on this subject, though even that is more apparent than real; also the teachers of constitutional law and history in the high schools claim to be exactly informed on these matters, and to be capable of passing on their knowledge to their students; and the further down the ladder of schools one goes, the more one finds, naturally enough, people's doubts of their own knowledge vanishing, and a sea of semi-education swirling sky-high around a few precepts that have been drilled into people's minds for centuries, precepts which, though they have lost nothing of their eternal truth, remain eternally invisible in this fog of confusion.

But it is precisely about the empire that one should in my opinion be asking the common people first, since after all they are the empire's final support. Here, I must confess, I can only speak once more for my native place. Except for the nature gods, and their ritual which fills the whole year in such beautiful and rich alternation, we think only about the Emperor. But not about the present one; or rather we would think about the present one if we knew who he was or knew anything definite about him. True – and it is the sole curiosity that fills us – we are always trying to get information on this subject, but, strange as it may sound, it is almost impossible to discover anything, either from pilgrims, though they have wandered through much of our land, or from near or distant villages, or from sailors, though they have navigated not only our little stream, but also the sacred rivers. One hears a great many things, true, but can gather nothing definite.

So vast is our land that no fable could do justice to its size, the heavens can scarcely span it. And Peking is only a dot in it, and the imperial palace less than a dot. And again the Emperor, as such, is unquestionably mighty throughout all the hierarchies of the world. But the living Emperor, a man like us, lies much like us on a couch which is indeed of generous proportions, yet still comparatively narrow and short. Like us he sometimes stretches himself and when he is very tired yawns with his delicately cut mouth. But how should we know anything about that – thousands of miles away in the south – almost on the borders of the Tibetan Highlands? And besides, any tidings, even if they did reach us, would arrive far too late, would have become obsolete long before they reached us. The Emperor is always surrounded by the brilliant and yet sinister throng of nobles and courtiers, the counterweight to the imperial power, perpetually labouring to topple the ruler from his seat with their poisoned arrows. The Empire is immortal, but the Emperor himself totters and falls from his throne, yes, whole dynasties sink in the end and breathe their last in one death rattle. Of these struggles and sufferings the people will never know; like tardy arrivals, like strangers in a city, they stand at the end of some densely thronged side street peacefully munching the food they have brought with them, while far away in front, in the Market Square at the heart of the city, the execution of their ruler is proceeding.

There is a parable that describes this situation very well: The Emperor, so it runs, has sent a message expressly to you, the miserable subject, the insignificant shadow cowering in the remotest distance before the imperial sun; the Emperor from his deathbed has sent a message to you expressly. He has commanded the messenger to kneel down by the bed, and has whispered the message to him; so much store did he lay on it that he ordered the messenger to whisper it back into his ear again. Then by a nod of the head he has confirmed that it is right. Yes, before the assembled spectators of his death – all the obstructing walls have been broken down, and on the spacious and loftily mounting open staircases stand in a ring the great princes of the Empire – before all these he has delivered his message. The messenger immediately sets out on his journey; a powerful, an indefatigable man, a swimmer without equal; now pushing with his right arm, now with his left, he cleaves a way for himself through the throng; if he encounters resistance he points to his breast, where the symbol of the sun glitters; and indeed he makes faster progress than would any other man. But the multitudes are so vast; their numbers have no end. If he could reach the open fields how fast he would fly, and soon doubtless you would hear the majestic hammering of his fists on your door. But instead how vainly does he wear out his strength; still he is only making his way through the chambers of the innermost palace; never will he get to the end of them; and if he succeeded in that nothing would be gained; he must next fight his way down the stairs; and if he succeeded in that nothing would be gained; the courts would still have to be crossed; and after the courts the second outer palace; and once more stairs and courts; and once more another palace; and so on for thousands of years; and if at last

24

he should burst through the outermost gate – but never, never can that happen – the imperial capital would lie before him, the centre of the world, crammed to bursting with its own sediment. Nobody could fight his way through here, let alone with a message from a dead man to a nonentity. But you sit at your window when evening falls and dream it to yourself.

Just so, as hopelessly and as hopefully, do our people regard the Emperor. They do not know what Emperor is reigning, and there exist doubts regarding even the name of the dynasty. In school a great deal is taught about the dynasties with the dates of succession, but the universal uncertainty in this matter is so great that even the best scholars are drawn into it. Long-dead emperors are set on the throne in our villages, and one that only lives on in song recently had a proclamation of his read out by the priest before the altar. Battles that are old history are new to us, and one's neighbour rushes in with a jubilant face to tell the news. The wives of the emperors, pampered and overweening, seduced from noble custom by wily courtiers, swelling with ambition, vehement in their greed, uncontrollable in their lust, practise their abominations ever anew. The more deeply they are buried in time the more glaring are the colours in which their deeds are painted, and with a loud cry of woe our village eventually hears how an Empress drank her husband's blood in long draughts thousands of years ago.

Thus, then, do our people deal with departed emperors, but the living they confuse among the dead. If once, only once in a man's lifetime, an imperial official on his tour of the provinces should arrive by chance at our village, make certain announcements in the name of the ruler, scrutinize the tax lists, examine the school children, inquire of the priest regarding our doings and affairs, and then, before he steps into his sedan chair, should sum up his impressions in verbose admonitions to the assembled commune – then a smile flits over every face, people throw surreptitious glances at each other, and bend over their children so as not to be observed by the official. Why, they think to themselves, he's speaking of a dead man as if he were alive, this Emperor of his died long ago, the dynasty is blotted out, the good official is having his joke with us, but we will behave as if we did not notice it, so as not to offend him. But we shall obey in earnest no one but our present ruler, for not to do so would be a crime. And behind the departing sedan chair of the official there rises in might as ruler of the village some figure fortuitously exalted from an urn already crumbled to dust.

If from such appearances anyone should draw the conclusion that in reality we have no Emperor, he would not be far from the truth. Over and over again it must be repeated: There is perhaps no people more faithful to the Emperor than ours in the south, but the Emperor derives no advantage from our fidelity. True, the sacred dragon stands on the little column at the end of our village, and ever since the beginning of human memory it has breathed out its fiery breath in the direction of Peking in token of homage – but Peking itself is far stranger to the people in our village than the next world. Can there really be a village where the houses stand side by side, covering all the fields for a greater distance than one can see from our hills, and can there be dense crowds of people packed between these houses day and night? We find it more difficult to picture such a city than to believe that Peking and its Emperor are one, a cloud, say, peacefully voyaging beneath the sun in the course of the ages.

Now the result of holding such opinions is a life on the whole free and unconstrained. By no means immoral, however; hardly ever have I found in my travels such pure morals as in my native village. But yet a life that is subject to no contemporary law, and attends only to the exhortations and warnings that come to us from olden times.

I guard against generalizations, and do not assert that in all the ten thousand villages in my province it is so, far less in all the five hundred provinces of China. Yet perhaps I may venture to assert on the basis of the many writings on this subject which I have read, as well as from my own observation – the building of the wall in particular, with its abundance of human material, provided a man of sensibility with the opportunity of traversing the souls of almost all the provinces – on the basis of all this, then, perhaps I may venture to assert that the prevailing attitude to the Emperor shows persistently and universally something fundamentally in common with that of our village. Now I have no wish whatever to represent this attitude as a virtue; on the contrary. True, the essential responsibility for it lies with the government, which in the most ancient empire in the world has not yet succeeded in developing, or has neglected to develop, the institution of the empire to such precision that its workings extend directly and unceasingly to the farthest frontiers of the land. On the other hand, however, there is also involved a certain feebleness of faith and imaginative power on the part of the people, that prevents them from raising the empire out of its stagnation in Peking and clasping it in all its palpable living reality to their own breasts, which yet desire nothing better than but once to feel that touch and then to die. This attitude then is certainly no virtue. All the more remarkable is it that this very weakness should seem to be one of the greatest unifying influences among our people . . .

Into this world there now penetrated the news of the building of the wall. It too came late, some thirty years after its announcement. It was on a summer evening. I, ten years old, was standing with my father on the riverbank. In keeping with the importance of this much-discussed hour, I can recall the smallest details. My father was holding me by the hand, something he was fond of doing to the end of his days, and running his other hand up and down his long, very thin pipe, as though it were a flute. His sparse, rigid beard was raised in the air, for as he enjoyed his pipe he was gazing up across the river, towards the sky. As a result his pigtail, object of the children's veneration, sank lower, rustling faintly on the gold-embroidered silk of his holiday gown. At that moment a bark drew up before us, the boatman beckoned to my father to come down the embankment, while he himself climbed up toward him. They met halfway, the boatman whispered something in my father's ear, in order to come quite close he had embraced him. I could not understand what they said, I only saw that my father did not seem to believe the news, that the boatman tried to insist upon its truth, that when my father still refused to believe it the boatman, with the passion of sailors, almost tore the garment from his chest to prove the truth, whereupon my father fell silent and the boatman jumped noisily into the bark and sailed away. Deep in thought my father turned toward me, knocked his pipe out and stuck it in his belt, stroked my cheek, and pulled my head toward him. That is what I liked best, it made me very happy, and so we came home. There the rice-pap was already steaming on the table, several guests had assembled, the wine was just being poured into the goblets. Paying no attention to any of this and having advanced no farther than the threshold, my father started telling what he had heard. Of the exact words I have of course no recollection, but owing to the exceptional circumstances which cast a spell even over the child, the meaning became so clear to me that I venture nevertheless to give some version of what my father said. I am doing so because it was very characteristic of the popular point of view. My father said something like this: 'A strange boatman — I know all those who usually pass by here, but this one was a stranger – has just told me that a great wall is going to be built to protect the Emperor. For it seems that infidel tribes, and demons among them, often assemble before the imperial palace and shoot their black arrows at the Emperor.'

Leopards in the Temple

Leopards break into the temple and drink to the dregs what is in the sacrificial pitchers; this is repeated over and over again; finally it can be calculated in advance, and it becomes a part of the ceremony.

Jackals and Arabs

We were camping in the oasis. My companions were asleep. The tall, white figure of an Arab passed by; he had been seeing to the camels and was on his way to his own sleeping place.

I threw myself on my back in the grass; I tried to fall asleep; I could not; a jackal howled in the distance; I sat up again. And what had been so far away was all at once quite near. Jackals were swarming around me, eyes gleaming dull gold and vanishing again, lithe bodies moving nimbly and rhythmically, as if at the crack of a whip.

One jackal came from behind me, nudging right under my arm, pressing against me, as if he needed my warmth, and then stood before me and spoke to me almost eye to eye.

'I am the oldest jackal far and wide. I am delighted to have met you here at last. I had almost given up hope, since we have been waiting endless years for you; my mother waited for you, and her mother, and all our foremothers right back to the first mother of all the jackals. It is true, believe me!'

'That is surprising,' said I, forgetting to kindle the pile of firewood which lay ready to smoke away jackals, 'that is very surprising for me to hear. It is by pure chance that I have come here from the far North, and I am making only a short tour of your country. What do you jackals want, then?'

As if emboldened by this perhaps too-friendly inquiry the ring of jackals closed in on me; all were panting and open-mouthed.

'We know,' began the eldest, 'that you have come from the North; that is just what we base our hopes on. You Northerners have the kind of intelligence that is not to be found among Arabs. Not a spark of intelligence, let me tell you, can be struck from their cold arrogance. They kill animals for food, and carrion they despise.'

'Not so loud,' said I, 'there are Arabs sleeping nearby.'

'You are indeed a stranger here,' said the jackal, 'or you would know that never in the history of the world has any jackal been afraid of an Arab. Why should we fear them? Is it not misfortune enough for us to be exiled among such creatures?'

'Maybe, maybe,' said I, 'matters so far outside my province I am not competent to judge; it seems to me a very old quarrel; I suppose it's in the blood, and perhaps will only end with it.'

'You are very clever,' said the old jackal; and they all began to pant more quickly; the air pumped out of their lungs although they were standing still; a rank smell which at times I had to set my teeth to endure streamed from their open

33

jaws, 'you are very clever; what you have just said agrees with our old tradition. So we shall draw blood from them and the quarrel will be over.'

'Oh!' said I, more vehemently than I intended, 'they'll defend themselves; they'll shoot you down in dozens with their muskets.'

'You misunderstand us,' said he, 'a human failing which persists apparently even in the far North. We're not proposing to kill them. All the water in the Nile couldn't cleanse us of that. Why, the mere sight of their living flesh makes us turn tail and flee into cleaner air, into the desert, which for that very reason is our home.'

And all the jackals around, including many newcomers from farther away, dropped their muzzles between their forelegs and wiped them with their paws; it was as if they were trying to conceal a disgust so overpowering that I felt like leaping over their heads to get away.

'Then what are you proposing to do?' I asked, trying to rise to my feet; but I could not get up; two young beasts behind me had locked their teeth through my coat and shirt; I had to go on sitting. 'These are your trainbearers,' explained the old jackal, quite seriously, 'a mark of honour.' 'They must let go!' I cried, turning now to the old jackal, now to the youngsters. 'They will, of course,' said the old one, 'if that is your wish. But it will take a little time, for they have got their teeth well in, as is our custom, and must first loosen their jaws bit by bit.

Meanwhile, give ear to our petition.' 'Your conduct hasn't exactly inclined me to grant it,' said I. 'Don't hold it against us that we are clumsy,' said he, and now for the first time had recourse to the natural plaintiveness of his voice, 'we are poor creatures, we have nothing but our teeth; whatever we want to do, good or bad, we can tackle it only with our teeth.' 'Well, what do you want?' I asked, not much mollified.

'Sir,' he cried, and all the jackals howled together; very remotely it seemed to resemble a melody. 'Sir, we want you to end this quarrel that divides the world. You are exactly the man whom our ancestors foretold as born to do it. We want to be troubled no more by Arabs; room to breathe; a skyline cleansed of them; no more bleating of sheep knifed by an Arab; every beast to die a natural death; no interference till we have drained the carcass empty and picked its bones clean. Cleanliness, nothing but cleanliness is what we want' – and now they were all lamenting and sobbing – 'how can you bear to live in such a world, O noble heart and kindly bowels? Filth is their white; filth is their black; their beards are a horror; the very sight of their eye sockets makes one want to spit; and when they lift an arm, the murk of hell yawns in the armpit. And so, sir, and so, dear sir, by means of your all-powerful hands slit their throats through with these scissors!' And in answer to a jerk of his head a jackal came trotting up with a small pair of sewing scissors, covered with ancient rust, dangling from an eyetooth.

'Well, here's the scissors at last, and high time to stop!' cried the Arab leader of our caravan who had crept upwind toward us and now cracked his great whip.

The jackals fled in haste, but at some little distance rallied in a close huddle, all the brutes so tightly packed and rigid that they looked as if penned in a small fold girt by flickering will-o'-the-wisps.

'So you've been treated to this entertainment too, sir,' said the Arab, laughing as gaily as the reserve of his race permitted. 'You know, then, what the brutes are after?' I asked. 'Of course,' said he, 'it's common knowledge; so long as Arabs exist, that pair of scissors goes wandering through the desert and will wander with us to the end of our days. Every European is offered it for the great work; every European is just the man that Fate has chosen for them. They have the most lunatic hopes, these beasts; they're just fools, utter fools. That's why we like them; they are our dogs; finer dogs than any of yours. Watch this, now, a camel died last night and I have had it brought here.'

Four men came up with the heavy carcass and threw it down before us. It had hardly touched the ground before the jackals lifted up their voices. As if irresistibly drawn by cords each of them began to waver forward, crawling on his belly. They had forgotten the Arabs, forgotten their hatred, the all-obliterating immediate presence of the stinking carrion bewitched them. One was already at the camel's throat, sinking his teeth straight into an artery. Like a vehement small pump endeavouring with as much determination as hopefulness to extinguish some raging fire, every muscle in his body twitched and laboured at the task. In a trice they were all on top of the carcass, labouring in common, piled mountain-high.

And now the caravan leader lashed his cutting whip criss-cross over their backs. They lifted their heads; half swooning in ecstasy; saw the Arabs standing before them; felt the sting of the whip on their muzzles; leaped and ran backwards a stretch. But the camel's blood was already lying in pools, reeking to heaven, the carcass was torn wide open in many places. They could not resist it; they were back again; once more the leader lifted his whip; I stayed his arm.

'You are right, sir,' said he, 'we'll leave them to their business; besides, it's time to break camp. Well, you've seen them. Marvellous creatures, aren't they? And how they hate us!'

A Report to an Academy

Honoured Members of the Academy!

You have done me the honour of inviting me to give your Academy an account of the life I formerly led as an ape.

I regret that I cannot comply with your request to the extent you desire. It is now nearly five years since I was an ape, a short space of time, perhaps, according to the calendar, but an infinitely long time to gallop through at full speed, as I have done, more or less accompanied by excellent mentors, good advice, applause, and orchestral music, and yet essentially alone, since all my escorters, to keep the image, kept well off the course. I could never have achieved what I have done had I been stubbornly set on clinging to my origins, to the remembrances of my youth. In fact, to give up being stubborn was the supreme commandment I laid upon myself; free ape as I was, I submitted myself to that yoke. In revenge, however, my memory of the past has closed the door against me more and more. I could have returned at first, had human beings allowed it, through an archway as wide as the span of heaven over the earth, but as I spurred myself on in my forced career, the opening narrowed and shrank behind me; I felt more comfortable in the world of men and fitted it better; the strong wind that blew after me out of my past began to slacken; today it is only a gentle puff of air that plays around my heels; and the opening in the distance, through which it comes and through which I once came myself, has grown so small that, even if my strength and my will power sufficed to get me back to it, I should have to scrape the very skin from my body to crawl through. To put it plainly, much as I like expressing myself in images, to put it plainly: your life as apes, gentlemen, insofar as something of that kind lies behind you, cannot be farther removed from you than mine is from me. Yet everyone on earth feels a tickling at the heels; the small chimpanzee and the great Achilles alike.

But to a lesser extent I can perhaps meet your demand, and indeed I do so with the greatest pleasure. The first thing I learned was to give a handshake; a handshake betokens frankness; well, today, now that I stand at the very peak of my career, I hope to add frankness in words to the frankness of that first handshake. What I have to tell the Academy will contribute nothing essentially new, and will fall far behind what you have asked of me and what with the best will in the world I cannot communicate – nonetheless, it should indicate the line an erstwhile ape has had to follow in entering and establishing himself in the world of men. Yet I could not risk putting into words even such insignificant information as I am going to give you if I were not quite sure of myself and if my position on all the great variety stages of the civilized world had not become quite unassailable.

I belong to the Gold Coast. For the story of my capture I must depend on the evidence of others. A hunting expedition sent out by the firm of Hagenbeck — by the way, I have drunk many a bottle of good red wine since then with the leader of that expedition — had taken up its position in the bushes by the shore when I came down for a drink at evening among a troop of apes. They shot at us; I was the only one that was hit; I was hit in two places.

Once in the cheek; a slight wound; but it left a large, naked, red scar which earned me the name of Red Peter, a horrible name, utterly inappropriate, which only some ape could have thought of, as if the only difference between me and the performing ape Peter, who died not so long ago and had some small local reputation, were the red mark on my cheek. This by the way.

The second shot hit me below the hip. It was a severe wound, it is the cause of my limping a little to this day. I read an article recently by one of the ten thousand windbags who vent themselves concerning me in the newspapers, saying: my ape nature is not yet quite under control; the proof being that when visitors come to see me, I have a predilection for taking down my trousers to show them where the shot went in. The hand which wrote that should have its fingers shot away one by one. As for me, I can take my trousers down before anyone if I like; you would find nothing but a well-groomed fur and the scar made – let me be particular in the choice of a word for this particular purpose, to avoid misunderstanding – the scar made by a wanton shot. Everything is open and aboveboard; there is nothing to conceal; when the plain truth is in question, great minds discard the niceties of refinement. But if the writer of the article were to take down his trousers before a visitor, that would be quite another story, and I will let it stand to his credit that he does not do it. In return, let him leave me alone with his delicacy!

After these two shots I came to myself – and this is where my own memories gradually begin – between decks in the Hagenbeck steamer, inside a cage. It was not a four-sided barred cage; it was only a three-sided cage nailed to a locker; the locker made the fourth side of it. The whole construction was too low for me to stand up in and too narrow to sit down in. So I had to squat with my knees bent and trembling all the time, and also, since probably for a time I wished to see no one, and to stay in the dark, my face was turned toward the locker while the bars of the cage cut into my flesh behind. Such a method of confining wild beasts is supposed to have its advantages during the first days of captivity, and out of my own experiences I cannot deny that from the human point of view this is really the case.

But that did not occur to me then. For the first time in my life I could see no way out; at least no direct way out; directly in front of me was the locker, board fitted close to board. True, there was a gap running right through the boards which I greeted with the blissful howl of ignorance when I first discovered it, but the hole was not even wide enough to stick one's tail through and not all the strength of an ape could enlarge it.

I am supposed to have made uncommonly little noise, as I was later informed, from which the conclusion was drawn that I would either soon die or if I managed to survive the first critical period would be very amenable to training. I did survive this period. Hopelessly sobbing, painfully hunting for fleas, apathetically licking a cocoanut, beating my skull against the locker, sticking out my tongue at anyone who came near me – that was how I filled in time at first in my new life. But over and above it all only the one feeling: no way out. Of course what I felt then as an ape I can represent now only in human terms, and therefore I misrepresent it, but although I cannot reach back to the truth of the old ape life, there is no doubt that it lies somewhere in the direction I have indicated.

Until then I had had so many ways out of everything, and now I had none. I was pinned down. Had I been nailed down, my right to free movement would not have been lessened. Why so? Scratch your flesh raw between your toes, but you won't find the answer. Press yourself against the bar behind you till it nearly cuts you in two, you won't find the answer. I had no way out but I had to devise one, for without it I could not live. All the time facing that locker – I should certainly have perished. Yet as far as Hagenbeck was concerned, the place for apes was in front of a locker – well then, I had to stop being an ape. A fine, clear train of thought, which I must have constructed somehow with my belly, since apes think with their bellies.

I fear that perhaps you do not quite understand what I mean by 'way out'. I use the expression in its fullest and most popular sense. I deliberately do not use the word 'freedom'. I do not mean the spacious feeling of freedom on all sides. As an ape, perhaps, I knew that, and I have met men who yearn for it. But for my part I desired such freedom neither then nor now. In passing: may I say that all too often men are betrayed by the word 'freedom'. And as freedom is counted among the most sublime feelings, so the corresponding disillusionment can be also sublime. In variety theatres I have often watched, before my turn came on, a couple of acrobats performing on trapezes high in the roof. They swung themselves, they rocked to and fro, they sprang into the air, they floated into each other's arms, one hung by the hair from the teeth of the other. 'And that too is human freedom,' I thought, 'self-controlled movement.' What a mockery of holy Mother Nature! Were the apes to see such a spectacle, no theatre walls could stand the shock of their laughter.

No, freedom was not what I wanted. Only a way out; right or left, or in any direction; I made no other demand; even should the way out prove to be an illusion; the demand was a small one, the disappointment could be no bigger. To get out somewhere, to get out! Only not to stay motionless with raised arms, crushed against a wooden wall.

Today I can see it clearly; without the most profound inward

43

calm I could never have found my way out. And indeed perhaps I owe all that I have become to the calm that settled within me after my first few days in the ship. And again for that calmness it was the ship's crew I had to thank.

They were good creatures, in spite of everything. I find it still pleasant to remember the sound of their heavy footfalls which used to echo through my half-dreaming head. They had a habit of doing everything as slowly as possible. If one of them wanted to rub his eyes, he lifted a hand as if it were a drooping weight. Their jests were coarse, but hearty. Their laughter had always a gruff bark in it that sounded dangerous but meant nothing. They always had something in their mouths to spit out and did not care where they spat it. They always grumbled that they got fleas from me; yet they were not seriously angry about it; they knew that my fur fostered fleas, and that fleas jump; it was a simple matter of fact to them. When they were off duty some of them often used to sit down in a semicircle around me; they hardly spoke but only grunted to each other; smoked their pipes, stretched out on lockers; smacked their knees as soon as I made the slightest movement; and now and then one of them would take a stick and tickle me where I liked being tickled. If I were to be invited today to take a cruise on that ship I should certainly refuse the invitation, but just as certainly the memories I could recall between its decks would not all be hateful.

The calmness I acquired among these people kept me above all from trying to escape. As I look back now, it seems to me I must have had at least an inkling that I had to find a way out or die, but that my way out could not be reached through flight. I cannot tell now whether escape was possible, but I believe it must have been; for an ape it must always be possible. With my teeth as they are today I have to be careful even in simply cracking nuts, but at that time I could certainly have managed by degrees to bite through the lock of my cage. I did not do it. What good would it have done me? As soon as I had poked out my head I should have been caught again and put in a worse cage; or I might have slipped among the other animals without being noticed, among the pythons, say, who were opposite me, and so breathed out my life in their embrace; or supposing I had actually succeeded in sneaking out as far as the deck and leaping overboard, I should have rocked for a little on the deep sea and then been drowned. Desperate remedies. I did not think it out in this human way, but under the influence of my surroundings I acted as if I had thought it out.

I did not think things out; but I observed everything quietly. I watched these men go to and fro, always the same faces, the same movements, often it seemed to me there was only the same man. So this man or these men walked about unimpeded. A lofty goal faintly dawned before me. No one promised me that if I became like them the bars of my cage would be taken away. Such promises for apparently impossible contingencies are not given. But if one achieves the impossible, the promises appear later retrospectively precisely where one had looked in vain for them before. Now, these men in themselves had no great attraction for me. Had I been devoted to the aforementioned idea of freedom, I should certainly have preferred the deep sea to the way out that suggested itself in the heavy faces of these men. At any rate, I watched them for a long time before I even thought of such things, indeed, it was only the mass weight of my observations that impelled me in the right direction.

It was so easy to imitate these people. I learned to spit in the very first days. We used to spit in each other's faces; the only difference was that I licked my face clean afterwards and they did not. I could soon smoke a pipe like an old hand; and if I also pressed my thumb into the bowl of the pipe, a roar of appreciation went up between-decks; only it took me a very long time to understand the difference between a full pipe and an empty one.

My worst trouble came from the schnapps bottle. The smell of it revolted me; I forced myself to it as best I could; but it took weeks for me to master my repulsion. This inward conflict, strangely enough, was taken more seriously by the crew than anything else about me. I cannot distinguish the men from each other in my recollection, but there was one of them who came again and again, alone or with friends, by day, by night, at all kinds of hours; he would post himself before me with the bottle and give me instructions. He could not understand me, he wanted to solve the enigma of my being. He would slowly uncork the bottle and then look at me to see if I had followed him; I admit that I always watched him with wildly eager, too eager attention; such a student of humankind no human teacher ever found on earth. After the bottle was uncorked he lifted it to his mouth; I followed it with my eyes right up to his jaws; he would nod, pleased with me, and set the bottle to his lips; I, enchanted with my gradual enlightenment, squealed and scratched myself comprehensively wherever scratching was called for; he rejoiced, tilted the bottle, and took a drink; I, impatient and desperate to emulate him, befouled myself in my cage, which again gave him great satisfaction; and then, holding the bottle at arm's length and bringing it up with a swing, he would empty it at one draught, leaning back at an exaggerated angle for my better instruction. I, exhausted by too much effort, could follow him no farther and hung limply to the bars, while he ended his theoretical exposition by rubbing his belly and grinning.

After theory came practice. Was I not already quite exhausted by my theoretical instruction? Indeed I was; utterly exhausted. That was part of my destiny. And yet I would take hold of the proffered bottle as well as I was able; uncork it, trembling; this successful action would gradually inspire me with new energy; I would lift the bottle, already following my original model almost exactly; put it to my lips and – and then throw it down in disgust, utter disgust, although it was empty and filled only with the smell of the spirit, throw it down on the floor in disgust. To the sorrow of my teacher, to the greater sorrow of myself;

47

neither of us being really comforted by the fact that I did not forget, even though I had thrown away the bottle, to rub my belly most admirably and to grin.

Far too often my lesson ended in that way. And to the credit of my teacher, he was not angry; sometimes indeed he would hold his burning pipe against my fur, until it began to smoulder in some place I could not easily reach, but then he would himself extinguish it with his own kind, enormous hand; he was not angry with me, he perceived that we were both fighting on the same side against the nature of apes and that I had the more difficult task.

What a triumph it was then both for him and for me, when one evening before a large circle of spectators – perhaps there was a celebration of some kind, a gramophone was playing, an officer was circulating among the crew – when on this evening, just as no one was looking, I took hold of a schnapps bottle that had been carelessly left standing before my cage, uncorked it in the best style, while the company began to watch me with mounting attention, set it to my lips without hesitation, with no grimace, like a professional drinker, with rolling eyes and full throat, actually and truly drank it empty; then threw the bottle away, not this time in despair but as an artistic performer; forgot, indeed, to rub my belly; but instead of that, because I could not help it, because my senses were reeling, called a brief and unmistakable 'Hallo!' breaking into human speech, and with this outburst broke into the human community, and felt its echo: 'Listen, he's talking!' like a caress over the whole of my sweat-drenched body.

I repeat: there was no attraction for me in imitating human beings; I imitated them because I needed a way out, and for no other reason. And even that triumph of mine did not achieve much. I lost my human voice again at once; it did not come back for months; my aversion for the schnapps bottle returned again with even greater force. But the line I was to follow had in any case been decided, once for all.

When I was handed over to my first trainer in Hamburg I soon realized that there were two alternatives before me: the Zoological Gardens or the variety stage. I did not hesitate. I said to myself: do your utmost to get onto the variety stage; the Zoological Gardens means only a new cage; once there, you are done for.

And so I learned things, gentlemen. Ah, one learns when one has to; one learns when one needs a way out; one learns at all costs. One stands over oneself with a whip; one flays oneself at the slightest opposition. My ape nature fled out of me, head over heels and away, so that my first teacher was almost himself turned into an ape by it, had soon to give up teaching and was taken away to a mental hospital. Fortunately he was soon let out again.

But I used up many teachers, indeed, several teachers at once. As I became more confident of my abilities, as the public took an interest in my progress and my future began to look bright, I engaged teachers for myself, established them in five communicating rooms, and took lessons from them all at once by dint of leaping from one room to the other.

That progress of mine! How the rays of knowledge penetrated from all sides into my awakening brain! I do not deny it: I found it exhilarating. But I must also confess: I did not overestimate it, not even then, much less now. With an effort which up till now has never been repeated I managed to reach the cultural level of an average European. In itself that might be nothing to speak of, but it is something insofar as it has helped me out of my cage and opened a special way out for me, the way of humanity. There is an excellent idiom: to fight one's way through the thick of things; that is what I have done, I have fought through the thick of things. There was nothing else for me to do, provided always that freedom was not to be my choice.

As I look back over my development and survey what I have achieved so far, I do not complain, but I am not complacent either. With my hands in my trouser pockets, my bottle of wine on the table, I half lie and half sit in my rocking chair and gaze out of the window: if a visitor arrives, I receive him with propriety. My manager sits in the anteroom; when I ring, he comes and listens to what I have to say. Nearly every evening I give a performance, and I have a success that could hardly be increased. When I come home late at night from banquets, from scientific receptions, from social gatherings, there sits waiting for me a half-trained little chimpanzee and I take comfort from her as apes do. By day I cannot bear to see her; for she has the insane look of the bewildered half-broken animal in her eye; no one else sees it, but I do, and I cannot bear it. On the whole, at any rate, I have achieved what I set out to achieve. But do not tell me that it was not worth the trouble. In any case, I am not appealing for any man's verdict, I am only imparting knowledge, I am only making a report. To you also, honoured Members of the Academy, I have only made a report.

A Report to an Academy:
Two Fragments

I

We all know Rotpeter, just as half the world knows him. But when he came to our town for a guest performance, I decided to get to know him personally. It is not difficult to be admitted. In big cities where everyone in the know clamours to watch celebrities breathe from as close as possible, great difficulties may be encountered; but in our town one is content to marvel at the marvellous from the pit. Thus I was the only one so far, as the hotel servant told me, to have announced his visit. Herr Busenau, the impresario, received me with extreme courtesy. I had not expected to meet a man so modest, indeed almost timid. He was sitting in the anteroom of Rotpeter's apartment, eating an omelette. Although it was morning he already sat there in the evening clothes in which he appears at the performances. Hardly had he caught sight of me – me the unknown, the unimportant guest – when he, possessor of highly distinguished medals, king of trainers, honorary doctor of great universities, jumped up, shook me by both hands, urged me to sit down, wiped his spoon on the tablecloth, and amiably offered it to me so that I might finish his omelette. He would not accept my grateful refusal and promptly tried to feed me. I had some trouble calming him down and warding him off, as well as his spoon and plate.

'Very kind of you to have come,' he said with a strong foreign accent. 'Most kind. You've also come at the right time, for alas Rotpeter cannot always receive. Seeing people is often repugnant to him; on these occasions no one, it does not matter who he may be, is admitted; then I, even I can see him only on business, so to speak, on the stage. And immediately after the performance I have to disappear, he drives home alone, locks himself in his room, and usually remains like that until the following evening. He always has a big hamper of fruit in his bedroom, this is what he lives on at these times. But I, who of course dare not let him out of my sight, always rent the apartment opposite his and watch him from behind curtains.'

2

When I sit opposite you like this, Rotpeter, listening to you talk, drinking your health, I really and truly forget – whether you take it as a compliment or not, it's the truth – that you are a chimpanzee. Only gradually, when I have forced myself out of my thoughts back to reality, do my eyes show me again whose guest I am.

Yes.

You're so silent suddenly, I wonder why? Just a moment ago you were pronouncing such astonishingly correct opinions about our town, and now you're so silent.

Silent?

Is something wrong? Shall I call the trainer? Perhaps you're in the habit of taking a meal at this hour?

No, no. It's quite all right. I can tell you what it was. Sometimes I'm overcome with such an aversion to human beings that I can barely refrain from retching. This, of course, has nothing to do with the individual human being, least of all with your charming presence. It concerns all human beings. There's nothing extraordinary about this. Suppose, for instance, that you were to live continuously with apes, you'd probably have similar attacks, however great your self-control. Actually, it's not the smell of human beings that repels me so much, it's the human smell which I have contracted and which mingles with the smell from my native land. Smell for yourself! Here on my chest! Put your nose deeper into the fur! Deeper, I say!

I'm sorry, but I can't smell anything special. Just the ordinary smell of a well-groomed body, that's all. The nose of a city-dweller, of course, is no fair test. You, no doubt, can scent thousands of things that evade us.

54

Once upon a time, sir, once upon a time. That's over.

Since you brought it up yourself, I dare to ask: How long have you actually been living among us?

Five years. On the fifth of April it will be five years.

Terrific achievement. To cast off apehood in five years and gallop through the whole evolution of mankind! Certainly no one has ever done that before! On this racecourse you have no rival.

It's a great deal, I know, and sometimes it surpasses even my understanding. In tranquil moments, however, I feel less exuberant about it. Do you know how I was caught?

I've read everything that's been printed about you. You were shot at and then caught.

Yes, I was hit twice, once here in the cheek – the wound of course was far larger than the scar you see – and the second time below the hip. I'll take my trousers down so you can see that scar, too. Here then was where the bullet entered; this was the severe, decisive wound. I fell from the tree and when I came to I was in a cage between decks.

In a cage! Between decks! It's one thing to read your story, and quite another to hear you tell it!

And yet another, sir, to have experienced it. Until then I had never known what it means to have no way out. It was not a four-sided barred cage, it had only three sides nailed to a locker, the locker forming the fourth side. The whole contrivance was so low that I could not stand upright, and so narrow that I could not even sit down. All I could do was squat there with bent knees.

In my rage I refused to see anyone, and so remained facing the locker; for days and nights I squatted there with trembling knees while behind me the bars cut into my flesh. This manner of confining wild animals is considered to have its advantages during the first days of captivity, and from my experience I cannot deny that from the human point of view this actually is the case. But at that time I was not interested in the human point of view. I had the locker in front of me. Break the boards, bite a hole through them, squeeze yourself through an opening which in reality hardly allows you to see through it and which, when you first discover it, you greet with the blissful howl of ignorance! Where do you want to go? Beyond the boards the forest begins . . .

The Negro

The Negro who, having gone mad from homesickness, was taken home from the World Exhibition and, in his village, surrounded by the lamentations of the tribe, with the most solemn face, by way of tradition and duty, demonstrated the pranks that delighted the European public, who believed they were the rites and customs of Africa.

A Crossbreed

I have a curious animal, half kitten, half lamb. It is a legacy from my father. But it only developed in my time; formerly it was far more lamb than kitten. Now it is both in about equal parts. From the cat it takes its head and claws, from the lamb its size and shape; from both its eyes, which are wild and flickering, its hair, which is soft, lying close to its body, its movements, which partake both of skipping and slinking. Lying on the window sill in the sun it curls up in a ball and purrs; out in the meadow it rushes about like mad and is scarcely to be caught. It flees from cats and makes to attack lambs. On moonlight nights its favourite promenade is along the eaves. It cannot mew and it loathes rats. Beside the hen coop it can lie for hours in ambush, but it has never yet seized an opportunity for murder.

I feed it on milk; that seems to suit it best. In long draughts it sucks the milk in through its fanglike teeth. Naturally it is a great source of entertainment for children. Sunday morning is the visiting hour. I sit with the little beast on my knees, and the children of the whole neighbourhood stand around me.

Then the strangest questions are asked, which no human being could answer: Why there is only one such animal, why I rather than anybody else should own it, whether there was ever an animal like it before and what would happen if it died, whether it feels lonely, why it has no children, what it is called, etc.

I never trouble to answer, but confine myself without further explanation to exhibiting my possession. Sometimes the children bring cats with them; once they actually brought two lambs. But against all their hopes there was no scene of recognition. The animals gazed calmly at each other with their animal eyes, and obviously accepted their reciprocal existence as a divine fact.

Sitting on my knees, the beast knows neither fear nor lust of pursuit. Pressed against me it is happiest. It remains faithful to the family that brought it up. In that there is certainly no extraordinary mark of fidelity, but merely the true instinct of an animal which, though it has countless step-relations in the world, has perhaps not a single blood relation, and to which consequently the protection it has found with us is sacred.

Sometimes I cannot help laughing when it sniffs around me and winds itself between my legs and simply will not be parted from me. Not content with being lamb and cat, it almost insists on being a dog as well. Once when, as may happen to anyone, I could see no way out of my business problems and all that they involved, and was ready to let everything go, and in this mood was lying in my rocking chair in my room, the beast on my knees, I happened to glance down and saw tears dropping from its huge whiskers. Were they mine, or were they the animal's? Had this cat, along with the soul of a lamb, the ambitions of a human being? I did not inherit much from my father, but this legacy is quite remarkable.

It has the restlessness of both beasts, that of the cat and that of the lamb, diverse as they are. For that reason its skin feels too tight for it. Sometimes it jumps up on the armchair beside me, plants its front legs on my shoulder, and put its muzzle to my ear. It is as if it were saying something to me, and as a matter of fact it turns its head afterwards and gazes in my face to see the impression its communication has made. And to oblige it I behave as if I had understood, and nod. Then it jumps to the floor and dances about with joy.

Perhaps the knife of the butcher would be a release for this animal; but as it is a legacy I must deny it that. So it must wait until the breath voluntarily leaves its body, even though it sometimes gazes at me with a look of human understanding, challenging me to do the thing of which both of us are thinking.

The Cares of a Family Man

Some say the word 'Odradek' is of Slavonic origin, and try to account for it on that basis. Others again believe it to be of German origin, only influenced by Slavonic. The uncertainty of both interpretations allows one to assume with justice that neither is accurate, especially as neither of them provides an intelligent meaning of the word.

No one, of course, would occupy himself with such studies if there were not a creature called Odradek. At first glance it looks like a flat star-shaped spool for thread, and indeed it does seem to have thread wound upon it; to be sure, they are only old, broken-off bits of thread, knotted and tangled together, of the most varied sorts and colours. But it is not only a spool, for a small wooden crossbar sticks out of the middle of the star, and another small rod is joined to that at a right angle. By means of this latter rod on one side and one of the points of the star on the other, the whole thing can stand upright as if on two legs.

One is tempted to believe that the creature once had some sort of intelligible shape and is now only a broken-down remnant. Yet this does not seem to be the case; at least there is no sign of it; nowhere is there an unfinished or unbroken surface to suggest anything of the kind; the whole thing looks senseless enough, but in its own way perfectly finished. In any case, closer scrutiny is impossible, since Odradek is extraordinarily nimble and can never be laid hold of.

He lurks by turns in the garret, the stairway, the lobbies, the entrance hall. Often for months on end he is not to be seen; then he has presumably moved into other houses; but he always comes faithfully back to our house again. Many a time when you go out of the door and he happens just to be leaning directly beneath you against the banisters you feel inclined to speak to him. Of course, you put no difficult questions to him, you treat him – he is so diminutive that you cannot help it – rather like a child. 'Well, what's your name?' you ask him. 'Odradek,' he says. 'And where do you live?' – 'No fixed abode,' he says and laughs; but it is only the kind of laughter that has no lungs behind it. It sounds rather like the rustling of fallen leaves. And that is usually the end of the conversation. Even these answers are not always forthcoming; often he stays mute for a long time, as wooden as his appearance.

I ask myself, to no purpose, what is likely to happen to him? Can he possibly die? Anything that dies has had some kind of aim in life, some kind of activity, which has worn out; but that does not apply to Odradek. Am I to suppose, then, that he will always be rolling down the stairs, with ends of thread trailing after him, right before the feet of my children, and my children's children? He does no harm to anyone that one can see; but the idea that he is likely to survive me I find almost painful.

A Life

A stinking bitch, mother of countless whelps, in places already rotting, but everything to me in my childhood, a faithful creature that follows me unfailingly, which I cannot bring myself to beat, from which I retreat step by step and which nevertheless, if I do not decide otherwise, will push me into the corner between the walls, the corner that I already see, there to decompose completely, upon me and with me, right to the end – is it an honour for me? – the purulent and wormy flesh of her tongue upon my hand.

III

At Night

Deeply lost in the night. Just as one sometimes lowers one's head to reflect, thus to be utterly lost in the night. All around people are asleep. It is just play acting, an innocent self-deception, that they sleep in houses, in safe beds, under a safe roof, stretched out or curled up on mattresses, in sheets, under blankets; in reality they have flocked together as they had once upon a time and again later in a deserted region, a camp in the open, a countless number of men, an army, a people, under a cold sky on cold earth, collapsed where once they had stood, forehead pressed on the arm, face to the ground, breathing quietly. And you are watching, are one of the watchmen, you find the next one by brandishing a burning stick from the brushwood pile beside you. Why are you watching? Someone must watch, it is said. Someone must be there.

Morning

To awaken on a cold autumn morning full of yellowish light. To force your way through the half-shut window and while still in front of the panes, before you fall, to hover, arms extended, belly arched, legs curving backward, like the figures on the bows of ships in old times.

The Helmsman

'Am I not the helmsman here?' I called out. 'You?' asked a tall, dark man and passed his hands over his eyes as though to banish a dream. I had been standing at the helm in the dark night, a feeble lantern burning over my head, and now this man had come and tried to push me aside. And as I would not yield, he put his foot on my chest and slowly crushed me while I still clung to the hub of the helm, wrenching it around in falling. But the man seized it, pulled it back in place, and pushed me away. I soon collected myself, however, ran to the hatchway which gave onto the mess quarters, and cried out: 'Men! Comrades! Come here, quick! A stranger has driven me away from the helm!' Slowly they came up, climbing the companion ladder, tired, swaying, powerful figures. 'Am I the helmsman?' I asked. They nodded, but they had eyes only for the stranger, stood around him in a semicircle, and when, in a commanding voice, he said: 'Don't disturb me!' they gathered together, nodded at me, and withdrew down the companion ladder. What kind of people are these? Do they ever think, or do they only shuffle pointlessly over the earth?

The Bridge

I was stiff and cold, I was a bridge, I lay over a ravine. My toes on one side, my fingers clutching the other, I had clamped myself fast into the crumbling clay. The tails of my coat fluttered at my sides. Far below brawled the icy trout stream. No tourist strayed to this impassable height, the bridge was not yet traced on any map. So I lay and waited; I could only wait. Without falling, no bridge, once spanned, can cease to be a bridge.

It was toward evening one day – was it the first, was it the thousandth? I cannot tell – my thoughts were always in confusion and perpetually moving in a circle. It was toward evening in summer, the roar of the stream had grown deeper, when I heard the sound of a human step! To me, to me. Straighten yourself, bridge, make ready, rail-less beams, to hold up the passenger entrusted to you. If his steps are uncertain, steady them unobtrusively, but if he stumbles show what you are made of and like a mountain god hurl him across to land.

He came, he tapped me with the iron point of his stick,

68

then he lifted my coat-tails with it and put them in order upon me. He plunged the point of his stick into my bushy hair and let it lie there for a long time, forgetting me no doubt while he wildly gazed around him. But then – I was just following him in thought over mountain and valley – he jumped with both feet on the middle of my body. I shuddered with wild pain, not knowing what was happening. Who was it? A child? A dream? A wayfarer? A suicide? A tempter? A destroyer? And I turned around so as to see him. A bridge to turn around! I had not yet turned quite around when I already began to fall. I fell and in a moment I was torn and transpierced by the sharp rocks which had always gazed up at me so peacefully from the rushing water.

The Next Village

My grandfather used to say: 'Life is astoundingly short. To me, looking back over it, life seems so foreshortened that I scarcely understand, for instance, how a young man can decide to ride over to the next village without being afraid that – not to mention accidents – even the span of a normal happy life may fall far short of the time needed for such a journey.'

The Knock at the Manor Gate

It was summer, a hot day. With my sister I was passing the gate
of a great house on our way home. I cannot tell now whether she
knocked on the gate out of mischief or out of absence of mind,
or merely threatened it with her fist and did not knock at all. A
hundred paces further on along the road, which here turned to
the left, began the village. We did not know it very well, but
no sooner had we passed the first house when people appeared
and made friendly or warning signs to us; they were themselves
apparently terrified, bowed down with terror. They pointed
toward the manor house that we had passed and reminded us
of the knock on the gate. The proprietor of the manor would
charge us with it, the interrogation would begin immediately.
I remained quite calm and also tried to calm my sister's fears.
Probably she had not struck the door at all, and if she had,
nowhere in the world would that be a reason for prosecution.
I tried to make this clear to the people around us; they listened
to me but refrained from passing any opinion. Later they told

me that not only my sister, but I too, as her brother, would be charged. I nodded and smiled. We all gazed back at the manor, as one watches a distant smoke-cloud and waits for the flames to appear. And right enough we presently saw horsemen riding in through the wide-open gate. Dust rose, concealing everything, only the tops of the tall spears glittered. And hardly had the troop vanished into the manor courtyard before they seemed to have turned their horses again, for they were already on their way to us. I urged my sister to leave me, I myself would set everything right. She refused to leave me. I told her that she should at least change, so as to appear in better clothes before these gentlemen. At last she obeyed and set out on the long road to our home. Already the horsemen were beside us, and even before dismounting they inquired after my sister. She wasn't here at the moment, was the apprehensive reply, but she would come later. The answer was received almost with indifference; the important thing seemed their having found me. The chief members of the party appeared to be a young lively fellow, who was a judge, and his silent assistant, who was called Assmann. I was asked to enter the farmhouse. Shaking my head and hitching up my trousers, I slowly began to move, while the sharp eyes of the party scrutinized me. I still half believed that a word would be enough to free me, a city man, and with honour too, from this peasant folk. But when I had stepped over the threshold of the parlour the judge, who had hastened in front and was already awaiting me, said: 'I'm really sorry for this man.' And it was

72

beyond all possibility of doubt that by this he did not mean my present state, but something that was to happen to me. The room looked more like a prison cell than the parlour of a farmhouse. Great stone flags on the floor, dark, quite bare walls, into one of which an iron ring was fixed, in the middle something that looked half a pallet, half an operating table.

Could I still endure any other air than prison air? That is the great question, or rather it would be if I still had any prospect of release.

A Country Doctor

I was in great perplexity; I had to start on an urgent journey; a
seriously ill patient was waiting for me in a village ten miles off;
a thick blizzard of snow filled all the wide spaces between him
and me; I had a gig, a light gig with big wheels, exactly right
for our country roads; muffled in furs, my bag of instruments
in my hand, I was in the courtyard all ready for the journey;
but there was no horse to be had, no horse. My own horse had
died in the night, worn out by the fatigues of this icy winter;
my servant girl was now running around the village trying to
borrow a horse; but it was hopeless, I knew it, and I stood there
forlornly, with the snow gathering more and more thickly upon
me, more and more unable to move. In the gateway the girl
appeared, alone, and waved the lantern; of course, who would
lend a horse at this time for such a journey? I strode through
the courtyard once more; I could see no way out; in my confused
distress I kicked at the dilapidated door of the yearlong uninhabited pigsty. It flew open and flapped to and fro on its hinges.

A steam and smell as of horses came out from it. A dim stable lantern was swinging inside from a rope. A man, crouching on his hams in that low space, showed an open blue-eyed face. 'Shall I yoke up?' he asked, crawling out on all fours. I did not know what to say and merely stooped down to see what else was in the sty. The servant girl was standing beside me. 'You never know what you're going to find in your own house,' she said, and we both laughed. 'Hey there, Brother, hey there, Sister!' called the groom, and two horses, enormous creatures with powerful flanks, one after the other, their legs tucked close to their bodies, each well-shaped head lowered like a camel's, by sheer strength of buttocking squeezed out through the door hole which they filled entirely. But at once they were standing up, their legs long and their bodies steaming thickly. 'Give him a hand,' I said, and the willing girl hurried to help the groom with the harnessing. Yet hardly was she beside him when the groom clipped hold of her and pushed his face against hers. She screamed and fled back to me; on her cheek stood out in red the marks of two rows of teeth. 'You brute,' I yelled in fury, 'do you want a whipping?' but in the same moment reflected that the man was a stranger; that I did not know where he came from, and that of his own free will he was helping me out when everyone else had failed me. As if he knew my thoughts he took no offence at my threat but, still busied with the horses, only turned around once toward me. 'Get in,' he said then, and indeed: everything was ready. A magnificent pair of horses, I observed, such as I had never sat behind, and I climbed in happily. 'But I'll drive, you don't know the way,' I said. 'Of course,' said he, 'I'm not coming with you anyway, I'm staying with Rose.' 'No,' shrieked Rose, fleeing into the house with a justified presentiment that her fate was inescapable; I heard the door chain rattle as she put it up; I heard the key turn in the lock; I could see, moreover, how she put out the lights in the entrance hall and in further flight all through the rooms to keep herself from being discovered. 'You're coming with me,' I said to the groom, 'or I won't go, urgent as my journey is. I'm not thinking of paying for it by handing the girl over to you.' 'Gee up!' he said; clapped his hands; the gig whirled off like a log in a freshet; I could just hear the door of my house splitting and bursting as the groom charged at it and then I was deafened and blinded by a storming rush that steadily buffeted all my senses. But this only for a moment, since, as if my patient's farmyard had opened out just before my courtyard gate, I was already there; the horses had come quietly to a standstill; the blizzard had stopped; moonlight all around; my patient's parents hurried out of the house, his sister behind them; I was almost lifted out of the gig; from their confused ejaculations I gathered not a word; in the sickroom the air was almost unbreathable; the neglected stove was smoking; I wanted to push open a window; but first I had to look at my patient. Gaunt, without any fever, not cold, not warm, with vacant eyes, without a shirt, the youngster heaved himself up from under the feather bedding, threw his arms around my neck, and whispered in my ear: 'Doctor, let me die.' I glanced around the room; no one had heard it; the parents were leaning forward in silence waiting for my verdict; the sister had set a chair for my handbag; I opened the bag and hunted among my instruments; the boy kept clutching at me from his bed to remind me of his entreaty; I picked up a pair of tweezers, examined them in the candlelight, and laid them down again. 'Yes,' I thought blasphemously, 'in cases like this the gods are helpful, send the missing horse, add to it a second because of the urgency, and to crown everything bestow even a groom –' And only now did I remember Rose again; what was I to do, how could I rescue her, how could I pull her away from under that groom at ten miles' distance, with a team of horses I couldn't control? These horses, now, they had somehow slipped the reins loose, pushed the windows open from outside, I did not know how; each of them had stuck a head in at a window and, quite unmoved by the startled cries of the family, stood eyeing the patient. 'Better go back at once,' I thought, as if the horses were summoning me to the return journey, yet I permitted the patient's sister, who fancied that I was dazed by the heat, to take my fur coat from me. A glass of rum was poured out for me, the old man clapped me on the shoulder, a familiarity justified by this offer of his treasure. I shook my head; in the narrow confines of the old man's thoughts I felt ill; that was my only reason for refusing the drink. The mother stood by the bedside and cajoled me toward it; I yielded, and, while one of the horses whinnied loudly to the ceiling, laid my head to the boy's breast, which shivered under my wet beard. I confirmed what I already knew; the boy was quite sound, something a little wrong with his circulation, saturated with coffee by his solicitous mother, but sound and best turned out of bed with one shove. I am no world reformer and so I let him lie. I was the district doctor and did my duty to the uttermost, to the point where it became almost too much. I was badly paid and yet generous and helpful to the poor. I had still to see that Rose was all right, and then the boy might have his way and I wanted to die too. What was I doing there in that endless winter! My horse was dead, and not a single person in the village would lend me another. I had to get my team out of the pigsty; if they hadn't chanced to be horses I should have had to travel with swine. That was how it was. And I nodded to the family. They knew nothing about it, and, had they known, would not have believed it. To write prescriptions is easy, but to come to an understanding with people is hard. Well, this should be the end of my visit, I had once more been called out needlessly, I was used to that, the whole district made my life a torment with my night bell, but that I should have to sacrifice Rose this time as well, the pretty girl who had lived in my house for years almost without my noticing her — that sacrifice was too much to ask, and I had somehow to get it reasoned out in my head with the help of what craft I could muster, in order not to let fly at this family, which with the best will in the world could not restore Rose to me. But as I shut my bag and put an arm out for my fur coat, the family meanwhile standing together, the father sniffing at the glass of rum in his hand, the mother, apparently disappointed in me – why, what do people expect? – biting her lips with tears in her eyes, the sister fluttering a blood-soaked towel, I was somehow ready to admit conditionally that the boy might be ill after all. I went toward him, he welcomed me smiling as if I were bringing him the most nourishing invalid broth – ah, now both horses were whinnying together; the noise, I suppose, was ordained by heaven to assist my examination of the patient – and this time I discovered that the boy was indeed ill. In his right side, near the hip, was an open wound as big as the palm of my hand. Rose-red, in many variations of shade, dark in the hollows, lighter at the edges, softly granulated, with irregular clots of blood, open as a surface mine to the daylight. That was how it looked from a distance. But on a closer inspection there was another complication. I could not help a low whistle of surprise. Worms, as thick and as long as my little finger, themselves rose-red and blood-spotted as well, were wriggling from their fastness in the interior of the wound toward the light, with small white heads and many little legs. Poor boy, you were past helping. I had discovered your great wound; this blossom in your side was destroying you. The family was pleased; they saw me busying myself; the sister told the mother, the mother the father, the father told several guests who were coming in, through the moonlight at the open door, walking on tiptoe, keeping their balance with outstretched arms.

'Will you save me?' whispered the boy with a sob, quite blinded by the life within his wound. That is what people are like in my district. Always expecting the impossible from the doctor. They have lost their ancient beliefs; the parson sits at home and unravels his vestments, one after another; but the doctor is supposed to be omnipotent with his merciful surgeon's hand. Well, as it pleases them; I have not thrust my services on them; if they misuse me for sacred ends, I let that happen to me too; what better do I want, old country doctor that I am, bereft of my servant girl! And so they came, the family and the village elders, and stripped my clothes off me; a school choir with the teacher at the head of it stood before the house and sang these words to an utterly simple tune:

> Strip his clothes off, then he'll heal us,
> If he doesn't, kill him dead!
> Only a doctor, only a doctor.

Then my clothes were off and I looked at the people quietly, my fingers in my beard and my head cocked to one side. I was altogether composed and equal to the situation and remained so, although it was no help to me, since they now took me by the head and feet and carried me to the bed. They laid me down in it next to the wall, on the side of the wound. Then they all left the room; the door was shut; the singing stopped; clouds covered the moon; the bedding was warm around me;

the horses' heads in the open windows wavered like shadows. 'Do you know,' said a voice in my ear, 'I have very little confidence in you. Why, you were only blown in here, you didn't come on your own feet. Instead of helping me, you're cramping me on my deathbed. What I'd like best is to scratch your eyes out.' 'Right,' I said, 'it is a shame. And yet I am a doctor. What am I to do? Believe me, it is not too easy for me either.' 'Am I supposed to be content with this apology? Oh, I must be, I can't help it. I always have to put up with things. A fine wound is all I brought into the world; that was my sole endowment.' 'My young friend,' said I, 'your mistake is: you have not a wide enough view. I have been in all the sickrooms, far and wide, and I tell you: your wound is not so bad. Done in a tight corner with two strokes of the axe. Many a one proffers his side and can hardly hear the axe in the forest, far less that it is coming nearer to him.' 'Is that really so, or are you deluding me in my fever?' 'It is really so, take the word of honour of an official doctor.' And he took it and lay still. But now it was time for me to think of escaping. The horses were still standing faithfully in their places. My clothes, my fur coat, my bag were quickly collected; I didn't want to waste time dressing; if the horses raced home as they had come, I should only be springing, as it were, out of this bed into my own. Obediently a horse backed away from the window; I threw my bundle into the gig; the fur coat missed its mark and was caught on a hook only by the sleeve. Good enough. I swung myself onto the horse. With the reins loosely trailing, one horse barely fastened to the other, the gig swaying behind, my fur coat last of all in the snow. 'Gee up!' I said, but there was no galloping; slowly, like old men, we crawled through the snowy wastes; a long time echoed behind us the new but faulty song of the children:

> O be joyful, all you patients,
> The doctor's laid in bed beside you!

Never shall I reach home at this rate; my flourishing practice is done for; my successor is robbing me, but in vain, for he cannot take my place; in my house the disgusting groom is raging; Rose is his victim; I do not want to think about it anymore. Naked, exposed to the frost of this most unhappy of ages, with an earthly vehicle, unearthly horses, old man that I am, I wander astray. My fur coat is hanging from the back of the gig, but I cannot reach it, and none of my limber pack of patients lifts a finger. Betrayed! Betrayed! A false alarm on the night bell once answered – it cannot be made good, not ever.

An Old Manuscript

It looks as if much had been neglected in our country's system of defence. We have not concerned ourselves with it until now and have gone about our daily work; but things that have been happening recently begin to trouble us.

I have a cobbler's workshop in the square that lies before the Emperor's palace. Scarcely have I taken my shutters down, at the first glimmer of dawn, when I see armed soldiers already posted in the mouth of every street opening on the square. But these soldiers are not ours, they are obviously nomads from the North. In some way that is incomprehensible to me they have pushed right into the capital, although it is a long way from the frontier. At any rate, here they are; it seems that every morning there are more of them.

As is their nature, they camp under the open sky, for they abominate dwelling houses. They busy themselves sharpening swords, whittling arrows, and practising horsemanship. This peaceful square, which was always kept so scrupulously clean, they have made literally into a stable. We do try every now and then to run out of our shops and clear away at least the worst of the filth, but this happens less and less often, for the labour is in vain and brings us besides into danger of falling under the hoofs of the wild horses or of being crippled with lashes from the whips.

Speech with the nomads is impossible. They do not know our language, indeed they hardly have a language of their own. They communicate with each other much as jackdaws do. A screeching as of jackdaws is always in our ears. Our way of living and our institutions they neither understand nor care to understand. And so they are unwilling to make sense even out of our sign language. You can gesture at them till you dislocate your jaws and your wrists and still they will not have understood you and will never understand. They often make grimaces; then the whites of their eyes turn up and foam gathers on their lips, but they do not mean anything by that, not even a threat; they do it because it is their nature to do it. Whatever they need, they take. You cannot call it taking by force. They grab at something and you simply stand aside and leave them to it.

From my stock, too, they have taken many good articles. But I cannot complain when I see how the butcher, for instance, suffers across the street. As soon as he brings in any meat the nomads snatch it all from him and gobble it up. Even their horses devour flesh; often enough a horseman and his horse are lying side by side, both of them gnawing at the same joint, one at either end. The butcher is nervous and does not dare to stop his deliveries of meat. We understand that, however, and subscribe money to keep him going. If the nomads got no meat, who knows what they might think of doing; who knows anyhow what they may think of, even though they get meat every day.

Not long ago the butcher thought he might at least spare himself the trouble of slaughtering, and so one morning he brought along a live ox. But he will never dare to do that again. I lay for a whole hour flat on the floor at the back of my workshop with my head muffled in all the clothes and rugs and pillows I had simply to keep from hearing the bellowing of that ox, which the nomads were leaping on from all sides, tearing morsels out of its living flesh with their teeth. It had been quiet for a long time before I risked coming out; they were lying overcome around the remains of the carcass like drunkards around a wine cask.

This was the occasion when I fancied I actually saw the Emperor himself at a window of the palace; usually he never enters these outer rooms but spends all his time in the innermost garden; yet on this occasion he was standing, or so at least it seemed to me, at one of the windows, watching with bent head the goings-on before his residence.

'What is going to happen?' we all ask ourselves. 'How long can we endure this burden and torment? The Emperor's palace has drawn the nomads here but does not know how to drive them away again. The gate stays shut; the guards, who used to be always marching out and in with ceremony, keep close behind barred windows. It is left to us artisans and tradesmen to save our country; but we are not equal to such a task; nor have we ever claimed to be capable of it. This is a misunderstanding of some kind; and it will be the ruin of us.

The Refusal

Our little town does not lie on the frontier, nowhere near; it is so far from the frontier, in fact, that perhaps no one from our town has ever been there; desolate highlands have to be crossed as well as wide fertile plains. To imagine even part of the road makes one tired, and more than part one just cannot imagine. There are also big towns on the road, each far larger than ours. Ten little towns like ours laid side by side, and ten more forced down from above, still would not produce one of these enormous, overcrowded towns. If one does not get lost on the way one is bound to lose oneself in these towns, and to avoid them is impossible on account of their size.

But what is even further from our town than the frontier, if such distances can be compared at all – it's like saying that a man of three hundred years is older than one of two hundred – what is even further than the frontier is the capital. Whereas we do get news of the frontier wars now and again, of the capital we learn next to nothing – we civilians that is, for of course the government officials have very good connections with the capital; they can get news from there in as little as three months, so they claim at least.

Now it is remarkable, and it continually surprises me afresh, how we in our town humbly submit to all orders issued in the capital. For centuries no political change has been brought about by the citizens themselves. In the capital great rulers have superseded one another – indeed, even dynasties have been deposed or annihilated, and new ones have started; in the past century even the capital itself was destroyed, a new one was founded far away from it, later on this too was destroyed and the old one rebuilt, yet none of this had any influence on our little town. Our officials have always remained at their posts; the highest officials came from the capital, the less high came at least from outside, and the lowest from among ourselves – that is how it has always been and it has suited us. The highest official is the chief tax-collector, he has the rank of colonel, and is known as such. The present one is an old man; I've known him for years, because he was already a colonel when I was a child. At first he rose very fast in his career, but then he seems to have advanced no further; actually, for our little town his rank is good enough, a higher rank would be out of place. When I try to recall him I see him sitting on the veranda of his house in the market square, leaning back, pipe in mouth. Above him from the roof flutters the imperial flag; on the sides of the veranda, which is so big that minor military manoeuvres are sometimes held there, washing hangs out to dry. His grandchildren, in beautiful silk clothes, play around him; they are not allowed down in the market square, the children there are considered unworthy of them, but the grandchildren are attracted by the square, so they thrust their heads between the posts of the banister and when the children below begin to quarrel they join in the quarrel from above.

This colonel, then, commands the town. I don't think he has ever produced a document entitling him to this position; very likely he does not possess such a thing. Maybe he really is chief tax-collector, but is that all? Does that entitle him to rule over all the other departments in the administration as well? True, his office is very important for the government, but for the citizens it is hardly the most important. One is almost under the impression that the people here say: 'Now that you've taken all we possess, please take us as well.' In reality, of course, it was not he who seized power, nor is he a tyrant. It has just come about over the years that the chief tax-collector is automatically the top official, and the colonel accepts the tradition just as we do.

Yet while he lives among us without laying too much stress on his official position, he is something quite different from the ordinary citizen. When a delegation comes to him with a request, he stands there like the wall of the world. Behind him is nothingness, one imagines hearing voices whispering in the background, but this is probably a delusion; after all, he represents the end of all things, at least for us. At these receptions he really was worth seeing. Once as a child I was present when a delegation of citizens arrived to ask him for a government subsidy because the poorest quarter of the town had been burned to the ground. My father, the blacksmith, a man well respected in the community, was a member of the delegation and had taken me along. There's nothing exceptional about this, everyone rushes to spectacles of this kind, one can hardly distinguish the actual delegation from the crowd. Since these receptions usually take place on the veranda, there are even people who climb up by ladder from the market square and take part in the goings-on from over the banister. On this occasion about a quarter of the veranda had been reserved for the colonel, the crowd filling the rest of it. A few soldiers kept watch, some of them standing around him in a semicircle. Actually a single soldier would have been quite enough, such is our fear of them. I don't know exactly where these soldiers come from, in any case from a long way off, they all look very much alike, they wouldn't even need a uniform. They are small, not strong but agile people, the most striking thing about them is the prominence of their teeth which almost overcrowd their mouths, and a certain restless twitching of their small narrow eyes. This makes them the terror of the children, but also their delight, for again and again the children long to be frightened by these teeth, these eyes, so as to be able to run away in horror. Even grown-ups probably never quite lose this childish terror, at least it continues to have an effect. There are, of course, other factors contributing to it. The soldiers speak a dialect utterly incomprehensible to us, and they can hardly get used to ours – all of which produces a certain shut-off, unapproachable quality corresponding, as it happens, to their character, for they are silent, serious, and rigid. They don't actually do anything evil, and yet they are almost unbearable in an evil sense. A soldier, for example, enters a shop, buys some trifling object, and stays there leaning against the counter; he listens to the conversations, probably does not understand them, and yet gives the impression of understanding; he himself does not say a word, just stares blankly at the speaker, then back at the listeners, all the while keeping his hand on the hilt of the long knife in his belt. This is revolting, one loses the desire to talk, the customers start leaving the shop, and only when it is quite empty does the soldier also leave. Thus wherever the soldiers appear, our lively people grow silent. That's what happened this time, too. As on all solemn occasions the colonel stood upright, holding in front of him two poles of bamboo in his outstretched hands. This is an ancient custom implying more or less that he supports the law, and the law supports him. Now everyone knows, of course, what to expect up on the veranda, and yet each time people take fright all over again. On this occasion, too, the man chosen to speak could not begin; he was already standing opposite the colonel when his courage failed him and, muttering a few excuses, he pushed his way back into the crowd. No other suitable person willing to speak could be found, albeit several unsuitable ones offered themselves; a great commotion ensued and messengers were sent in search of various citizens who were well-known speakers. During all this time the colonel stood there motionless, only his chest moving visibly up and down to his breathing. Not that he breathed with difficulty, it was just that he breathed so conspicuously, much as frogs breathe – except that with them it is normal, while here it was exceptional. I squeezed myself through the grown-ups and watched him through a gap between two soldiers, until one of them kicked me away with his knee. Meanwhile the man originally chosen to speak had regained his composure and, firmly held up by two fellow citizens, was delivering his address. It was touching to see him smile throughout this solemn speech describing a grievous misfortune – a most humble smile which strove in vain to elicit some slight reaction on the colonel's face. Finally he formulated the request – I think he was only asking for a year's tax exemption, but possibly also for timber from the imperial forests at a reduced price. Then he bowed low, remaining in this position for some time, as did everyone else except the colonel, the soldiers, and a number of officials in the background. To the child it seemed ridiculous that the people on the ladders should climb down a few rungs so as not to be seen during the decisive pause and now and again peer inquisitively over the floor of the veranda. After this had lasted quite a while an official, a little man, stepped up to the colonel and tried to reach the latter's height by standing on his toes. The colonel, still motionless save for his deep breathing, whispered something in his ear, whereupon the little man clapped his hands and everyone rose. 'The petition has been refused,' he announced. 'You may go.' An undeniable sense of relief passed through the crowd, everyone surged out, hardly a soul paying any special attention to the colonel, who, as it were, had turned once more into a human being like the rest of us. I still caught one last glimpse of him as he wearily let go of the poles, which fell to the ground, then sank into an armchair produced by some officials, and promptly put his pipe in his mouth.

This whole occurrence is not isolated, it's in the general run of things. Indeed, it does happen now and again that minor petitions are granted, but then it invariably looks as though the colonel had done it as a powerful private person on his own responsibility, and it had to be kept all but a secret from the government – not explicitly of course, but that is what it feels like. No doubt in our little town the colonel's eyes, so far as we know, are also the eyes of the government, and yet there is a difference which it is impossible to comprehend completely.

In all important matters, however, the citizens can always count on a refusal. And now the strange fact is that without this refusal one simply cannot get along, yet at the same time these official occasions designed to receive the refusal are by no means a formality. Time after time one goes there full of expectation and in all seriousness and then one returns, if not exactly strengthened or happy, nevertheless not disappointed or tired.

As a matter of fact there is, so far as my observations go, a certain age group that is not content – these are the young people roughly between seventeen and twenty. Quite young fellows, in fact, who are utterly incapable of foreseeing the consequences of even the least significant, far less a revolutionary, idea. And it is among just them that discontent creeps in.

The Test

I am a servant, but there is no work for me. I am timid and don't push myself to the fore, indeed I don't even push myself into line with the others, but that is only one reason for my non-employment, it's even possible that it has nothing to do with my non-employment, in any case the main thing is that I am not called upon to serve, others have been called yet they have not tried harder than I, indeed perhaps they have not even felt the desire to be called, whereas I, at least sometimes feel it very strongly.

So I lie on the pallet in the servants' hall, stare at the beams in the ceiling, fall asleep, wake up, and promptly fall asleep again. Occasionally I walk over to the tavern where they sell a sour beer, occasionally I have even poured away a glass in disgust, but then I go back to it again. I like sitting there because from behind the closed little window, without the possibility of being discovered, I can see across to the windows of our house. Not that one sees very much there, to my knowledge only the windows of the corridors look out on the street, and moreover not even those of the corridors leading to the master apartments. It is also possible that I am mistaken; but someone, without my having asked him, once said so, and the general impression of this house front confirms this. Only rarely are the windows opened, and when this does occur it is done by a servant who may then lean against the balustrade to look down for a while. It follows therefore that these are corridors where he cannot be taken by surprise. As a matter of fact I am not personally acquainted with these servants; those who are permanently employed upstairs sleep elsewhere, not in my room.

Once when I arrived at the tavern, a guest was sitting at my observation post. I did not dare look at him closely and was about to turn around in the doorway and leave. The guest, however, called me over, and it turned out that he too was a servant whom I had once seen somewhere before, but without having spoken to him. 'Why do you want to run away? Sit down and have a drink. I'll pay.' So I sat down. He asked me several things, but I couldn't answer, indeed I didn't even understand his questions. So I said: 'Perhaps you are sorry now that you invited me, so I'd better go,' and I was about to get up. But he stretched his hand out over the table and pressed me down. 'Stay,' he said, 'that was only a test. He who does not answer the questions has passed the test.'

The Village Schoolmaster

Those, and I am one of them, who find even a small ordinary-sized mole disgusting, would probably have died of disgust if they had seen the giant mole that a few years back was observed in the neighbourhood of one of our villages, which achieved a certain transitory celebrity on account of the incident. Today it has long since sunk back into oblivion again, and in that only shares the obscurity of the whole incident, which has remained quite inexplicable, but which people, it must be confessed, have also taken no great pains to explain; and as a result of an incomprehensible apathy in those very circles that should have concerned themselves with it, and who in fact have shown enthusiastic interest in far more trifling matters, the affair has been forgotten without ever being adequately investigated. In any case, the fact that the village could not be reached by the railroad was no excuse. Many people came from great distances out of pure curiosity, there were even foreigners among them; it was only those who should have shown something more than curiosity that refrained from coming. In fact, if a few quite simple people, people whose daily work gave them hardly a moment of leisure – if these people had not quite disinterestedly taken up the affair, the rumour of this natural phenomenon would probably have never spread beyond the locality. Indeed, rumour itself, which usually cannot be held within bounds, was actually sluggish in this case; if it had not literally been given a shove it would not have spread. But even that was no valid reason for refusing to inquire into the affair; on the contrary this second phenomenon should have been investigated as well. Instead the old village schoolmaster was left to give the sole written account in black and white of the incident, and though he was an excellent man in his own profession, neither his abilities nor his training equipped him to produce an exhaustive description that could be used as a foundation by others, far less, therefore, an actual explanation of the occurrence. His little pamphlet was printed, and a good many copies were sold to visitors to the village about that time; it also received some public recognition, but the teacher was wise enough to perceive that his fragmentary labours, in which no one supported him, were basically without value. If in spite of that he did not relax in them, and made the question his lifework, though it naturally became more hopeless from year to year, that only shows on the one hand how powerful an effect the appearance of the giant mole was capable of producing, and on the other how much stamina and fidelity to his convictions may be found in an old and obscure village schoolmaster. But that he suffered deeply from the cold attitude of the recognized authorities is proved by a brief brochure with which he followed up his pamphlet several years later, by which time hardly anyone could remember what it was all about. In this brochure he complained of the lack of understanding that he had encountered in people where it was least to be expected; complaints that carried conviction less by the skill with which they were expressed than by their honesty. Of such people he said very appositely: 'It is not I, but they, who talk like old village schoolmasters.' And among other things he adduced the pronouncement of a scholar to whom he had gone expressly about his affair. The name of the scholar was not mentioned, but from various circumstances we could guess who it was. When the teacher had managed with great difficulty to secure admittance, after announcing himself for weeks on end, he perceived at once from the very way in which he was greeted that the savant had already acquired a rooted prejudice against the matter. The absent-mindedness with which he listened to the long report which the teacher, pamphlet in hand, delivered to him, can be gauged from a remark that he let fall after a pause for ostensible reflection: 'The soil in your neighbourhood is particularly black and rich. Consequently it provides the moles with particularly rich nourishment, and so they grow to an unusual size.'

'But not to such a size as that!' exclaimed the teacher, and he measured off two yards on the wall, somewhat exaggerating the length of the mole in exasperation. 'Oh, and why not?' replied the scholar, who obviously looked upon the whole affair as a great joke. With this verdict the teacher had to return to his home. He tells how his wife and six children were waiting for him by the roadside in the snow, and how he had to admit to them the final collapse of his hopes.

When I read of the scholar's attitude toward the old man I was not yet acquainted with the teacher's pamphlet. But I at once resolved myself to collect and correlate all the information I could discover regarding the case. If I could not employ physical force against the scholar, I could at least write a defence of the teacher, or more exactly, of the good intentions of an honest but uninfluential man. I admit that I rued this decision later, for I soon saw that its execution was bound to involve me in a very strange predicament. On the one hand my own influence was far from sufficient to effect a change in learned or even public opinion in the teacher's favour, while on the other the teacher was bound to notice that I was less concerned with his main object, which was to prove that the giant mole had actually been seen, than to defend his honesty, which must naturally be self-evident to him and in need of no defence. Accordingly, what was bound to happen was this: I would be misunderstood by the teacher, though I wanted to collaborate with him, and instead of helping him I myself would probably require support, which was most unlikely to appear. Besides, my decision would impose a great burden of work upon me. If I wanted to convince people I could not invoke the teacher, since he himself had not been able to convince them. To read his pamphlet could only have led me astray, and so I refrained from reading it until I should have finished my own labours. More, I did not even get in touch with the teacher. True, he heard of my inquiries through intermediaries, but he did not know whether I was working for him or against him. In fact he probably assumed the latter, though he denied it later on; for I have proof of the fact that he put various obstacles in my way. It was quite easy for him to do that, for of course I was compelled to undertake anew all the inquiries he had already made, and so he could always steal a march on me. But that was the only objection that could be justly made to my method, an unavoidable reproach, but one that was palliated by the caution and self-abnegation with which I drew my conclusions. But for the rest my pamphlet was quite uninfluenced by the teacher, perhaps on this point, indeed, I showed all too great a scrupulosity; from my words one might have thought nobody had ever inquired into the case before, and I was the first to interrogate those who had seen or heard of the mole, the first to correlate the evidence, the first to draw conclusions. When later I read the schoolmaster's pamphlet – it had a very circumstantial title: 'A mole, larger in size than ever seen before' – I found that we actually did not agree on certain important points, though we both believed we had proved our main point, namely, the existence of the mole. These differences prevented the establishment of the friendly relations with the schoolmaster that

I had been looking forward to in spite of everything. On his side there developed a feeling almost of hostility. True, he was always modest and humble in his bearing toward me, but that only made his real feelings the more obvious. In other words, he was of the opinion that I had thoroughly damaged both him and his cause, and that my belief that I had been or could be of assistance to him was simplicity at best, but more likely presumption or artifice. He was particularly fond of saying that all his previous enemies had shown their hostility either not at all, or in private, or at most by word of mouth, while I had considered it necessary to have my censures straightway published. Moreover, the few opponents of his who had really occupied themselves with the subject, if but superficially, had at least listened to his, the schoolmaster's, views before they had given expression to their own: while I, on the strength of unsystematically assembled and in part misunderstood evidence, had published conclusions which, even if they were correct as regarded the main point, must evoke incredulity, and among the public no less than the educated. But the faintest hint that the existence of the mole was unworthy of credence was the worst thing that could happen in this case. To these reproaches, veiled as they were, I could easily have found an answer – for instance, that his own pamphlet achieved the very summit of the incredible – it was less easy, however, to make headway against his continual suspicion, and that was the reason why I was very reserved in my dealings with him. For in his heart he was convinced that I wanted to rob him of the fame of being the first man publicly to vindicate the mole.

Now of course he really enjoyed no fame whatever, but only an absurd notoriety that was shrinking more and more, and for which I had certainly no desire to compete. Besides, in the foreword to my pamphlet I had expressly declared that the teacher must stand for all time as the discoverer of the mole – and he was not even that – and that only my sympathy with his unfortunate fate had spurred me on to write. 'It is the aim of this pamphlet' – so I ended up all too melodramatically, but it corresponded with my feelings at that time – 'to help in giving the schoolmaster's book the wide publicity it deserves. If I succeed in that, then may my name, which I regard as only transiently and indirectly associated with this question, be blotted from it at once.' Thus I disclaimed expressly any major participation in the affair; it was almost as if I had foreseen in some manner the teacher's unbelievable reproaches. Nevertheless he found in that very passage a handle against me, and I do not deny that there was a faint show of justice in what he said or rather hinted; indeed I was often struck by the fact that he showed almost a keener penetration where I was concerned than he had done in his pamphlet. For he maintained that my foreword was double-faced. If I was really concerned solely to give publicity to his pamphlet, why had I not occupied myself exclusively with him and his pamphlet, why had I not pointed out its virtues, its irrefutability, why had I not confined myself to insisting on the significance of the discovery and making that clear, why had I instead tackled the discovery itself, while completely ignoring the pamphlet? Had not the discovery been made already? Was there still anything left to be done in that direction? But if I really thought that it was necessary for me to make the discovery all over again, why had I disassociated myself from the discovery so solemnly in my foreword? One might put that down to false modesty, but it was something worse. I was trying to belittle the discovery, I was drawing attention to it merely for the purpose of depreciating it; I had inquired into it only to lay it aside; the affair had perhaps quietened down somewhat, and now I was making a noise about it again, but at the same time making the schoolmaster's position more difficult than ever. What did he care whether his honesty was vindicated or not? All that he was concerned with was the thing itself, and with that alone. But I was only of disservice to it, for I did not understand it, I did not prize it at its true value, I had no real feeling for it. It was infinitely above my intellectual capacity. He sat before me and looked at me, his old wrinkled face quite composed, and yet this was what he was thinking. Yet it was not true that he was only concerned with the thing itself: actually he was very greedy for fame, and wanted to make money out of the business too, which, however, considering his large family, was very understandable. Nevertheless my interest in the affair seemed so trivial compared with his own, that he felt he could claim to be completely disinterested without deviating very seriously from the truth. And indeed my inner doubts refused to be quite calmed by my telling myself that the man's reproaches were really due to the fact that he clung to his mole, so to speak, with both hands, and was bound to look upon anyone who laid even a finger on it as a traitor. For that was not true; his attitude was not to be explained by greed, or at any rate by greed alone, but rather by the touchiness which his great labours and their complete unsuccess had bred in him. Yet even his touchiness did not explain everything. Perhaps my interest in the affair was really too trivial. The schoolmaster was used to lack of interest in strangers. He regarded it as a universal evil, but no longer suffered from its individual manifestations. Now a man had appeared who, strangely enough, took up the affair; and even he did not understand it. Attacked from this side I can make no defence. I am no zoologist; yet perhaps I would have thrown myself into the case with my whole heart if I had discovered it; but I had not discovered it. Such a gigantic mole is certainly a prodigy, yet one cannot expect the continuous and undivided attention of the whole world to be accorded it, particularly if its existence is not completely and irrefutably established, and in any case it cannot be produced. And I admit too that even if I had been the discoverer I would probably never have come forward so gladly and voluntarily in defence of the mole as I had in that of the schoolmaster.

Now the misunderstanding between me and the schoolmaster would probably have quickly cleared up if my pamphlet had achieved success. But success was not forthcoming. Perhaps the book was not well enough written, not persuasive enough; I am a businessman, it may be that the composition of such a pamphlet was still further beyond my limited powers than those of the teacher, though in the kind of knowledge required I was greatly superior to him. Besides, my unsuccess may be explicable in other ways; the time at which the pamphlet appeared may have been inauspicious. The discovery of the mole, which had failed to penetrate to a wide public at the time it took place, was not so long past on the one hand as to be completely forgotten, and thus capable of being brought alive again by my pamphlet, while on the other hand enough time had elapsed quite to exhaust the trivial interest that had originally existed. Those who took my pamphlet at all seriously told themselves, in that bored tone which from the first had characterized the debate, that now the old useless labours on this wearisome question were to begin all over again; and some even confused my pamphlet with the schoolmaster's. In a leading agricultural journal appeared the following comment, fortunately at the very end, and in small print: 'The pamphlet on the giant mole has once more been sent to us. Years ago we remember having had a hearty laugh over it. Since then it has not become more intelligible, nor we more hard of understanding. But we simply refuse to laugh at it a second time. Instead, we would ask our teaching associations whether more useful work cannot be found for our village schoolmasters than hunting out giant moles.' An unpardonable confusion of identity. They had read neither the first nor the second pamphlet, and the two perfunctorily scanned expressions, 'giant mole' and 'village schoolmaster,' were sufficient for these gentlemen, as representatives of publicly esteemed interest, to pronounce on the subject. Against this attack measures might have been attempted and with success, but the lack of understanding between the teacher and myself kept me from venturing upon them. I tried instead to keep the review from his knowledge as long as I could. But he very soon discovered it, as I recognized from a sentence in one of his letters, in which he announced his intention of visiting me for the Christmas holidays. He wrote: 'The world is full of malice, and people smooth the path for it,' by which he wished to convey that I was one of the malicious, but, not content with my own innate malice, wished also to make the world's path smooth for it: in other words, was acting in such a way as to arouse the general malice and help it to victory. Well, I summoned the resolution I required, and was able to await him calmly, and calmly greet him when he arrived, this time a shade less polite in his bearing than usual; he carefully drew out the journal from the breast pocket of his old-fashioned padded overcoat, and opening it handed it to me. 'I've seen it,' I replied, handing the journal back unread. 'You've seen it,' he said with a sigh; he had the old teacher's habit of repeating the other person's answers. 'Of course I won't take this lying down!' he went on, tapping the journal excitedly with his finger and glancing up sharply at me, as if I were of a different mind; he certainly had some idea of what I was about to say, for I think I have noticed, not so much from his words as from other indications, that he often has a genuine intuition of my intentions, though he never yields to them but lets himself be diverted. What I said to him I can set down almost word for word, for I made a note of it shortly after our interview. 'Do what you like,' I said, 'our ways part from this moment. I fancy that that is neither unexpected nor unwelcome news to you. The review in this journal is not the real reason for my decision; it has merely finally confirmed it. The real reason is this: originally I thought my intervention might be of some use to you, while now I cannot but recognize that I have damaged you in every direction. Why it has turned out so I cannot say; the causes of success and unsuccess are always ambiguous; but don't look for the sole explanation in my shortcomings. Consider: you too had the best intentions, and yet, if one regards the matter objectively, you failed. I don't intend it as a joke, for it would be a joke against myself, when I say that your connection with me must unfortunately be counted among your failures. It is neither cowardice nor treachery, if I withdraw from the affair now. Actually it involves a certain degree of self-renunciation; my pamphlet itself proves how much I respect you personally, in a certain sense you have become my teacher, and I have almost grown fond of the mole itself. Nevertheless I have decided to step aside; you are the discoverer, and all that I can do is to prevent you from gaining possible fame, while I attract failure and pass it on to you. At least that is your own opinion. Enough of that. The sole expiation that I can make is to beg your forgiveness and, should you require it, to publish openly, that is, in this journal, the admission I have just made to you.'

These were my words; they were not entirely sincere, but what was sincere in them was obvious enough. My explanation had the effect upon him that I had roughly anticipated. Most old people have something deceitful, something mendacious, in their dealings with people younger than themselves; you live at peace with them, imagine you are on the best of terms with them, know their ruling prejudices, receive continual assurances of amity, take the whole thing for granted; and when something decisive happens and those peaceful relations, so long nourished, should come into effective operation, suddenly these old people rise before you like strangers, show that they have deeper and stronger convictions, and now for the first time literally unfurl their banner, and with terror you read upon it the new decree. The reason for this terror lies chiefly in the fact that what the old say now is really far more just and sensible than what they had said before; it is as if even the self-evident had degrees of validity, and their words now were more self-evident than ever. But the final deceit lies in the fact that what they are saying now is basically what they have always said, and yet that it was never possible to see it coming. I must have probed deeply into the schoolmaster, seeing that his next words did not entirely take me by surprise. 'Child,' he said, laying his hand on mine and patting it gently, 'how did you ever take it into your head to go into this affair? The very first I heard of it I talked it over with my wife.' He pushed his chair back from the table, got up, spread out his arms, and stared at the floor, as if his tiny little wife were standing there and he were speaking to her. '"We've struggled on alone," I said to her, "for many years; now, it seems, a noble protector has risen for us in the city, a fine businessman, Mr So-and-so. We should congratulate ourselves, shouldn't we? A businessman in the city isn't to be sniffed at; when an ignorant peasant believes us and says so it doesn't help us, for what a peasant may say or do is of no account; whether he says the old village schoolmaster is right, or spits to show his contempt, the net result is the same. And if instead of one peasant ten thousand should stand up for us, the result, if possible, would only be still worse. A businessman in the city, on the other hand, that's something else again; a man like that has connections, things he says in passing, as it were, are taken up and repeated, new patrons interest themselves in the question, one of them, it may be, remarks: You can learn even from old village schoolmasters, and next day whole crowds of people are saying it to one another, people you would never imagine saying such things, to look at them. Next, money is found to finance the business, one gentleman goes around collecting for it and the others shower subscriptions on him; they decide that the village schoolmaster must be dragged from his obscurity; they arrive, they don't bother about his external appearance, but take him to their bosoms, and since his wife and children hang onto him, they are taken along too. Have you ever watched city people? They chatter without stopping. When there's a whole lot of them together you can hear their chatter running from right to left and back again, and up and down, this way and that. And so, chattering away, they push us into the coach, so that we've hardly time to bow to everybody. The gentleman on the coachman's seat puts his glasses straight, flourishes his whip, and off we go. They all wave a parting greeting to the village, as if we were still there and not sitting among them. The more impatient city people drive out in carriages to meet us. As we approach they get up from their seats and crane their necks. The gentleman who collected the money arranges everything methodically and in order. When we drive into the city we are a long procession of carriages. We think the public welcome is over; but it really only begins when we reach our hotel. In a city an announcement attracts a great many people. What interests one interests all the rest immediately. They take their views from one another and promptly make those views their own. All the people who haven't managed to drive out and meet us in carriages are waiting in front of the hotel; others could have driven out, but they were too self-conscious. They're waiting too. It's extraordinary, the way that the gentleman who collected the money keeps his eye on everything and directs everything.'"

I had listened coolly to him, indeed I had grown cooler and cooler while he went on. On the table I had piled up all the copies of my pamphlet in my possession. Only a few were missing, for during the past week I had sent out a circular demanding the return of all the copies distributed, and had received most of them back. True, from several quarters I had got very polite notes saying that So-and-so could not remember having received such a pamphlet, and that, if it had actually arrived, he was sorry to confess that he must have lost it. Even that was gratifying; in my heart I desired nothing better. Only one reader begged me to let him keep the pamphlet as a curiosity, pledging himself, in accordance with the spirit of my circular, to show it to no one for twenty years. The village teacher had not yet seen my circular. I was glad that his words made it so easy for me to show it to him. I could do that without anxiety in any case, however, as I had drawn it up very circumspectly, keeping his interests in mind the whole time. The crucial passage in the circular ran as follows: 'I do not ask for the return of the pamphlet because I retract in any way the opinions defended there or wish them to be regarded as erroneous or even undemonstrable on any point. My request has purely personal and moreover very urgent grounds; but no conclusion whatever must be drawn from it as regards my attitude to the whole matter. I beg to draw your particular attention to this, and would be glad also if you would make the fact better known.'

For the time being I kept my hand over the circular and said: 'You reproach me in your heart because things have not turned out as you hoped. Why do that? Don't let us embitter our last moments together. And do try to see that, though you've made a discovery, it isn't necessarily greater than every other discovery, and consequently the injustice you suffer under any greater than other injustices. I don't know the ways of learned societies, but I can't believe that in the most favourable circumstances you would have been given a reception even remotely resembling the one you seem to have described to your wife. While I myself still hoped that something might come of my pamphlet, the most I expected was that perhaps the attention of a professor might be drawn to our case, that he might commission some young student to inquire into it, that this student might visit you and check in his own fashion your and my inquiries once more on the spot, and that finally, if the results seemed to him worth consideration – we must not forget that all young students are full of scepticism – he might bring out a pamphlet of his own in which your discoveries would be put on a scientific basis. All the same, even if that hope had been realized nothing very much would have been achieved. The student's pamphlet, supporting such queer opinions, would probably be held up to ridicule. If you take this agricultural journal as a sample, you can see how easily that may happen; and scientific periodicals are still more ruthless in such matters. And that's quite understandable; pro-fessors bear a great responsibility toward themselves, toward science, toward posterity; they can't take every new discovery to their bosoms straight away. We others have the advantage of them there. But I'll leave that out of account and assume that the student's pamphlet has found acceptance. What would happen next? You would probably receive honourable mention, and that might perhaps benefit your profession too; people would say: "Our village schoolmasters have sharp eyes"; and this journal, if journals have a memory or a conscience, would be forced to make you a public apology; also some well-intentioned professor would be found to secure a scholarship for you; it's possible they might even get you to come to the city, find a post for you in some school, and so give you a chance of using the scientific resources of a city so as to improve yourself. But if I am to be quite frank, I think they would content themselves with merely trying to do all this. They would summon you and you would appear, but only as an ordinary petitioner like hundreds of others, and not in solemn state; they would talk to you and praise your honest efforts, but they would see at the same time that you were an old man, that it was hopeless for anyone to begin to study science at such an age, and moreover that you had hit upon your discovery more by chance than by design, and had besides no ambition to extend your labours beyond this one case. For these reasons they would probably send you back to your village again. Your discovery, of course, would be carried further, for it is not so trifling that, once having achieved recognition, it could be forgotten again. But you would not hear much more about it, and what you heard you would scarcely understand. Every new discovery is assumed at once into the sum total of knowledge, and with that ceases in a sense to be a discovery;

it dissolves into the whole and disappears, and one must have a trained scientific eye even to recognize it after that. For it is related to fundamental axioms of whose existence we don't even know, and in the debates of science it is raised on these axioms into the very clouds. How can we expect to understand such things? Often as we listen to a discussion of this kind we may be under the impression that it is about your discovery, when it is about something quite different, and the next time, when we think it is about something else, and not about your discovery at all, it may turn out to be about that and that alone.'

'Well and good,' said the teacher, taking out his pipe and beginning to fill it with the tobacco that he carried loose in all his pockets. 'You took up this thankless business of your own free will, and now of your own free will you withdraw. It's all quite in order.'

'I'm not an obstinate man,' I said. 'Do you find anything to object to in my proposal?'

'No, absolutely nothing,' said the schoolmaster, and his pipe was already going. I could not bear the stink of his tobacco, and so I rose and began to walk up and down the room. From previous encounters I was used to the teacher's extreme taciturnity, and to the fact that in spite of it he never seemed to have any desire to stir from my room once he was in it. That had often disturbed me before. He wants something more, I always thought at such times, and I would offer him money, which indeed he invariably accepted. Yet he never went away before it suited his convenience. Generally his pipe was smoked out by that time, then he would ceremoniously and respectfully push his chair in to the table, make a detour around it, seize his walking stick from the corner, press my hand warmly, and go. But today his silent presence as he sat there was positively irksome. When one has bidden a last farewell to someone, as I had done, and he has declared this to be quite in order, surely the mutual formalities that remain should be got over as quickly as possible and one should not burden one's host purposelessly with one's silent presence. As I contemplated the stubborn little fellow from behind, while he sat at the table, it seemed an impossible idea to ever show him the door. His long stiff overcoat, which he never took off, stuck out around him in sharp folds, making him into a broad and massive form.

The Burrow

I have completed the construction of my burrow and it seems
to be successful. All that can be seen from outside is a big hole;
that, however, really leads nowhere; if you take a few steps you
strike against natural firm rock. I can make no boast of having
contrived this ruse intentionally; it is simply the remains of one
of my many abortive building attempts, but finally it seemed to
me advisable to leave this one hole without filling it in. True,
some ruses are so subtle that they defeat themselves, I know that
better than anyone, and it is certainly a risk to draw attention by
this hole to the fact that there may be something in the vicinity
worth inquiring into. But you do not know me if you think I
am afraid, or that I built my burrow simply out of fear. At a
distance of some thousand paces from this hole lies, covered by
a movable layer of moss, the real entrance to the burrow; it is
secured as safely as anything in this world can be secured; yet
someone could step on the moss or break through it, and then
my burrow would lie open, and anybody who liked – please

note, however, that certain fairly uncommon abilities would also be required – could make his way in and destroy everything for good. I know that very well, and even now, at the zenith of my life, I can scarcely pass an hour in complete tranquillity; at that one point in the dark moss I am vulnerable, and in my dreams I often see a greedy muzzle sniffing around it persistently. It will be objected that I could quite well have filled in this proper entrance too, with a thin layer of hard earth on top and with loose soil further down, so that it would not cost me much trouble to dig my way out again whenever I liked. But that plan is impossible; prudence itself demands that I should have a way of leaving at a moment's notice if necessary, prudence itself demands, as alas! so often, that one should risk one's life. All this involves very laborious calculation, and the sheer pleasure of the mind in its own keenness is often the sole reason why one keeps it up. I must have a way of leaving at a moment's notice, for, despite all my vigilance, may I not be attacked from some quite unexpected quarter? I live in peace in the inmost chamber of my burrow, and meanwhile the enemy may be boring his way slowly and stealthily towards me. I do not say that he has a better scent than I; probably he knows as little about me as I of him; but there are insatiable robbers who burrow blindly through the ground, and to whom the very size of my house gives the hope of hitting by chance on some of its far-flung passages. I certainly have the advantage of being in my own house and knowing all the passages and how they run; a robber may very easily become my victim and a succulent one too; but I am growing old; I am not as strong as many others, and my enemies are countless; it could well happen that in flying from one enemy I might run into the jaws of another. What might not happen, indeed, but in any case I must have the reassurance that somewhere there is an exit easy to reach and quite free, where I have to do nothing whatever to get out, lest while I am desperately burrowing away, even if it is at loose easy soil, I might suddenly – Heaven protect me! – feel the teeth of the pursuer in my flank. And it is not only by external enemies that I am threatened; there are also enemies in the bowels of the earth. I have never seen them, but legend tells of them and I firmly believe in them. They are creatures of the inner earth; not even legend can describe them; their very victims can scarcely have seen them; they come, you hear the scratching of their claws just under you in the ground, which is their element, and already you are lost. Here it is of no avail to console yourself with the thought that you are in your own house; far rather are you in theirs. Not even my exit could save me from them; indeed in all probability it would not save me in any case, but rather betray me; yet it is a hope, and I cannot live without it. Apart from this main exit I am also connected with the outer world by quite narrow, tolerably safe passages which provide me with good fresh air to breathe; they are the work of the field mice, I have made judicious use of them, transform-ing them into an organic part of my burrow; they also give me the possibility of scenting things from afar, and thus serve as a protection; all sorts of small fry, too, come running through them, and I devour these; so I can have a certain amount of subterranean hunting, sufficient for a modest way of life, without leaving my burrow at all; and that is naturally a great advantage.

But the most beautiful thing about my burrow is the stillness. Of course, this is deceptive. At any moment it may be shattered and all will be over. But for the present the silence is still there, for hours I can stroll through my passages and hear nothing except the rustling of some little creature, which I immediately reduce to silence between my jaws, or the pattering of soil, which draws my attention to the need for repair; otherwise all is still. The fragrance of the woods floats in, the place feels both warm and cool, sometimes I lie down and roll about in the passage with pure joy. It is good to have a burrow like mine for the approach of old age, to have settled oneself under cover as autumn sets in. Every hundred yards or so I have widened the passages into little round cells; there I can curl myself up in comfort and lie warm. There I sleep the sweet sleep of tranquillity, of satisfied desire, of achieved ambition; for I possess a house. I do not know whether it is a habit that still persists from former days, or whether the perils even of this house of mine are great enough to awaken me; but invariably every now and then I start up out of profound sleep and listen, listen into the stillness which reigns here unchanged day and night, smile contentedly, and then sink with loosened limbs into still profounder sleep. Poor homeless wanderers in the roads and woods, creeping for warmth into a heap of leaves or a herd of their comrades, delivered to all the perils of heaven and earth! I lie here in a room secured on every side – there are more than fifty such rooms in my burrow – and pass as much of my time as I choose between dozing and unconscious sleep.

Not quite in the centre of the burrow, carefully chosen to serve as a refuge in case of extreme danger from siege if not from immediate pursuit, lies the chief cell. While all the rest of the burrow is the outcome rather of intense intellectual than of physical labour, this Castle Keep was fashioned by the most arduous labour of my whole body. Several times, in the despair brought on by physical exhaustion, I was on the point of giving up the whole business, rolled about on my back and cursed the burrow, dragged myself outside and left the place lying open to all the world. I could afford to do that, for I had no longer any wish to return to it, until at last, after four hours or days, back I went repentantly, and when I saw that the burrow was unharmed I could almost have raised a hymn of thanksgiving, and in sincere gladness of heart started on the work anew. My labours on the Castle Keep were also made harder, and unnecessarily so (unnecessarily in that the burrow derived no real benefit from the additional work), by the fact that just at the place where, according to my calculations, the Castle Keep should be, the soil was very loose and sandy and had literally to be hammered and pounded into a firm state to serve as a wall for the rounded and beautifully vaulted chamber. But for such tasks the only tool I possess is my forehead. So I had to run with my forehead thousands and thousands of times, for whole days and nights, against the earth, and I was glad when the blood came, for that was a proof that the walls were beginning to harden; and in that way, as will perhaps be granted, I richly paid for my Castle Keep.

In the Castle Keep I assemble my stores; everything over and above my daily wants that I capture inside the burrow, and everything I bring back with me from my hunting expeditions outside, I pile up here. The place is so spacious that food for half a year scarcely fills it. Consequently I can spread my stores out well, walk about among them, play with them, enjoy their plenty and their various smells, and reckon up exactly how much they represent. I can thus always undertake rearrangements, and make my calculations and hunting plans for the future, taking into account the season of the year. There are times when I am so well provided for that in my indifference to food I never even touch the smaller fry that scuttle about the burrow, which, however, is probably imprudent of me. My constant preoccupation with defensive measures involves a frequent alteration or modification, though within narrow limits, of my views on how the building can best be organized for that end. Then it sometimes seems risky to make the Castle Keep the basis of defence; the ramifications of the burrow present me with manifold possibilities, and it seems more in accordance with prudence to divide up my stores somewhat, and put part of them in certain of the smaller rooms; thereupon I mark off every third room, let us say, as a reserve storeroom, or every fourth room as a main and every second as an auxiliary storeroom, and so forth. Or I ignore certain passages altogether and store no food in them, so as to throw any enemy off the scent, or I choose quite at random a very few rooms according to their distance from the main exit. Each of these new plans involves of course heavy work; I have to make my calculations and then carry my stores to their new places. True, I can do that at my leisure and without any hurry, and it is not at all unpleasant to carry such good food in your jaws, to lie down and rest whenever you like, and to nibble an occasional tasty titbit. But it is not so pleasant when, as sometimes happens, you suddenly fancy, starting up from your sleep, that the present distribution of your stores is completely and totally wrong, might lead to great dangers, and must be set right at once, no matter how tired or sleepy you may be; then I rush, then I fly, then I have no time for calculation; and although I was about to execute a perfectly new, perfectly exact plan, I now seize whatever my teeth hit upon and drag it or carry it away, sighing, groaning, stumbling, and even the most haphazard change in the present situation, which seems so terribly dangerous, can satisfy me. Until little by little full wakefulness sobers me, and I can hardly understand my panic haste, breathe in deeply the tranquillity of my house, which I myself have disturbed, return to my resting place, fall asleep at once in a new-won exhaustion, and on awakening find hanging from my jaws, say, a rat, as indubitable proof of night labours which already seem almost unreal. Then again there are times when the storing of all my food in one place seems the best plan of all. Of what use to me could my stores in the smaller rooms be, how much could I store there in any case? And whatever I put there would block the passage, and be a greater hindrance than help to me if I were pursued and had to fly. Besides, it is stupid but true that one's self-conceit suffers if one cannot see all one's stores together, and so at one glance know how much one possesses. And in dividing up my food in those various ways might not a great deal get lost? I can't be always scouring through all my passages and cross-passages so as to make sure that everything is in order. The idea of dividing up my stores is of course a good one, but only if one had several rooms similar to my Castle Keep. Several such rooms! Indeed! And who is to build them? In any case, they could not be worked into the general plan of my burrow at this late stage. But I will admit that that is a fault in my burrow; it is always a fault to have only one piece of anything. And I confess too that during the whole time I was constructing the burrow a vague idea that I should have more such cells stirred in my mind, vaguely, yet clearly enough if I had only welcomed it; I did not yield to it, I felt too feeble for the enormous labour it would involve, more, I felt too feeble even to admit to myself the necessity for that labour, and comforted myself as best I could with the vague hope that a building which in any other case would clearly be inadequate, would in my own unique, exceptional, favoured case suffice, presumably because providence was interested in the preservation of my forehead, that unique instrument. So I have only one Castle Keep, but my dark premonitions that one would not suffice have faded. However that may be, I must content myself with the one big chamber, the smaller ones are simply no substitute for it, and so, when this conviction has grown on me, I begin once more to haul all my stores back from them to the Castle Keep. For some time afterwards I find a certain comfort in having all the passages and rooms free, in seeing my stores growing in the Castle Keep and emitting their variegated and mingled smells, each of which delights me in its own fashion, and every one of which I can distinguish even at a distance, as far as the very remotest passages. Then I usually enjoy periods of particular tranquillity, in which I change my sleeping place by stages, always working in toward the centre of the burrow, always steeping myself more profoundly in the mingled smells, until at last I can no longer restrain myself and one night rush into the Castle Keep, mightily fling myself upon my stores, and glut myself with the best that I can seize until I am completely gorged. Happy but dangerous hours; anyone who knew how to exploit them could destroy me with ease and without any risk. Here too the absence of a second or third large storeroom works to my detriment; for it is the single huge accumulated mass of food that seduces me. I try to guard myself in various ways against this danger; the distribution of my stores in the smaller rooms is really one of these expedients; but unfortunately, like other such expedients, it leads through renunciation to still greater greed, which, overruling my intelligence, makes me arbitrarily alter my plans of defence to suit its ends.

To regain my composure after such lapses I make a practice of reviewing the burrow, and after the necessary improvements have been carried out, frequently leave it, though only for a short spell. Even at such moments the hardship of being without it for a long time seems too punitive to me, yet I recognize clearly the need for occasional short excursions. It is always with a certain solemnity that I approach the exit again. During my spells of home life I avoid it, steer clear even of the outer windings of the corridor that leads to it; besides, it is no easy job to wander about out there, for I have contrived there a whole little maze of passages; it was there that I began my burrow, at a time when I had no hope of ever completing it according to my plans; I began, half in play, at that corner, and so my first joy in labour found riotous satisfaction there in a labyrinthine burrow which at the time seemed to me the crown of all burrows, but which I judge today, perhaps with more justice, to be too much of an idle *tour de force*, not really worthy of the rest of the burrow, and though perhaps theoretically brilliant – here is my main entrance, I said in those days, ironically addressing my invisible enemies and seeing them all already caught and stifled in the outer labyrinth – is in reality a flimsy piece of jugglery that would hardly withstand a serious attack or the struggles of an enemy fighting for his life. Should I reconstruct this part of my burrow? I keep on postponing the decision, and the labyrinth will probably remain as it is. Apart from the sheer hard work that I should have to face, the task would also be the most dangerous imaginable. When I began the burrow I could work away at it in comparative peace of mind, the risk wasn't much greater than any other risk; but to attempt that today would be to draw the whole world's attention, and gratuitously, to my burrow; today the whole thing is impossible. I am almost glad of that, for I still have a certain sentiment about this first achievement of mine. And if a serious attack were attempted, what pattern of entrance at all would be likely to save me? An entrance can deceive, can lead astray, can give the attacker no end of worry, and the present one too can do that at a pinch. But a really serious attack has to be met by an instantaneous mobilization of all the resources in the burrow and all the forces of my body and soul – that is self-evident. So this entrance can very well remain where it is. The burrow has so many unavoidable defects imposed by natural causes that it can surely stand this one defect for which I am responsible, and which I recognize as a defect, even if only after the event. In spite of that, however, I do not deny that this fault worries me from time to time, indeed always. If on my customary rounds I avoid this part of the burrow, the fundamental reason is that the sight of it is painful to me, because I don't want to be perpetually reminded of a defect in my house, even if that defect is only too disturbingly present in my mind. Let it continue to exist ineradicably at the entrance; I can at least refuse to look at it as long as that is possible. If I merely walk in the direction of the entrance, even though I may be separated from it by several passages and rooms, I find myself sensing an atmosphere of great danger, actually as if my hair were growing thin and in a moment might fly off and leave me bare and shivering, exposed to the howls of my enemies. Yes, the mere thought of the door itself, the end of the domestic protection, brings such feelings with it, yet it is the labyrinth leading up to it that torments me most of all. Sometimes I dream that I have reconstructed it, transformed it completely, quickly, in a night, with a giant's strength, nobody having noticed, and now it is impregnable; the nights in which such dreams come to me are the sweetest I know, tears of joy and deliverance still glisten on my beard when I awaken.

So I must thread the tormenting complications of this labyrinth physically as well as mentally whenever I go out, and I am both exasperated and touched when, as sometimes happens, I lose myself for a moment in my own maze, and the work of my hands seems to be still doing its best to prove its sufficiency to me, its maker, whose final judgment has long since been passed on it. But then I find myself beneath the mossy covering, which has been left untouched for so long – for I stay for long spells in my house – that it has grown fast to the soil around it, and now only a little push with my head is needed and I am in the upper world. For a long time I do not dare to make that little movement, and if it were not that I would have to traverse the labyrinth once more, I would certainly leave the matter for the time being and turn back again. Just think. Your house is protected and self-sufficient. You live in peace, warm, well nourished, master, sole master of all your manifold passages and rooms, and all this you are prepared – not to give up, of course – but to risk it, so to speak; you nurse the confident hope, certainly, that you will regain it; yet is it not a dangerous, a far too dangerous stake that you are playing for? Can there be any reasonable grounds for such a step? No, for such acts as these there can be no reasonable grounds. But all the same, I then cautiously raise the trap door and slip outside, let it softly fall back again, and fly as fast as I can from the treacherous spot.

Yet I am not really free. True, I am no longer confined by narrow passages, but hunt through the open woods, and feel new powers awakening in my body for which there was no room, as it were, in the burrow, not even in the Castle Keep, though it had been ten times as big. The food too is better up here; though hunting is more difficult, success more rare, the results are more valuable from every point of view; I do not deny all this; I appreciate it and take advantage of it at least as fully as anyone else, and probably more fully, for I do not hunt like a vagrant out of mere idleness or desperation, but calmly and methodically. Also I am not permanently doomed to this free life, for I know that my term is measured, that I do not have to hunt here forever, and that, whenever I am weary of this life and wish to leave it, Someone, whose invitation I shall not be able to withstand, will, so to speak, summon me to him. And so I can pass my time here quite without care and in complete enjoyment, or rather I could, and yet I cannot. My burrow takes up too much of my thoughts. I fled from the entrance fast enough, but soon I am back at it again. I seek out a good hiding place and keep watch on the entrance of my house – this time from outside – for whole days and nights. Call it foolish if you like; it gives me infinite pleasure and reassures me. At such times it is as if I were not so much looking at my house as at myself sleeping, and had the joy of being in a profound slumber and simultaneously of keeping vigilant guard over myself. I am privileged, as it were, not only to dream about the spectres of the night in all the helplessness and blind trust of sleep, but also at the same time to confront them in actuality with the calm judgment of the fully awake. And strangely enough I discover that my situation is not so bad as I had often thought, and will probably think again when I return to my house. In this connection – it may be in others too, but in this one especially – these excursions of mine are truly indispensable. Carefully as I have chosen an out-of-the-way place for my door, the traffic that passes it is nevertheless, if one takes a week's observation, very great; but so it is, no doubt, in all inhabited regions, and probably it is actually better to hazard the risks of dense traffic, whose very impetus carries it past, than to be delivered in complete solitude to the first persistently searching intruder. Here enemies are numerous and their allies and accomplices still more numerous, but they fight one another, and while thus employed rush past my burrow without noticing it. In all my time I have never seen anyone investigating the actual door of my house, which is fortunate both for me and for him, for I would certainly have launched myself at his throat, forgetting everything else in my anxiety for the burrow. True, creatures come, in whose vicinity I dare not remain, and from whom I have to fly as soon as I scent them in the distance; on their attitude to the burrow I really can't pronounce with certainty, but it is at least a re-assurance that when I presently return I never find any of them there, and the entrance is undamaged. There have been happy periods in which I could almost assure myself that the enmity of the world toward me had ceased or been assuaged, or that the strength of the burrow had raised me above the destructive struggle of former times. The burrow has probably protected me in more ways than I thought or dared think while I was inside it. This fancy used to have such a hold over me that sometimes I have been seized by the childish desire never to return to the burrow again, but to settle down somewhere close to the entrance, to pass my life watching the entrance, and gloat perpetually upon the reflection – and in that find my happiness – how steadfast a protection my burrow would be if I were inside it. Well, one is soon roughly awakened from childish dreams. What does this protection which I am looking at here from the outside amount to after all? Dare I estimate the danger which I run inside the burrow from observations which I make when outside? Can my enemies, to begin with, have any proper awareness of me if I am not in my burrow? A certain awareness of me they certainly have, but not full awareness. And is not that full awareness the real definition of a state of danger? So the experiments I attempt here are only half-experiments or even less, calculated merely to reassure my fears and by giving me false reassurance to lay me open to great perils. No, I do not watch over my own sleep, as I imagined; rather it is I who sleep, while the destroyer watches. Perhaps he is one of those who pass the entrance without seeming to notice it, concerned merely to ascertain, just like myself, that the door is still untouched and waits for their attack, and only pass because they know that the master of the house is out, or because they are quite aware that he is guilelessly lying on the watch in the bushes close by. And I leave my post of observation and find I have had enough of this outside life; I feel that there is nothing more that I can learn here, either now or at any time. And I long to say a last goodbye to everything up here, to go down into my burrow never to return again, let things take their course, and not try to retard them with my profitless vigils. But spoiled by seeing for such a long time everything that happened around the entrance, I find great difficulty in summoning the resolution to carry out the actual descent, which might easily draw anyone's attention, and without knowing what is happening behind my back and behind the door after it is fastened. I take advantage of stormy nights to get over the necessary preliminaries, and quickly bundle in my spoil; that seems to have come off, but whether it has really come off will only be known when I myself have made the descent; it will be known, but not by me, or by me, but too late. So I give up the attempt and do not make the descent. I dig an experimental burrow, naturally at a good distance from the real entrance, a burrow just as long as myself, and seal it also with a covering of moss. I creep into my hole, close it after me, wait patiently, keep vigil for long or short spells, and at various hours of the day, then fling off the moss, issue from my hole, and summarize my observations. These are extremely heterogeneous, and both good and bad; but I have never been able to discover a universal principle or an infallible method of descent. In consequence of all this I have not yet summoned the resolution to make my actual descent, and am thrown into despair at the necessity of doing it soon. I almost screw myself to the point of deciding to emigrate to distant parts and take up my old comfortless life again, which had no security whatever, but was one indiscriminate succession of perils, yet in consequence prevented one from perceiving and fearing particular perils, as I am constantly reminded by comparing my secure burrow with ordinary life. Certainly such a decision would be an arrant piece of folly, produced simply by living too long in senseless freedom; the burrow is still mine, I have only to take a single step and I am safe. And I tear myself free from all my doubts and by broad daylight rush to the door, quite resolved to raise it now; but I cannot, I rush past it and fling myself into a thorn bush, deliberately, as a punishment, a punishment for some sin I do not know of. Then, at the last moment, I am forced to admit to myself that I was right after all, and that it was really impossible to go down into the burrow without exposing the thing I love best, for a little while at least, to all my enemies, on the ground, in the trees, in the air. And the danger is by no means a fanciful one, but very real. It need not be any particular enemy that is provoked to pursue me, it may very well be some chance innocent little creature, some disgusting little beast which follows me out of curiosity, and thus, without knowing it, becomes the leader of all the world against me; nor need it be even that, it may be – and that would be just as bad, indeed in some respects worse – it may be someone of my own kind, a connoisseur and prizer of burrows, a hermit, a lover of peace, but all the same a filthy scoundrel who wishes to be housed where he has not built. If he were actually to arrive now, if in his obscene lust he were to discover the entrance and set about working at it, lifting the moss; if he were actually to succeed, if he were actually to wriggle his way in in my stead, until only his hindquarters still showed; if all this were actually to happen, so that at last, casting all prudence to the winds, I might in my blind rage leap on him, maul him, tear the flesh from his bones, destroy him, drink his blood, and fling his corpse among the rest of my spoil, but above all – that is the main thing – were at last back in my burrow once more, I would have it in my heart to greet the labyrinth itself with rapture; but first I would draw the moss covering over me, and I would want to rest, it seems to me, for all the remainder of my life. But nobody comes and I am left to my own resources. Perpetually obsessed by the sheer difficulty of the attempt, I lose much of my timidity, I no longer attempt even to appear to avoid the entrance, but make a hobby of prowling around it; by now it is almost as if I were the enemy spying out a suitable opportunity for successfully breaking in. If I only had someone I could trust to keep watch at post of observation; then of course I could descend in perfect peace of mind. I would make an agreement with this trusty confederate of mine that he would keep a careful note of the state of things during my descent and for quite a long time afterwards, and if he saw any sign of danger knock on the moss covering, and if he saw nothing do nothing. With that a clean sweep would be made of all my fears, no residue would be left, or at most my confidant. For would he not demand some counter-service from me; would he not at least want to see the burrow? That in itself, to let anyone freely into my burrow, would be exquisitely painful to me. I built it for myself, not for visitors, and I think I would refuse to admit him, not even though he alone made it possible for me to get into the burrow would I let him in. But I simply could not admit him, for either I must let him go in first by himself, which is simply unimaginable, or we must both descend at the same time, in which case the advantage I am supposed to derive from him, that of being kept watch over, would be lost.

And what trust can I really put in him? Can I trust one whom I have had under my eyes just as fully when I can't see him, and the moss covering separates us? It is comparatively easy to trust anyone if you are supervising him or at least can supervise him; perhaps it is possible even to trust someone at a distance; but completely to trust someone outside the burrow when you are inside the burrow, that is, in a different world, that, it seems to me, is impossible. But such considerations are not in the least necessary; the mere reflection is enough that during or after my descent one of the countless accidents of existence might prevent my confidant from fulfilling his duty, and what incalculable results might not the smallest accident of that kind have for me? No, if one takes it by and large, I have no right to complain that I am alone and have nobody that I can trust. I certainly lose nothing by that and probably spare myself trouble. I can only trust myself and my burrow. I should have thought of that before and taken measures to meet the difficulty that worries me so much now. When I began the burrow it would at least have been partly possible. I should have so constructed the first passage that it had two entrances at a moderate distance from each other, so that after descending through the one entrance with that slowness which is unavoidable, I might rush at once through the passage to the second entrance, slightly raise the moss covering, which would be so arranged as to make that easy, and from there keep watch on the position for several days and nights. That would have been the only right way of doing it.

True, the two entrances would double the risk, but that consideration need not delay me, for one of the entrances, serving merely as a post of observation, could be quite narrow. And with that I lose myself in a maze of technical speculations, I begin once more to dream my dream of a completely perfect burrow, and that somewhat calms me; with closed eyes I behold with delight perfect or almost perfect structural devices for enabling me to slip out and in unobserved. While I lie there thinking such things I admire these devices very greatly, but only as technical achievements, not as real advantages; for this freedom to slip out and in at will, what does it amount to? It is the mark of a restless nature, of inner uncertainty, disreputable desires, evil propensities that seem still worse when one thinks of the burrow, which is there at one's hand and can flood one with peace if one only remains quite open and receptive to it. For the present, however, I am outside it seeking some possibility of returning, and for that the necessary technical devices would be very desirable. But perhaps not so very desirable after all. Is it not a very grave injustice to the burrow to regard it in moments of nervous panic as a mere hole into which one can creep and be safe? Certainly it is a hole among other things, and a safe one, or should be, and when I picture myself in the midst of danger, then I insist with clenched teeth and all my will that the burrow should be nothing but a hole set apart to save me, and that it should fulfil that clearly defined function with the greatest possible efficiency, and I am ready to absolve it from every other duty. Now the truth of the matter – and one has no eye for that in times of great peril, and only by a great effort even in times when danger is threatening – is that in reality the burrow does provide a considerable degree of security, but by no means enough, for is one ever free from anxieties inside it? These anxieties are different from ordinary ones, prouder, richer in content, often long repressed, but in their destructive effects they are perhaps much the same as the anxieties that existence in the outer world gives rise to. Had I constructed the burrow exclusively to assure my safety I would not have been disappointed, it is true; nevertheless the relation between the enormous labour involved and the actual security it would provide, at least insofar as I could feel it and profit by it, would not have been in my favour. It is extremely painful to have to admit such things to oneself, but one is forced to do it, confronted by that entrance over there which now literally locks and bars itself against me, the builder and possessor. Yet the burrow is not a mere hole for taking refuge in. When I stand in the Castle Keep surrounded by my piled-up stores, surveying the ten passages which begin there, raised and sunken passages, vertical and rounded passages, wide and narrow passages, as the general plan dictates, and all alike still and empty, ready by their various routes to conduct me to all the other rooms, which are also still and empty – then all thought of mere safety is far from my mind, then I know that here is my castle, which I have wrested from the refractory soil with tooth and claw, with pounding and hammering blows, my castle which can never belong to anyone else, and is so essentially mine that I can calmly accept in it even my enemy's mortal stroke at the final hour, for my blood will ebb away here in my own soil and not be lost. And what but that is the meaning of the blissful hours which I pass, now peacefully slumbering, now happily keeping watch, in these passages, these passages which suit me so well, where one can stretch oneself out in comfort, roll about in childish delight, lie and dream, or sink into blissful sleep. And the smaller rooms, each familiar to me, so familiar that in spite of their complete similarity I can clearly distinguish one from the other with my eyes shut by the mere feel of the wall: they enclose me more peacefully and warmly than a bird is enclosed in its nest. And all, all still and empty.

But if that is the case, why do I hang back? Why do I dread the thought of the intruding enemy more than the possibility of never seeing my burrow again? Well, the latter alternative is fortunately an impossibility; there is no need for me even to take thought to know what the burrow means to me; I and the burrow belong so indissolubly together that in spite of all my fears I could make myself quite comfortable out here, and not even need to overcome my repugnance and open the door; I could be quite content to wait here passively, for nothing can part us for long, and somehow or other I shall quite certainly find myself in my burrow again. But on the other hand how much time may pass before then, and how many things may happen in that time, up here no less than down there? And it lies with me solely to curtail that interval and to do what is necessary at once.

And then, too exhausted to be any longer capable of thought, my head hanging, my legs trembling with fatigue, half asleep, feeling my way rather than walking, I approach the entrance, slowly raise the moss covering, slowly descend, leaving the door open in my distraction for a needlessly long time, and presently remember my omission, and get out again to make it good – but what need was there to get out for that? All that was needed was to draw to the moss covering; right; so I creep in again and now at last draw to the moss covering. Only in this state, and in this state alone, can I achieve my descent. So at last I lie down beneath the moss on the top of my bloodstained spoil and can now enjoy my longed-for sleep. Nothing disturbs me, no one has tracked me down, above the moss everything seems to be quiet thus far at least, but even if all were not quiet I question whether I could stop to keep watch now; I have changed my place, I have left the upper world and am in my burrow, and I feel its effect at once. It is a new world, endowing me with new powers, and what I felt as fatigue up there is no longer that here. I have returned from a journey dog-tired with my wanderings, but the sight of the old house, the thought of all the things that are waiting to be done, the necessity at least to cast a glance at all the rooms, but above all to make my way immediately to the Castle Keep; all this transforms my fatigue into ardent zeal; it is as though at the moment when I set foot in the burrow I had wakened from a long and profound sleep. My first task is a very laborious one and requires all my attention; I mean getting my spoil through the narrow and thin-walled passages of the labyrinth. I shove with all my might, and the work gets done too, but far too slowly for me; to hasten it I drag part of my flesh supply back again and push my way over it and through it; now I have only a portion of my spoil before me and it is easier to make progress; but my road is so blocked by all this flesh in these narrow passages, through which it is not always easy for me to make my way even when I am alone, that I could quite easily smother among my own stores; sometimes I can only rescue myself from their pressure by eating and drinking a clear space for myself. But the work of transport is successful, I finish it in quite a reasonable time, the labyrinth is behind me, I reach an ordinary passage and breathe freely, push my spoil through a communication passage into a main passage expressly designed for the purpose, a passage sloping down steeply to the Castle Keep. What is left to be done is not really work at all; my whole load rolls and flows down the passage almost of itself. The Castle Keep at last! At last I can dare to rest. Everything is unchanged, no great mishap seems to have occurred, the few little defects that I note at a first glance can soon be repaired; first, however, I must go my long round of all the passages, but that is no hardship, that is merely to commune again with friends, as I often did in the old days or – I am not so very old yet, but my memory of many things is already quite confused – as I often did, or as I have often heard that it was done. Now I begin with the second passage, purposefully slow, now that I have seen the Castle Keep I have endless time – inside the burrow I always have endless time – for everything I do there is good and important and satisfies me somehow. I begin with the second passage, but break off in the middle and turn into the third passage and let it take me back again to the Castle Keep, and now of course I have to begin at the second passage once more, and so I play with my task and lengthen it out and smile to myself and enjoy myself and become quite dazed with all the work in front of me, but never think of turning aside from it. It is for your sake, ye passages and rooms, and you, Castle Keep, above all, that I have come back, counting my own life as nothing in the balance, after stupidly trembling for it for so long, and postponing my return to you. What do I care for danger now that I am with you? You belong to me, I to you, we are united; what can harm us? What if my foes should be assembling even now up above there and their muzzles be preparing to break through the moss? And with its silence and emptiness the burrow answers me, confirming my words. But now a feeling of lassitude overcomes me and in some favourite room I curl myself up tentatively, I have not yet surveyed everything by a long way, though still resolved to examine everything to the very end; I have no intention of sleeping here, I have merely yielded to the temptation of making myself comfortable and pretending I want to sleep, I merely wish to find out if this is as good a place for sleeping as it used to be. It is, but it is a better place for sleep than for waking, and I remain lying where I am in deep slumber.

I must have slept for a long time. I was only wakened when I had reached the last light sleep which dissolves of itself, and it must have been very light, for it was an almost inaudible whistling noise that wakened me. I recognized what it was immediately; the small fry, whom I had allowed far too much latitude, had burrowed a new channel somewhere during my absence, this channel must have chanced to intersect an older one, the air was caught there, and that produced the whistling noise. What an indefatigably busy lot these small fry are, and what a nuisance their diligence can be! First I shall have to listen at the walls of my passages and locate the place of disturbance by experimental excavations, and only then will I be able to get rid of the noise. However, this new channel may be quite welcome as a further means of ventilation, if it can be fitted into the plan of the burrow. But after this I shall keep a much sharper eye on the small fry than I used to; I shall spare none of them.

As I have a good deal of experience in investigations of this kind the work probably will not take me long and I can start upon it at once; there are other jobs awaiting me, it is true, but this is the most urgent. I must have silence in my passages. This noise, however, is a comparatively innocent one; I did not hear it at all when I first arrived, although it must certainly have been there; I must first feel quite at home before I could hear it; it is, so to speak, audible only to the ear of the householder. And it is not even constant, as such noises usually are; there are long pauses, obviously caused by stoppages of the current of air. I start on my investigations, but I can't find the right place to begin at, and though I cut a few trenches I do it at random; naturally that has no effect, and the hard work of digging and the still harder work of filling the trenches up again and beating the earth firm is so much labour lost. I don't seem to be getting any nearer to the place where the noise is, it goes on always on the same thin note, with regular pauses, now a sort of whistling, but again like a kind of piping. Now I could leave it to itself for the time being; it is very disturbing, certainly, but there can hardly be any doubt that its origin is what I took it to be at first; so it can scarcely become louder, on the contrary, such noises may quite well – though until now I have never had to wait so long for that to happen – may quite well vanish of themselves in the course of time through the continued labours of these little burrowers; and apart from that, often chance itself puts one on the track of the disturbance, where systematic investigation has failed for a long time. In such ways I comfort myself, and resolve simply to continue my tour of the passages, and visit the rooms, many of which I have not even seen yet since my return, and enjoy myself contemplating the Castle Keep now and then between times; but my anxiety will not let me, and I must go on with my search. These little creatures take up much, far too much, time that could be better employed. In such cases as the present it is usually the technical problem that attracts me; for example, from the noise, which my ear can distinguish in all its finest shades, so that it has a perfectly clear outline to me, I deduce its cause, and now I am on fire to discover whether my conclusion is valid. And with good reason, for as long as that is not established I cannot feel safe, even if it were merely a matter of discovering where a grain of sand that had fallen from one of the walls had rolled to. And a noise such as this is by no means a trifling matter, regarded from that angle. But whether trifling or important, I can find nothing, no matter how hard I search, or it may be that I find too much. This had to happen just in my favourite room, I think to myself, and I walk a fair distance away from it, almost halfway along the passage leading to the next room; I do this more as a joke, pretending to myself that my favourite room is not alone to blame, but that there are disturbances elsewhere as well, and with a smile on my face I begin to listen; but soon I stop smiling, for, right enough, the same whistling meets me here too. It is really nothing to worry about; sometimes I think that nobody but myself would hear it; it is true, I hear it now more and more distinctly, for my ear has grown keener through practice; though in reality it is exactly the same noise wherever I may hear it, as I have convinced myself by comparing my impressions. Nor is it growing louder; I recognize this when I listen in the middle of the passage instead of pressing my ear against the wall. Then it is only with an effort, indeed with great intentness, that I can more guess at than hear the merest trace of a noise now and then. But it is this very uniformity of the noise everywhere that disturbs me most, for it cannot be made to agree with my original assumption. Had I rightly divined the cause of the noise, then it must have issued with greatest force from some given place, which it would be my task to discover, and after that have grown fainter and fainter. But if my hypothesis does not meet the case, what can the explanation be? There still remains the possibility that there are two noises, that up to now I have been listening at a good distance from the two centres, and that while its noise increases, when I draw near to one of them, the total result remains approximately the same for the ear in consequence of the lessening volume of sound from the other centre. Already I have almost fancied sometimes, when I have listened carefully, that I could distinguish, if very indistinctly, differences of tone which support this new assumption. In any case I must extend my sphere of investigation much farther than I have done. Accordingly I descend the passage to the Castle Keep and begin to listen there. Strange, the same noise there too. Now it is a noise produced by the burrowing of some species of small fry who have infamously exploited my absence; in any case they have no intention of doing me harm, they are simply busied with their own work, and so long as no obstacle comes in their way they will keep on in the direction they have taken: I know all this, yet that they should have dared to approach the very Castle Keep itself is incomprehensible to me and fills me with agitation, and confuses the faculties which I need so urgently for the work before me. Here I have no wish to discover whether it is the unusual depth at which the Castle Keep lies, or its great extent and correspondingly powerful air suction, calculated to scare burrowing creatures away, or the mere fact that it is the Castle Keep, that by some channel or other has penetrated to their dull minds. In any case, I have never noticed any sign of burrowing in the walls of the Castle Keep until now. Crowds of little beasts have come here, it is true, attracted by the powerful smells; here I have had a constant hunting ground, but my quarry has always burrowed a way through in the upper passages, and come running down here, somewhat fearfully, but unable to withstand such a temptation. But now, it seems, they are burrowing in all the passages. If I had only carried out the best of the grand plans I thought out in my youth and early manhood, or rather, if I had only had the strength to carry them out, for there would have been no lack of will. One of these favourite plans of mine was to isolate the Castle Keep from its surroundings, that is to say, to restrict the thickness of its walls to about my own height, and leave a free space of about the same width all around the Castle Keep, except for a narrow foundation, which unfortunately would have to be left to bear up the whole. I had always pictured this free space, and not without reason, as the loveliest imaginable haunt. What a joy to lie pressed against the rounded outer wall, pull oneself up, let oneself slide down again, miss one's footing and find oneself on firm earth, and play all those games literally upon the Castle Keep and not inside it; to avoid the Castle Keep, to rest one's eyes from it whenever one wanted, to postpone the joy of seeing it until later and yet not have to do without it, but literally hold it safe between one's claws, a thing that is impossible if you have only an ordinary open entrance to it; but above all to be able to stand guard over it, and in that way to be so completely compensated for renouncing the actual sight of it that, if one had to choose between staying all one's life in the Castle Keep or in the free space outside it, one would choose the latter, content to wander up and down there all one's days and keep guard over the Castle Keep. Then there would be no noises in the walls, no insolent burrowing up to the very Keep itself; then peace would be assured there and I would be its guardian; then I would not have to listen with loathing to the burrowing of the small fry, but with delight to something that I cannot hear now at all: the murmurous silence of the Castle Keep.

But that beautiful dream is past and I must set to work, almost glad that now my work has a direct connection with the Castle Keep, for that wings it. Certainly, as I can see more and more clearly, I need all my energies for this task, which at first seemed quite a trifling one. I listen now at the walls of the Castle Keep, and wherever I listen, high or low, at the roof or the floor, at the entrance or in the corners, everywhere, everywhere, I hear the same noise. And how much time, how much care must be wasted in listening to that noise, with its regular pauses. One can, if one wishes, find a tiny deceitful comfort in the fact that here in the Castle Keep, because of its vastness, one hears nothing at all, as distinguished from the passages, when one stands back from the walls. Simply as a rest and a means to regain my composure I often make this experiment, listen intently and am overjoyed when I hear nothing. But the question still remains, what can have happened? Confronted with this phenomenon my original explanation completely falls to the ground. But I must also reject other explanations which present themselves to me. One could assume, for instance, that the noise I hear is simply that of the small fry themselves at their work. But all my experience contradicts this; I cannot suddenly begin to hear now a thing that I have never heard before though it was always there. My sensitiveness to disturbances in the burrow has perhaps become greater with the years, yet my hearing has by no means grown keener. It is of the very nature of small fry not to be heard. Would I have tolerated them otherwise? Even at the risk of starvation I would have exterminated them. But perhaps – this idea now insinuates itself – I am concerned here with some animal unknown to me. That is possible. True, I have observed the life down here long and carefully enough, but the world is full of diversity and is never wanting in painful surprises. Yet it cannot be a single animal, it must be a whole swarm that has suddenly fallen upon my domain, a huge swarm of little creatures, which, as they are audible, must certainly be bigger than the small fry, but yet cannot be very much bigger, for the sound of their labours is itself very faint. It may be, then, a swarm of unknown creatures on their wanderings, who happen to be passing by my way, who disturb me, but will presently cease to do so. So I could really wait for them to pass, and need not put myself to the trouble of work that will be needless in the end. Yet if these creatures are strangers, why is it that I never see any of them? I have already dug a host of trenches, hoping to catch one of them, but I can find not a single one. Then it occurs to me that they may be quite tiny creatures, far tinier than any I am acquainted with, and that it is only the noise they make that is greater. Accordingly I investigate the soil I have dug up, I cast the lumps into the air so that they break into quite small particles, but the noise-makers are not among them. Slowly I come to realize that by digging such small fortuitous trenches I achieve nothing; in doing that I merely disfigure the walls of my burrow, scratching hastily here and there without taking time to fill up the holes again; at many places already there are heaps of earth which block my way and my view. Still, that is only a secondary worry; for now I can neither wander about my house, nor review it, nor rest; often already I have fallen asleep at my work in some hole or other, with one paw clutching the soil above me, from which in a semi-stupor I have been trying to tear a lump. I intend now to alter my methods. I shall dig a wide and carefully constructed trench in the direction of the noise and not cease from digging until, independent of all theories, I find the real cause of the noise. Then I shall eradicate it, if that is within my power, and if it is not, at least I shall know the truth. That truth will bring me either peace or despair, but whether the one or the other, it will be beyond doubt or question. This decision strengthens me. All that I have done till now seems to me far too hasty; in the excitement of my return, while I had not yet shaken myself free from the cares of the upper world, and was not yet completely penetrated by the peace of the burrow, but rather hypersensitive at having had to renounce it for such a long time, I was thrown into complete confusion of mind by an unfamiliar noise. And what was it? A faint whistling, audible only at long intervals, a mere nothing to which I don't say that one could actually get used, for no one could get used to it, but which one could, without actually doing anything about it at once, observe for a while; that is, listen every few hours, let us say, and patiently register the results, instead of, as I had done, keeping one's ear fixed to the wall and at every hint of noise tearing out a lump of earth, not really hoping to find anything, but simply so as to do something to give expression to one's inward agitation. All that will be changed now, I hope. And then, with furious shut eyes, I have to admit to myself that I hope nothing of the kind, for I am still trembling with agitation just as I was hours ago, and if my reason did not restrain me I would probably like nothing better than to start stubbornly and defiantly digging, simply for the sake of digging, at some place or other, whether I heard anything there or not; almost like the small fry, who burrow either without any object at all or simply because they eat the soil. My new and reasonable plan both tempts me and leaves me cold. There is nothing in it to object to, I at least know of no objection; it is bound, so far as I can see, to achieve my aim. And yet at bottom I do not believe in it; I believe in it so little that I do not even fear the terrors which its success may well bring, I do not believe even in a dreadful denouement; indeed it seems to me that I have been thinking ever since the first appearance of the noise of such a methodical trench, and have not begun upon it until now simply because I put no trust in it. In spite of that I shall of course start on the trench; I have no other alternative; but I shall not start at once, I shall postpone the task for a little while. If reason is to be reinstated on the throne, it must be completely reinstated; I shall not rush blindly into my task. In any case I shall first repair the damage that I have done to the burrow with my wild digging; that will take a good long time, but it is necessary; if the new trench is really to reach its goal it will probably be long, and if it should lead to nothing at all it will be endless; in any case this task means a longish absence from the burrow, though an absence by no means so painful as an absence in the upper world, for I can interrupt my work whenever I like and pay a visit to my house; and even if I should not do that the air of Castle Keep will be wafted to me and surround me while I work; nevertheless it means leaving the burrow and surrendering myself to an uncertain fate, and consequently I want to leave the burrow in good order behind me; it shall not be said that I, who am fighting for its peace, have myself destroyed that peace without reinstating it at once. So I begin by shovelling the soil back into the holes from which it was taken, a kind of work I am familiar with, that I have done countless times almost without regarding it as work, and at which, particularly as regards the final pressing and smoothing down – and this is no empty boast, but the simple truth – I am unbeatable. But this time everything seems difficult, I am too distracted, every now and then, in the middle of my work, I press my ear to the wall and listen, and without taking any notice let the soil that I have just lifted trickle back into the passage again. The final embellishments, which demand a stricter attention, I can hardly achieve at all. Hideous protuberances, disturbing cracks remain, not to speak of the fact that the old buoyancy simply cannot be restored again to a wall patched up in such a way. I try to comfort myself with the reflection that my present work is only temporary. When I return after peace has been restored I shall repair everything properly: work will be mere play to me then. Oh yes, work is mere play in fairy tales, and this comfort of mine belongs to the realm of fairy tales too. It would be far better to do the work thoroughly now, at once, far more reasonable than perpetually to interrupt it and wander off through the passages to discover new sources of noise, which is easy enough, all that is needed being to stop at any point one likes and listen. And that is not the end of my useless discoveries. Sometimes I fancy that the noise has stopped, for it makes long pauses; sometimes such a faint whistling escapes one, one's own blood is pounding all too loudly in one's ears; then two pauses come one after another, and for a while one thinks that the whistling has stopped forever. I listen no longer, I jump up, all life is transfigured; it is as if the fountains from which flows the silence of the burrow were unsealed. I refrain from verifying my discovery at once, I want first to find someone to whom in all good faith I can confide it, so I rush to the Castle Keep, I remember, for I and everything in me has awakened to new life, that I have eaten nothing for a long time, I snatch something or other from among my store of food half buried under the debris and hurriedly begin to swallow it while I hurry back to the place where I made my incredible discovery, I only want to assure myself about it incidentally, perfunctorily, while I am eating; I listen, but the most perfunctory listening shows at once that I was shamefully deceived: away there in the distance the whistling still remains unshaken. And I spit out my food, and would like to trample it underfoot, and go back to my task, not caring which I take up; anyplace where it seems to be needed, and there are enough places like that, I mechanically start on something or other, just as if the overseer had appeared and I must make a pretence of working for his benefit. But hardly have I begun to work in this fashion when it may happen that I make a new discovery. The noise seems to have become louder, not much louder, of course – here it is always a matter of the subtlest shades – but all the same sufficiently louder for the ear to recognize it clearly. And this growing-louder is like a coming-nearer; still more distinctly than you hear the increasing loudness of the noise, you can literally see the step that brings it closer to you. You leap back from the wall, you try to grasp at once all the possible consequences that this discovery will bring with it. You feel as if you had never really organized the burrow for defence against attack; you had intended to do so, but despite all your experience of life the danger of an attack, and consequently the need to organize the place for defence, seemed remote – or rather not remote (how could it possibly be!) – but infinitely less important than the need to put it in a state where one could live peacefully; and so that consideration was given priority in everything relating to the burrow. Many things in this direction might have been done without affecting the plan of the whole; most incomprehensibly they have been neglected. I have had a great deal of luck all those years, luck has spoiled me; I have had anxieties, but anxiety leads to nothing when you have luck to back you.

The thing to do, really to do now, would be to go carefully over the burrow and consider every possible means of defending it, work out a plan of defence and a corresponding plan of construction, and then start on the work at once with the vigour of youth. That is the work that would really be needed, for which, I may add, it is now far too late in the day; yet that is what would really be needed, and not the digging of a grand experimental trench, whose only real result would be to deliver me hand and foot to the search for danger, out of the foolish fear that it will not arrive quickly enough of itself. Suddenly I cannot comprehend my former plan. I can find no slightest trace of reason in what had seemed so reasonable; once more I lay aside my work and even my listening; I have no wish to discover any further signs that the noise is growing louder; I have had enough of discoveries; I let everything slide; I would be quite content if I could only still the conflict going on within me. Once more I let my passages lead me where they will, I come to more and more remote ones that I have not yet seen since my return, and that are quite unsullied by my scratching paws, and whose silence rises up to meet me and sinks into me. I do not surrender to it, I hurry on, I do not know what I want, probably simply to put off the hour. I stray so far that I find myself at the labyrinth; the idea of listening beneath the moss covering tempts me; such distant things, distant for the moment, chain my interest. I push my way up and listen. Deep stillness; how lovely it is here, outside there nobody troubles about my burrow, everybody has his own affairs, which have no connection with me; how have I managed to achieve this? Here under the moss covering is perhaps the only place in my burrow now where I can listen for hours and hear nothing. A complete reversal of things in the burrow; what was once the place of danger has become a place of tranquillity, while the Castle Keep has been plunged into the melee of the world and all its perils. Still worse, even here there is no peace in reality, here nothing has changed; silent or vociferous, danger lies in ambush as before above the moss, but I have grown insensitive to it, my mind is far too much taken up with the whistling in my walls. Is my mind really taken up with it? It grows louder, it comes nearer, but I wriggle my way through the labyrinth and make a couch for myself up here under the moss; it is almost as if I were already leaving the house to the whistler, content if I can only have a little peace up here. To the whistler? Have I come, then, to a new conclusion concerning the cause of the noise? But surely the noise is caused by the channels bored by the small fry? Is not that my considered opinion? It seems to me that I have not retreated from it thus far. And if the noise is not caused directly by these channels, it is indirectly. And even if it should have no connection with them whatever, one is not at liberty to make *a priori* assumptions, but must wait until one finds the cause, or it reveals itself. One could play with hypotheses, of course, even at this stage; for instance, it is possible that there has been a water burst at some distance away, and what seems a piping or whistling to me is in reality a gurgling. But apart from the fact that I have no experience in that sphere – the groundwater that I found at the start I drained away at once, and in this sandy soil it has never returned – apart from this fact the noise is undeniably a whistling and simply not to be translated into a gurgling. But what avail all exhortations to be calm; my imagination will not rest, and I have actually come to believe – it is useless to deny it to myself – that the whistling is made by some beast, and moreover not by a great many small ones, but by a single big one. Many signs contradict this. The noise can be heard everywhere and always at the same strength, and moreover uniformly, both by day and night. At first, therefore, one cannot but incline to the hypothesis of a great number of little animals; but as I must have found some of them during my digging and I have found nothing, it only remains for me to assume the existence of a great beast, especially as the things that seem to contradict the hypothesis are merely things which make the beast, not so much impossible, as merely dangerous beyond all one's powers of conception. For that reason alone have I resisted this hypothesis. I shall cease from this self-deception. For a long time already I have played with the idea that the beast can be heard at such a great distance because it works so furiously; it burrows as fast through the ground as another can walk on the open road; the ground still trembles at its burrowing when it has ceased; this reverberation and the noise of the boring itself unite into one sound at such a great distance, and I, as I hear only the last dying ebb of that sound, hear it always at the same uniform strength. It follows from this also that the beast is not making for me, seeing that the noise never changes; more likely it has a plan in view whose purpose I cannot decipher; I merely assume that the beast – and I make no claim whatever that it knows of my existence – is encircling me; it has probably made several circles around my burrow already since I began to observe it. The nature of the noise, the piping or whistling, gives me much food for thought. When I scratch and scrape in the soil in my own fashion the sound is quite different. I can explain the whistling only in this way: that the beast's chief means of burrowing is not its claws, which it probably employs merely as a secondary resource, but its snout or its muzzle, which, of course, apart from its enormous strength, must also be fairly sharp at the point. It probably bores its snout into the earth with one mighty push and tears out a great lump; while it is doing that I hear nothing; that is the pause; but then it draws in the air for a new push. This indrawal of its breath, which must be an earth-shaking noise, not only because of the beast's strength, but of its haste, its furious lust for work as well: this noise I hear then as a faint whistling. But quite incomprehensible remains the beast's capacity to work without stopping; perhaps the short pauses provide also the opportunity of snatching a moment's rest; but apparently the beast has never yet allowed itself a really long rest, day and night it goes on burrowing, always with the same freshness and vigour, always thinking of its object, which must be achieved with the utmost expedition, and which it has the ability to achieve with ease. Now I could not have foreseen such an opponent. But apart altogether from the beast's peculiar characteristics, what is happening now is only something which I should really have feared all the time, something against which I should have been constantly prepared: the fact that someone would come. By what chance can everything have flowed on so quietly and happily for such a long time? Who can have diverted my enemies from their path, and forced them to make a wide detour around my property? Why have I been spared for so long, only to be delivered to such terrors now? Compared with this, what are all the petty dangers in brooding over which I have spent my life! Had I hoped, as owner of the burrow, to be in a stronger position than any enemy who might chance to appear? But simply by virtue of being owner of this great vulnerable edifice I am obviously defenceless against any serious attack. The joy of possessing it has spoiled me, the vulnerability of the burrow has made me vulnerable; any wound to it hurts me as if I myself were hit. It is precisely this that I should have foreseen; instead of thinking only of my own defence – and how perfunctorily and vainly I have done even that – I should have thought of the defence of the burrow. Above all, provision should have been made for cutting off sections of the burrow, and as many as possible of them, from the endangered sections when they are attacked; this should have been done by means of improvised landslides, calculated to operate at a moment's notice; moreover these should have been so thick, and have provided such an effectual barrier, that the attacker would not even guess that the real burrow only began at the other side. More, these landslides should have been so devised that they not only concealed the burrow, but also entombed the attacker. Not the slightest attempt have I made to carry out such a plan, nothing at all has been done in this direction, I have been as thoughtless as a child, I have passed my manhood's years in childish games, I have done nothing but play even with the thought of danger, I have shirked really taking thought for actual danger. And there has been no lack of warning.

Nothing, of course, approaching the present situation has happened before; nevertheless there was an incident not unlike it when the burrow was only beginning. The main difference between that time and this is simply that the burrow was only beginning then . . . In those days I was literally nothing more than a humble apprentice, the labyrinth was only sketched out in rough outline, I had already dug a little room, but the proportions and the execution of the walls were sadly bungled; in short, everything was so tentative that it could only be regarded as an experiment, as something which, if one lost patience some day, one could leave behind without much regret. Then one day as I lay on a heap of earth resting from my labours – I have rested far too often from my labours all my life – suddenly I heard a noise in the distance. Being young at the time, I was less frightened than curious. I left my work to look after itself and set myself to listen; I listened and listened, and had no wish to fly up to my moss covering and stretch myself out there so that I might not have to hear. I did listen, at least. I could clearly recognize that the noise came from some kind of burrowing similar to my own; it was somewhat fainter, of course, but how much of that might be put down to the distance one could not tell. I was intensely interested, but otherwise calm and cool. Perhaps I am in somebody else's burrow, I thought to myself, and now the owner is boring his way toward me. If that assumption had proved to be correct I would have gone away, for I have never had any desire for conquest or bloodshed, and begun building somewhere else. But after all I was still young and still without a burrow, so I could remain quite cool. Besides, the further course of the noise brought no real cause for apprehension, except that it was not easy to explain. If whoever was boring there was really making for me, because he had heard me boring, then if he changed his direction, as now actually happened, it could not be told whether he did this because my pause for rest had deprived him of any definite point to make toward, or because – which was more plausible – he had himself changed his plans. But perhaps I had been deceived altogether, and he had never been actually making in my direction; at any rate the noise grew louder for a while as if he were drawing nearer, and being young at that time I probably would not have been displeased to see the burrower suddenly rising from the ground; but nothing of that kind happened, at a certain point the sound of boring began to weaken, it grew fainter and fainter, as if the burrower were gradually diverging from his first route, and suddenly it broke off altogether, as if he had decided now to take the diametrically opposite direction and were making straight away from me into the distance. For a long time I still went on listening for him in the silence, before I returned once more to my work. Now that warning was definite enough, but I soon forgot it, and it scarcely influenced my building plans.

Between that day and this lie my years of maturity, but is it not as if there were no interval at all between them? I still take long rests from my labours and listen at the wall, and the burrower has changed his intention anew, he has turned back, he is returning from his journey, thinking he has given me ample time in the interval to prepare for his reception. But on my side everything is worse prepared for than it was then; the great burrow stands defenceless, and I am no longer a young apprentice, but an old architect, and the powers I still have fail me when the decisive hour comes; yet old as I am it seems to me that I would gladly be still older, so old that I should never be able to rise again from my resting place under the moss. For to be honest I cannot endure the place, I rise up and rush, as if I had filled myself up there with new anxieties instead of peace, down into the house again. What was the state of things the last time I was here? Had the whistling grown fainter? No, it had grown louder. I listen at ten places chosen at random and clearly notice the deception; the whistling is just the same as ever, nothing has altered. Over there, there are no changes, there one is calm and not worried about time; but here every instant frets and gnaws at the listener. I go once more the long road to the Castle Keep, all my surroundings seem filled with agitation, seem to be looking at me, and then look away again so as not to disturb me, yet cannot refrain the very next moment from trying to read the saving solution from my expression. I shake my head, I have not yet found any solution. Nor do I go to the Castle Keep in pursuance of any plan. I pass the spot where I had intended to begin the experimental trench, I look it over once more, it would have been an admirable place to begin at, the trench's course would have been in the direction where lay the majority of the tiny ventilation holes, which would have greatly lightened my labours; perhaps I should not have had to dig very far, should not even have had to dig to the source of the noise; perhaps if I had listened at the ventilation holes it would have been enough. But no consideration is potent enough to animate me to this labour of digging. This trench will bring me certainty, you say? I have reached the stage where I no longer wish to have certainty. In the Castle Keep I choose a lovely piece of flayed red flesh and creep with it into one of the heaps of earth; there I shall have silence at least, such silence, at any rate, as still can be said to exist here. I munch and nibble at the flesh, think of the strange beast going its own road in the distance, and then again that I should enjoy my store of food as fully as possible, while I still have the chance. This last is probably the sole plan I have left that I can carry out. For the rest I try to unriddle the beast's plans. Is it on its wanderings, or is it working on its own burrow? If it is on its wanderings then perhaps an understanding with it might be possible. If it should really break through to the burrow I shall give it some of my stores and it will go on its way again. It will go its way again, a fine story! Lying in my heap of earth I can naturally dream of all sorts of things, even of an understanding with the beast, though I know well enough that no such thing can happen, and that at the instant when we see each other, more, at the moment when we merely guess at each other's presence, we shall both blindly bare our claws and

164

teeth, neither of us a second before or after the other, both of us filled with a new and different hunger, even if we should already be gorged to bursting. And with entire justice, for who, even if he were merely on his wanderings, would not change his itinerary and his plans for the future on catching sight of the burrow? But perhaps the beast is digging in its own burrow, in which case I cannot even dream of an understanding. Even if it should be such a peculiar beast that its burrow could tolerate a neighbour, my burrow could not tolerate a neighbour, at least not a clearly audible one. Now actually the beast seems to be a great distance away; if it would only withdraw a little farther the noise too would probably disappear; perhaps in that case everything would be peaceful again as in the old days; all this would then become a painful but salutary lesson, spurring me on to make the most diverse improvements on the burrow; if I have peace, and danger does not immediately threaten me, I am still quite fit for all sorts of hard work; perhaps, considering the enormous possibilities which its powers of work open before it, the beast has given up the idea of extending its burrow in my direction, and is compensating itself for that in some other one. That consummation also cannot, of course, be brought about by negotiation, but only by the beast itself, or by some compulsion exercised from my side. In both cases the decisive factor will be whether the beast knows about me, and if so what it knows. The more I reflect upon it the more improbable does it seem to me that the beast has even heard me; it is possible, though I can't imagine it, that it can have received news of me in some other way, but it has certainly never heard me. So long as I still knew nothing about it, it simply cannot have heard me, for at that time I kept very quiet, nothing could be more quiet than my return to the burrow; afterwards, when I dug the experimental trenches, perhaps it could have heard me, though my style of digging makes very little noise; but if it had heard me I must have noticed some sign of it, the beast must at least have stopped its work every now and then to listen. But all remained unchanged.

Josephine the Singer

Our singer is called Josephine. Anyone who has not heard her does not know the power of song. There is no one but is carried away by her singing, a tribute all the greater as we are not in general a music-loving race. Tranquil peace is the music we love best; our life is hard, we are no longer able, even on occasions when we have tried to shake off the cares of daily life, to rise to anything so high and remote from our usual routine as music. But we do not much lament that; we do not get even so far; a certain practical cunning, which admittedly we stand greatly in need of, we hold to be our greatest distinction, and with a smile born of such cunning we are wont to console ourselves for all shortcomings, even supposing – only it does not happen – that we were to yearn once in a way for the kind of bliss which music may provide. Josephine is the sole exception; she has a love for music and knows too how to transmit it; she is the only one; when she dies, music – who knows for how long – will vanish from our lives.

I have often thought about what this music of hers really means. For we are quite unmusical; how is it that we understand Josephine's singing or, since Josephine denies that, at least think we can understand it. The simplest answer would be that the beauty of her singing is so great that even the most insensitive cannot be deaf to it, but this answer is not satisfactory. If it were really so, her singing would have to give one an immediate and lasting feeling of being something out of the ordinary, a feeling that from her throat something is sounding which we have never heard before and which we are not even capable of hearing, something that Josephine alone and no one else can enable us to hear. But in my opinion that is just what does not happen, I do not feel this and have never observed that others feel anything of the kind. Among intimates we admit freely to one another that Josephine's singing, as singing, is nothing out of the ordinary.

Is it in fact singing at all? Although we are unmusical we have a tradition of singing; in the old days our people did sing; this is mentioned in legends and some songs have actually survived, which, it is true, no one can now sing. Thus we have an inkling of what singing is, and Josephine's art does not really correspond to it. So is it singing at all? Is it not perhaps just a piping? And piping is something we all know about, it is the real artistic accomplishment of our people, or rather no mere accomplishment but a characteristic expression of our life. We all pipe, but of course no one dreams of making out that our piping is an art, we pipe without thinking of it, indeed without noticing it, and there are even many among us who are quite unaware that piping is one of our characteristics. So if it were true that Josephine does not sing but only pipes and perhaps, as it seems to me at least, hardly rises above the level of our usual piping – yet, perhaps her strength is not even quite equal to our usual piping, whereas an ordinary farmhand can keep it up effortlessly all day long, besides doing his work – if that were all true, then indeed Josephine's alleged vocal skill might be disproved, but that would merely clear the ground for the real riddle which needs solving, the enormous influence she has.

After all, it is only a kind of piping that she produces. If you post yourself quite far away from her and listen, or, still better, put your judgment to the test, whenever she happens to be singing along with others, by trying to identify her voice, you will undoubtedly distinguish nothing but a quite ordinary piping tone, which at most differs a little from the others through being delicate or weak. Yet if you sit down before her, it is not merely a piping; to comprehend her art it is necessary not only to hear but to see her. Even if hers were only our usual workaday piping, there is first of all this peculiarity to consider, that here is someone making a ceremonial performance out of doing the usual thing. To crack a nut is truly no feat, so no one would ever dare to collect an audience in order to entertain it with nut-cracking. But if all the same one does do that and succeeds in entertaining the public, then it cannot be a matter of simple nut-cracking. Or it is a matter of nut-cracking, but it turns out that we have overlooked the art of cracking nuts because we were too skilled in it and that this newcomer to it first shows us its real nature, even finding it useful in making his effects to be rather less expert in nut-cracking than most of us.

Perhaps it is much the same with Josephine's singing; we admire in her what we do not at all admire in ourselves; in this respect, I may say, she is of one mind with us. I was once present when someone, as of course often happens, drew her attention to the folk piping everywhere going on, making only a modest reference to it, yet for Josephine that was more than enough. A smile so sarcastic and arrogant as she then assumed I have never seen; she, who in appearance is delicacy itself, conspicuously so even among our people who are prolific in such feminine types, seemed at that moment actually vulgar; she was at once aware of it herself, by the way, with her extreme sensibility, and controlled herself. At any rate she denies any connection between her art and ordinary piping. For those who are of the contrary opinion she has only contempt and probably unacknowledged hatred. This is not simple vanity, for the opposition, with which I too am half in sympathy, certainly admires her no less than the crowd does, but Josephine does not want mere admiration, she wants to be admired exactly in the way she prescribes, mere admiration leaves her cold. And when you take a seat before her, you understand her; opposition is possible only at a distance, when you sit before her, you know: this piping of hers is no piping.

Since piping is one of our thoughtless habits, one might think that people would pipe up in Josephine's audience too; her art makes us feel happy, and when we are happy we pipe; but her audience never pipes, it sits in mouselike stillness; as if we had become partakers in the peace we long for, from which our own piping at the very least holds us back, we make no sound. Is it her singing that enchants us or is it not rather the solemn stillness enclosing her frail little voice? Once it happened while Josephine was singing that some silly little thing in all innocence began to pipe up too. Now it was just the same as what we were hearing from Josephine; in front of us the piping sound that despite all rehearsal was still tentative and here in the audience the unself-conscious piping of a child; it would have been impossible to define the difference; but yet at once we hissed and whistled the interrupter down, although it would not really have been necessary, for in any case she would certainly have crawled away in fear and shame, whereas Josephine struck up her most triumphal notes and was quite beyond herself, spreading her arms wide and stretching her throat as high as it could reach.

That is what she is like always, every trifle, every casual incident, every nuisance, a creaking in the parquet, a grinding of teeth, a failure in the lighting incites her to heighten the effectiveness of her song; she believes anyhow that she is singing to deaf ears; there is no lack of enthusiasm and applause, but she has long learned not to expect real understanding, as she conceives it. So all disturbance is very welcome to her; whatever intervenes from outside to hinder the purity of her song, to be overcome with a slight effort, even with no effort at all, merely by confronting it, can help to awaken the masses, to teach them not perhaps understanding but awed respect.

And if small events do her such service, how much more do great ones. Our life is very uneasy, every day brings surprises, apprehensions, hopes, and terrors, so that it would be impossible for a single individual to bear it all did he not always have by day and night the support of his fellows; but even so it often becomes very difficult; frequently as many as a thousand shoulders are trembling under a burden that was really meant only for one pair. Then Josephine holds that her time has come. So there she stands, the delicate creature, shaken by vibrations especially below the breastbone, so that one feels anxious for her, it is as if she has concentrated all her strength on her song, as if from everything in her that does not directly subserve her singing all strength has been withdrawn, almost all power of life, as if she were laid bare, abandoned, committed merely to the care of good angels, as if while she is so wholly withdrawn and living only in her song a cold breath blowing upon her might kill her. But just when she makes such an appearance, we who are supposed to be her opponents are in the habit of saying: 'She can't even pipe; she has to put such a terrible strain on herself to force out not a song – we can't call it song – but some approximation to our usual customary piping.' So it seems to us, but this impression although, as I said, inevitable is yet fleeting and transient. We too are soon sunk in the feeling of the mass, which, warmly pressed body to body, listens with indrawn breath.

And to gather around her this mass of our people who are almost always on the run and scurrying hither and thither for reasons that are often not very clear, Josephine mostly needs to do nothing else than take up her stand, head thrown back, mouth half open, eyes turned upwards, in the position that indicates her intention to sing. She can do this where she likes, it need not be a place visible a long way off, any secluded corner pitched on in a moment's caprice will serve as well. The news that she is going to sing flies around at once and soon whole processions are on the way there. Now, sometimes, all the same, obstacles intervene, Josephine likes best to sing just when things are most upset, many worries and dangers force us then to take devious ways, with the best will in the world we cannot assemble ourselves as quickly as Josephine wants, and on occasion she stands there in ceremonial state for quite a time without a sufficient audience – then indeed she turns furious, then she stamps her feet, swearing in most unmaidenly fashion; she actually bites. But even such behaviour does no harm to her reputation; instead of curbing a little her excessive demands, people exert themselves to meet them; messengers are sent out to summon fresh hearers; she is kept in ignorance of the fact that this is being done; on the roads all around sentries can be seen posted who wave on newcomers and urge them to hurry; this goes on until at last a tolerably large audience is gathered.

What drives the people to make such exertions for Josephine's sake? This is no easier to answer than the first question about Josephine's singing, with which it is closely connected. One could eliminate that and combine them both in the second question, if it were possible to assert that because of her singing our people are unconditionally devoted to Josephine. But this is simply not the case; unconditional devotion is hardly known among us; ours are people who love slyness beyond everything, without any malice, to be sure, and childish whispering and chatter, innocent, superficial chatter, to be sure, but people of such a kind cannot go in for unconditional devotion, and that Josephine herself certainly feels, that is what she is fighting against with all the force of her feeble throat.

In making such generalized pronouncements, of course, one should not go too far, our people are all the same devoted to Josephine, only not unconditionally. For instance, they would not be capable of laughing at Josephine. It can be admitted: in Josephine there is much to make one laugh; and laughter for its own sake is never far away from us; in spite of all the misery of our lives quiet laughter is always, so to speak, at our elbows; but we do not laugh at Josephine. Many a time I have had the impression that our people interpret their relationship to Josephine in this way, that she, this frail creature, needing protection and in some way remarkable, in her own opinion remarkable for her gift of song, is entrusted to their care and they must look after her; the reason for this is not clear to anyone, only the fact seems to be established. But what is entrusted to one's care one does not laugh at; to laugh would be a breach of duty; the utmost malice which the most malicious of us wreak on Josephine is to say now and then: 'The sight of Josephine is enough to make one stop laughing.'

So the people look after Josephine much as a father takes into his care a child whose little hand — one cannot tell whether in appeal or command — is stretched out to him. One might think that our people are not fitted to exercise such paternal duties, but in reality they discharge them, at least in this case, admirably; no single individual could do what in this respect the people as a whole are capable of doing. To be sure, the difference in strength between the people and the individual is so enormous that it is enough for the nursling to be drawn into the warmth of their nearness and he is sufficiently protected. To Josephine, certainly, one does not dare mention such ideas. 'Your protection isn't worth an old song,' she says then. Sure, sure, old song, we think. And besides her protest is no real contradiction, it is rather a thoroughly childish way of doing, and childish gratitude, while a father's way of doing is to pay no attention to it.

Yet there is something else behind it which is not so easy to explain by this relationship between the people and Josephine. Josephine, that is to say, thinks just the opposite, she believes it is she who protects the people. When we are in a bad way politically or economically, her singing is supposed to save us, nothing less than that, and if it does not drive away the evil, at least gives us the strength to bear it. She does not put it in these words or in any other, she says very little anyhow, she is silent among the chatterers, but it flashes from her eyes, on her closed lips – few among us can keep their lips closed, but she can – it is plainly legible. Whenever we get bad news – and on many days bad news comes thick and fast at once, lies and half-truths included – she rises up at once, whereas usually she sits listlessly on the ground, she rises up and stretches her neck and tries to see over the heads of her flock like a shepherd before a thunderstorm. It is certainly a habit of children, in their wild, impulsive fashion, to make such claims, but Josephine's are not quite so unfounded as children's. True, she does not save us and she gives us no strength; it is easy to stage oneself as a saviour of our people, inured as they are to suffering, not sparing themselves, swift in decision, well acquainted with death, timorous only to the eye in the atmosphere of reckless daring which they constantly breathe, and as prolific besides as they are bold – it is easy, I say, to stage oneself after the event as the saviour of our people, who have always somehow managed to save themselves, although at the cost of sacrifices which make historians – generally speaking we ignore historical research entirely – quite horror-struck. And yet it is true that just in emergencies we hearken better than at other times to Josephine's voice. The menaces that loom over us make us quieter, more humble, more submissive to Josephine's domination; we like to come together, we like to huddle close to each other, especially on an occasion set apart from the troubles preoccupying us; it is as if we were drinking in all haste – yes, haste is necessary, Josephine too often forgets that – from a cup of peace in common before the battle. It is not so much a performance of songs as an assembly of the people, and an assembly where except for the small piping voice in front there is complete stillness; the hour is much too grave for us to waste it in chatter.

A relationship of this kind, of course, would never content Josephine. Despite all the nervous uneasiness that fills Josephine because her position has never been quite defined, there is still much that she does not see, blinded by her self-conceit, and she can be brought fairly easily to overlook much more, a swarm of flatterers is always busy about her to this end, thus really doing a public service – and yet to be only an incidental, unnoticed performer in a corner of an assembly of the people, for that, although in itself it would be no small thing, she would certainly not make us the sacrifice of her singing.

Nor does she need to, for her art does not go unnoticed. Although we are at bottom preoccupied with quite other things and it is by no means only for the sake of her singing that stillness prevails and many a listener does not even look up but buries his face in his neighbour's fur, so that Josephine up in front seems to be exerting herself to no purpose, there is yet something – it cannot be denied – that irresistibly makes its way into us from Josephine's piping. This piping, which rises up where everyone else is pledged to silence, comes almost like a message from the whole people to each individual; Josephine's thin piping amidst grave decisions is almost like our people's precarious existence amidst the tumult of a hostile world. Josephine exerts herself, a mere nothing in voice, a mere nothing in execution, she asserts herself and gets across to us; it does us good to think of that. A really trained singer, if ever such a one should be found among us, we could certainly not endure at such a time and we should unanimously turn away from the senselessness of any such performance. May Josephine be spared from perceiving that the mere fact of our listening to her is proof that she is no singer. An intuition of it she must have, else why does she so passionately deny that we do listen, only she keeps on singing and piping her intuition away.

But there are other things she could take comfort from: we do really listen to her in a sense, probably much as one listens to a trained singer; she gets effects which a trained singer would try in vain to achieve among us and which are only produced precisely because her means are so inadequate. For this, doubtless, our way of life is mainly responsible.

Among our people there is no age of youth, scarcely the briefest childhood. Regularly, it is true, demands are put forward that the children should be granted a special freedom, a special protection, that their right to be a little carefree, to have a little senseless giddiness, a little play, that this right should be respected and the exercise of it encouraged; such demands are put forward and nearly everyone approves them, there is nothing one could approve more, but there is also nothing, in the reality of our daily life, that is less likely to be granted, one approves these demands, one makes attempts to meet them, but soon all the old ways are back again. Our life happens to be such that a child, as soon as it can run about a little and a little distinguish one thing from another, must look after itself just like an adult; the areas on which, for economic reasons, we have to live in dispersion are too wide, our enemies too numerous, the dangers lying everywhere in wait for us too incalculable – we cannot shelter our children from the struggle for existence, if we did so, it would bring them to an early grave. These depressing considerations are reinforced by another, which is not depressing: the fertility of our race. One generation – and each is numerous – treads on the heels of another, the children have no time to be children. Other races may foster their children carefully, schools may be erected for their little ones, out of these schools the children may come pouring daily, the future of the race, yet among them it is always the same children that come out day after day for a long time. We have no schools, but from our race come pouring at the briefest intervals the innumerable swarms of our children, merrily lisping or chirping so long as they cannot yet pipe, rolling or tumbling along by sheer impetus so long as they cannot yet run, clumsily carrying everything before them by mass weight so long as they cannot yet see, our children! And not the same children, as in those schools, no, always new children again and again, without end, without a break, hardly does a child appear than it is no more a child, while behind it new childish faces are already crowding so fast and so thick that they are indistinguishable, rosy with happiness. Truly, however delightful this may be and however much others may envy us for it, and rightly, we simply cannot give a real childhood to our children. And that has its consequences. A kind of unexpended, ineradicable childishness pervades our people; in direct opposition to what is best in us, our infallible practical common sense, we often behave with the utmost foolishness, with exactly the same foolishness as children, senselessly, wastefully, grandiosely, irresponsibly, and all that often for the sake of some trivial amusement. And although our enjoyment of it cannot of course be so whole-hearted as a child's enjoyment, something of this survives in it without a doubt. From this childishness of our people Josephine too has profited since the beginning.

Yet our people are not only childish, we are also in a sense prematurely old. Childhood and old age come upon us not as upon others. We have no youth, we are all at once grown-up, and then we stay grown-up too long, a certain weariness and hopelessness spreading from that leaves a broad trail through our people's nature, tough and strong in hope that it is in general. Our lack of musical gifts has surely some connection with this; we are too old for music, its excitement, its rapture do not suit our heaviness, wearily we wave it away; we content ourselves with piping; a little piping here and there, that is enough for us. Who knows, there may be talents for music among us; but if there were, the character of our people would suppress them before they could unfold. Josephine on the other hand can pipe as much as she will, or sing or whatever she likes to call it, that does not disturb us, that suits us, that we can well put up with; any music there may be in it is reduced to the least possible trace; a certain tradition of music is preserved, yet without making the slightest demand upon us.

But our people, being what they are, get still more than this from Josephine. At her concerts, especially in times of stress, it is only the very young who are interested in her singing as singing, they alone gaze in astonishment as she purses her lips, expels the air between her pretty front teeth, half dies in sheer wonderment at the sounds she herself is producing and after such a swooning swells her performance to new and more incredible heights, whereas the real mass of the people – this is plain to see – are quite withdrawn into themselves. Here in the brief intervals between their struggles our people dream, it is as if the limbs of each were loosened, as if the harried individual once in a while could relax and stretch himself at ease in the great, warm bed of the community. And into these dreams Josephine's piping drops note by note; she calls it pearl-like, we call it staccato; but at any rate here it is in its right place, as nowhere else, finding the moment wait for it as music scarcely ever does. Something of our poor brief childhood is in it, something of lost happiness that can never be found again, but also something of active daily life, of its small gaieties, unaccountable and yet springing up and not to be obliterated. And indeed this is all expressed not in full round tones but softly, in whispers, confidentially, sometimes a little hoarsely. Of course it is a kind of piping. Why not? Piping is our people's daily speech, only many a one pipes his whole life long and does not know it, where here piping is set free from the fetters of daily life and it sets us free too for a little while. We certainly should not want to do without these performances.

But from that point it is a long, long way to Josephine's claim that she gives us new strength and so on and so forth. For ordinary people, at least, not for her train of flatterers. 'What other explanation could there be?' – they say with quite shameless sauciness – 'how else could you explain the great audiences, especially when danger is most imminent, which have even often enough hindered proper precautions being taken in time to avert danger.' Now, this last statement is unfortunately true, but can hardly be counted as one of Josephine's titles to fame, especially considering that when such large gatherings have been unexpectedly flushed by the enemy and many of our people left lying for dead, Josephine, who was responsible for it all, and indeed perhaps attracted the enemy by her piping, has always occupied the safest place and was always the first to whisk away quietly and speedily under cover of her escort. Still, everyone really knows that, and yet people keep running to whatever place Josephine decides on next, at whatever time she rises up to sing. One could argue from this that Josephine stands almost beyond the law, that she can do what she pleases, at the risk of actually endangering the community, and will be forgiven for everything. If this were so, even Josephine's claims would be entirely comprehensible, yes, in this freedom to be allowed her, this extraordinary gift granted to her and to no one else in direct contravention of the laws, one could see an admission of the fact that the people do not understand Josephine, just as she alleges, that they marvel helplessly at her art, feel themselves unworthy of it, try to assuage the pity she rouses in them by making really desperate sacrifices for her and, to the same extent that her art is beyond their comprehension, consider her personality and her wishes to lie beyond their jurisdiction. Well, that is simply not true at all, perhaps as individuals the people may surrender too easily to Josephine, but as a whole they surrender unconditionally to no one, and not to her either.

For a long time back, perhaps since the very beginning of her artistic career, Josephine has been fighting for exemption from all daily work on account of her singing; she should be relieved of all responsibility for earning her daily bread and being involved in the general struggle for existence, which – apparently – should be transferred on her behalf to the people as a whole. A facile enthusiast – and there have been such – might argue from the mere unusualness of this demand, from the spiritual attitude needed to frame such a demand, that it has an inner justification. But our people draw other conclusions and quietly refuse it. Nor do they trouble much about disproving the assumptions on which it is based. Josephine argues, for instance, that the strain of working is bad for her voice, that the strain of working is of course nothing to the strain of singing, but it prevents her from being able to rest sufficiently after singing and to recuperate for more singing, she has to exhaust her strength completely and yet, in these circumstances, can never rise to the peak of her abilities. The people listen to her arguments and pay no attention. Our people, so easily moved, sometimes cannot be moved at all. Their refusal is sometimes so decided that even Josephine is taken aback, she appears to submit, does her proper share of work, sings as best she can, but all only for a time, then with renewed strength – for this purpose her strength seems inexhaustible – she takes up the fight again.

Now it is clear that what Josephine really wants is not what she puts into words. She is honourable, she is not work-shy, shirking in any case is quite unknown among us, if her petition were granted she would certainly live the same life as before, her work would not at all get in the way of her singing nor would her singing grow any better – what she wants is public, unambiguous, permanent recognition of her art, going far beyond any precedent so far known. But while almost everything else seems within her reach, this eludes her persistently. Perhaps she should have taken a different line of attack from the beginning, perhaps she herself sees that her approach was wrong, but now she cannot draw back, retreat would be self-betrayal, now she must stand or fall by her petition.

If she really had enemies, as she avers, they could get much amusement from watching this struggle, without having to lift a finger. But she has no enemies, and even though she is often criticized here and there, no one finds this struggle of hers amusing. Just because of the fact that the people show themselves here in their cold, judicial aspect, which is otherwise rarely seen among us. And however one may approve it in this case, the very idea that such an aspect might be turned upon oneself some day prevents amusement from breaking in. The important thing, both in the people's refusal and in Josephine's petition, is not the action itself, but the fact that the people are capable of presenting a stony, impenetrable front to one of their own, and that it is all the more impenetrable because in other respects they show an anxious paternal care, and more than paternal care, for this very member of the people.

Suppose that instead of the people one had an individual to deal with: one might imagine that this man had been giving in to Josephine all the time while nursing a wild desire to put an end to his submissiveness one fine day; that he had made superhuman sacrifices for Josephine in the firm belief that there was a natural limit to his capacity for sacrifice; yes, that he had sacrificed more than was needful merely to hasten the process, merely to spoil Josephine and encourage her to ask for more and more until she did indeed reach the limit with this last petition of hers; and that he then cut her off with a final refusal which was curt because long held in reserve. Now, this is certainly not how the matter stands, the people have no need of such guile, besides, their respect for Josephine is well tried and genuine, and Josephine's demands are after all so far-reaching that any simple child could have told her what the outcome would be; yet it may be that such considerations enter into Josephine's way of taking the matter and so add a certain bitterness to the pain of being refused.

But whatever her ideas on the subject, she does not let them deter her from pursuing the campaign. Recently she has even intensified her attack; hitherto she has used only words as her weapons but now she is beginning to have recourse to other means, which she thinks will prove more efficacious but which we think will run her into greater dangers.

Many believe that Josephine is becoming so insistent because she feels herself growing old and her voice falling off, and so she thinks it high time to wage the last battle for recognition. I do not believe it. Josephine would not be Josephine if that were true. For her there is no growing old and no falling off in her voice. If she makes demands it is not because of outward circumstances but because of an inner logic. She reaches for the highest garland not because it is momentarily hanging a little lower but because it is the highest; if she had any say in the matter she would have it still higher.

This contempt for external difficulties, to be sure, does not hinder her from using the most unworthy methods. Her rights seem beyond question to her; so what does it matter how she secures them; especially since in this world, as she sees it, honest methods are bound to fail. Perhaps that is why she has transferred the battle for her rights from the field of song to another which she cares little about. Her supporters have let it be known that, according to herself, she feels quite capable of singing in such a way that all levels of the populace, even to the remotest corners of the opposition, would find it a real delight, a real delight not by popular standards, for the people affirm that they have always delighted in her singing, but a delight by her own standards. However, she adds, since she cannot falsify the highest standards nor pander to the lowest, her singing will have to stay as it is. But when it comes to her campaign for exemption from work, we get a different story; it is of course also a campaign on behalf of her singing, yet she is not fighting directly with the priceless weapon of her song, so any instrument she uses is good enough. Thus, for instance, the rumour went around that Josephine meant to cut short her grace notes if her petition were not granted. I know nothing about grace notes, and have never noticed any in Josephine's singing. But Josephine is going to cut short her grace notes, not, for the present, to cut them out entirely, only to cut them short. Presumably she has carried out her threat, although I for one have observed no difference in her performance. The people as a whole listened in the usual way without making any pronouncement on the grace notes, nor did their response to her petition vary by a jot. It must be admitted that Josephine's way of thinking, like her figure, is often very charming.

And so, for instance, after that performance, just as if her decision about the grace notes had been too severe or too sudden a move against the people, she announced that next time she would put in all the grace notes again. Yet after the next concert she changed her mind once more, there was to be definitely an end of these great arias with the grace notes, and until her petition was favourably regarded they would never recur. Well, the people let all these announcements, decisions and counter-decisions go in at one ear and out at the other, like a grown-up person deep in thought turning a deaf ear to a child's babble, fundamentally well disposed but not accessible.

Josephine, however, does not give in. The other day, for instance, she claimed that she had hurt her foot at work, so that it was difficult for her to stand up to sing; but since she could not sing except standing up, her songs would now have to be cut short. Although she limps and leans on her supporters, no one believes that she is really hurt. Granted that her frail body is extra sensitive, she is yet one of us and we are a race of workers; if we were to start limping every time we got a scratch, the whole people would never be done limping. Yet though she lets herself be led about like a cripple, though she shows herself in this pathetic condition oftener than usual, the people all the same listen to her singing thankfully and appreciatively as before, but do not bother much about the shortening of her songs.

Since she cannot very well go on limping forever, she thinks of something else, she pleads that she is tired, not in the mood for singing, feeling faint. And so we get a theatrical performance as well as a concert. We see Josephine's supporters in the background begging and imploring her to sing. She would be glad to oblige, but she cannot. They comfort and caress her with flatteries, they almost carry her to the selected spot where she is supposed to sing. At last, bursting inexplicably into tears, she gives way, but when she stands up to sing, obviously at the end of her resources, weary, her arms not widespread as usual but hanging lifelessly down, so that one gets the impression that they are perhaps a little too short – just as she is about to strike up, there, she cannot do it after all, an unwilling shake of the head tells us so and she breaks down before our eyes. To be sure, she pulls herself together again and sings, I fancy, much as usual; perhaps, if one has an ear for the finer shades of expression, one can hear that she is singing with unusual feeling, which is, however, all to the good. And in the end she is actually less tired than before, with a firm tread, if one can use such a term for her tripping gait, she moves off, refusing all help from her supporters and measuring with cold eyes the crowd which respectfully makes way for her.

That happened a day or two ago; but the latest is that she has disappeared, just at a time when she was supposed to sing. It is not only her supporters who are looking for her, many are devoting themselves to the search, but all in vain; Josephine has vanished, she will not sing; she will not even be cajoled into singing, this time she has deserted us entirely.

Curious, how mistaken she is in her calculations, the clever creature, so mistaken that one might fancy she has made no calculations at all but is only being driven on by her destiny, which in our world cannot be anything but a sad one. Of her own accord she abandons her singing, of her own accord she destroys the power she has gained over people's hearts. How could she ever have gained that power, since she knows so little about these hearts of ours? She hides herself and does not sing, but our people, quietly, without visible disappointment, a self-confident mass in perfect equilibrium, so constituted, even though appearances are misleading, that they can only bestow gifts and not receive them, even from Josephine, our people continue on their way.

Josephine's road, however, must go downhill. The time will soon come when her last notes sound and die into silence. She is a small episode in the eternal history of our people, and the people will get over the loss of her. Not that it will be easy for us; how can our gatherings take place in utter silence? Still, were they not silent even when Josephine was present? Was her actual piping notably louder and more alive than the memory of it will be? Was it even in her lifetime more than a simple memory? Was it not rather because Josephine's singing was already past losing in this way that our people in their wisdom prized it so highly?

So perhaps we shall not miss so very much after all, while Josephine, redeemed from the earthly sorrows which to her thinking lay in wait for all chosen spirits, will happily lose herself in the numberless throng of the heroes of our people, and soon, since we are no historians, will rise to the heights of redemption and be forgotten like all her brothers.

A Little Fable

'Alas,' said the mouse, 'the world is growing smaller every day. At the beginning it was so big that I was afraid, I kept running and running, and I was glad when at last I saw walls far away to the right and left, but these long walls have narrowed so quickly that I am in the last chamber already, and there in the corner stands the trap that I must run into.' 'You only need to change your direction,' said the cat, and ate it up.

IV

The True Path

The true path is along a rope that is not spanned high in the air, but only just above the ground. It seems intended more to cause stumbling than to be walked along.

The Noose

To be pulled in through the ground-floor window of a house by a rope tied around one's neck and to be yanked up, bloody and ragged, through all the ceilings, furniture, walls, and attics, without consideration, as if by a person who is paying no attention, until the empty noose, dropping the last fragments of me when it breaks through the roof tiles, is seen on the roof.

First Sorrow

A trapeze artist – this art, practised high in the vaulted domes of the great variety theatres, is admittedly one of the most difficult humanity can achieve – had so arranged his life that, as long as he kept working in the same building, he never came down from his trapeze by night or day, at first only from a desire to perfect his skill, but later because custom was too strong for him. All his needs, very modest needs at that, were supplied by relays of attendants who watched from below and sent up and hauled down again in specially constructed containers whatever he required. This way of living caused no particular inconvenience to the theatrical people, except that, when other turns were on the stage, his being still up aloft, which could not be dissembled, proved somewhat distracting, as also the fact that, although at such times he mostly kept very still, he drew a stray glance here and there from the public. Yet the management overlooked this, because he was an extraordinary and unique artist. And of course they recognized that this mode of life was no mere prank, and that only in this way could he really keep himself in constant practice and his art at the pitch of its perfection.

Besides, it was quite healthful up there, and when in the warmer seasons of the year the side windows all around the dome of the theatre were thrown open and sun and fresh air came pouring irresistibly into the dusky vault, it was even beautiful. True, his social life was somewhat limited, only sometimes a fellow acrobat swarmed up the ladder to him, and then they both sat on the trapeze, leaning left and right against the supporting ropes, and chatted, or builders' workmen repairing the roof exchanged a few words with him through an open window, or the fireman, inspecting the emergency lighting in the top gallery, called over to him something that sounded respectful but could hardly be made out. Otherwise nothing disturbed his seclusion; occasionally, perhaps, some theatre hand straying through the empty theatre of an afternoon gazed thoughtfully up into the great height of the roof, almost beyond eyeshot, where the trapeze artist, unaware that he was being observed, practised his art or rested.

The trapeze artist could have gone on living peacefully like that, had it not been for the inevitable journeys from place to place, which he found extremely trying. Of course his manager saw to it that his sufferings were not prolonged one moment more than necessary; for town travel, racing automobiles were used, which whirled him, by night if possible or in the earliest hours of the morning, through the empty streets at breakneck speed, too slow all the same for the trapeze artist's impatience; for railway journeys, a whole compartment was reserved, in which the trapeze artist, as a possible though wretched alternative to his usual way of living, could pass the time up on the luggage rack; in the next town on their circuit, long before he arrived, the trapeze was already slung up in the theatre and all the doors leading to the stage were flung wide open, all corridors kept free – yet the manager never knew a happy moment until the trapeze artist set his foot on the rope ladder and in a twinkling, at long last, hung aloft on his trapeze.

Despite so many journeys having been successfully arranged by the manager, each new one embarrassed him again, for the journeys, apart from everything else, got on the nerves of the artist a great deal.

Once when they were again travelling together, the trapeze artist lying on the luggage rack dreaming, the manager leaning back in the opposite window seat reading a book, the trapeze artist addressed his companion in a low voice. The manager was immediately all attention. The trapeze artist, biting his lips, said that he must always in future have two trapezes for his performance instead of only one, two trapezes opposite each other. The manager at once agreed. But the trapeze artist, as if to show that the manager's consent counted for as little as his refusal, said that never again would he perform on only one trapeze, in no circumstances whatever. The very idea that it might happen at all seemed to make him shudder. The manager, watchfully feeling his way, once more emphasized his entire agreement, two trapezes were better than one, besides it would be an advantage to have a second bar, more variety could be introduced into the performance. At that the trapeze artist suddenly burst into tears. Deeply distressed, the manager sprang to his feet and asked what was the matter, then getting no answer climbed up on the seat and caressed him, cheek to cheek, so that his own face was bedabbled by the trapeze artist's tears. Yet it took much questioning and soothing endearment until the trapeze artist sobbed: 'Only the one bar in my hands – how can I go on living!' That made it somewhat easier for the manager to comfort him; he promised to wire from the very next station for a second trapeze to be installed in the first town on their circuit; reproached himself for having let the artist work so long on only one trapeze; and thanked and praised him warmly for having at last brought the mistake to his notice. And so he succeeded in reassuring the trapeze artist, little by little, and was able to go back to his corner. But he himself was far from reassured, with deep uneasiness he kept glancing secretly at the trapeze artist over the top of his book. Once such ideas began to torment him, would they ever quite leave him alone? Would they not rather increase in urgency? Would they not threaten his very existence? And indeed the manager believed he could see, during the apparently peaceful sleep which had succeeded the fit of tears, the first furrows of care engraving themselves upon the trapeze artist's smooth, childlike forehead.

Up in the Gallery

If some frail, consumptive equestrienne in the circus were to be urged around and around on an undulating horse for months on end without respite by a ruthless, whip-flourishing ring-master, before an insatiable public, whizzing along on her horse, throwing kisses, swaying from the waist, and if this performance were likely to continue in the infinite perspective of a drab future to the unceasing roar of the orchestra and hum of the ventilators, accompanied by ebbing and renewed swelling bursts of applause which are really steam hammers – then, perhaps, a young visitor to the gallery might race down the long stairs through all the circles, rush into the ring, and yell: Stop! against the fanfares of the orchestra still playing the appropriate music.

But since that is not so; a lovely lady, pink and white, floats in between the curtains, which proud lackeys open before her; the ringmaster, deferentially catching her eye, comes toward her breathing animal devotion; tenderly lifts her up on the dapple-grey, as if she were his own most precious granddaughter about to start on a dangerous journey; cannot make up his mind to give the signal with his whip, finally masters himself enough to crack the whip loudly; runs along beside the horse, open-mouthed; follows with a sharp eye the leaps taken by its rider; finds her artistic skill almost beyond belief; calls to her with English shouts of warning; angrily exhorts the grooms who hold the hoops to be most closely attentive; before the great somersault lifts up his arms and implores the orchestra to be silent; finally lifts the little one down from her trembling horse, kisses her on both cheeks, and finds that all the ovation she gets from the audience is barely sufficient; while she herself, supported by him, right up on the tips of her toes, in a cloud of dust, with outstretched arms and small head thrown back, invites the whole circus to share her triumph — since that is so, the visitor to the gallery lays his face on the rail before him and, sinking into the closing march as into a heavy dream, weeps without knowing it.

The Whip

The animal wrests the whip from its master and whips itself in order to become master, not knowing that this is only a fantasy produced by a new knot in the master's whiplash.

The Snake Charmer

Sweet serpent, why do you stay so far away, come nearer, nearer still, enough, no further, stay there. For you, too, there are no frontiers. How am I to attain mastery over you if you recognize no frontiers? It will be hard work. I begin by asking you to curl yourself up. Curl yourself up, I said, and you stretch yourself. Don't you understand me? You don't understand me. But I speak very clearly: Curl up! No, you don't grasp it. So then I show you, here, with the staff. First of all you must describe a large circle, then inside, adjoining it, a second, and so forth. If then finally you are still holding your little head high, lower it slowly to the tune on the flute that I shall later play, and when I cease, you shall have become quiet too, with your head in the inmost circle.

The Snake

'Prepare the way for the snake!', came the shout. 'Prepare the way for the great Madame!' – 'We are ready,' came the answering shout, 'we are ready!' And we who were to prepare the way, renowned stone-crushers all, marched out of the woods. 'To work!', cried our ever-cheerful Commandant, 'to work, you snake-fodder!' Immediately we raised our hammers, and for miles around began the busiest of hammering. No pause was allowed, only a change from one hand to the other. The arrival of our snake was already promised for that evening; by then everything had to be hammered to dust; our snake could not tolerate even the smallest stone. Where is there another snake so fastidious? She is a snake without peer, she has been thoroughly pampered by our labour, and by now there is none to compare with her. We do not understand, indeed we deplore the fact that she still calls herself snake. She should call herself Madame, at least – though as Madame she is of course equally incomparable. But that is no concern of ours, our business is to make dust.

Joys

The joys of this life are not life's, but our fear of ascending into a higher life; the torments of this life are not life's, but our self-torment on account of that fear.

The Top

A certain philosopher used to hang about wherever children were at play. And whenever he saw a boy with a top, he would lie in wait. As soon as the top began to spin the philosopher went in pursuit and tried to catch it. He was not perturbed when the children noisily protested and tried to keep him away from their toy; so long as he could catch the top while it was still spinning, he was happy, but only for a moment; then he threw it to the ground and walked away. For he believed that the understanding of any detail, that of a spinning top, for instance, was sufficient for the understanding of all things. For this reason he did not busy himself with great problems, it seemed to him uneconomical; once the smallest detail was properly understood, then everything was understood, which was why he busied himself only with the spinning top. And whenever preparations were being made for the spinning of the top, he hoped that this time he would succeed: as soon as the top began to spin and he was running breathlessly after it, the hope would turn to certainty, but when he held the silly piece of wood in his hand, he felt nauseated, and the screaming of the children, which hitherto he had not heard and which now suddenly pierced his ears, chased him away; he reeled off like a top under a clumsy whip.

A Chinese Puzzle

Once there was a Chinese puzzle, a cheap simple toy, not much bigger than a pocket watch and without any sort of surprising contrivances. Cut into the flat wood, which was painted reddish-brown, there were some blue labyrinthine paths, which all led into a little hole. The ball, which was also blue, had to be got into one of the paths by means of tilting and shaking the box, and then into the hole. Once the ball was in the hole, the game was over, and if one wanted to start all over again, one had first to shake the ball out of the hole. The whole thing was covered over with a strong, convex glass, one could not put the puzzle in one's pocket and carry it about with one, and wherever one was, one could take it out and play with it.

If the ball was unemployed, it spent most of the time strolling to and fro, its hands clasped behind its back, on the plateau, avoiding the paths. It held the view that it was quite enough bothered with the paths during the game and that it had every right to recuperate on the open plain when no game was going on. Sometimes it would look up at the vaulted glass, but merely out of habit and quite without any intention of trying to make out anything up there. It had a rather straddling gait and maintained that it was not made for those narrow paths. That was partly true, for indeed the paths could hardly contain it, but it was also untrue, for the fact was that it was very carefully made to fit the width of the paths exactly, but the paths were certainly not meant to be comfortable for it, or else it would not have been a puzzle at all.

A Hunger Artist

During these last decades the interest in professional fasting has markedly diminished. It used to pay very well to stage such great performances under one's own management, but today that is quite impossible. We live in a different world now. At one time the whole town took a lively interest in the hunger artist; from day to day of his fast the excitement mounted; everybody wanted to see him at least once a day; there were people who bought season tickets for the last few days and sat from morning till night in front of his small barred cage; even in the night-time there were visiting hours, when the whole effect was heightened by torch flares; on fine days the cage was set out in the open air, and then it was the children's special treat to see the hunger artist; for their elders he was often just a joke that happened to be in fashion, but the children stood open-mouthed, holding each other's hands for greater security, marvelling at him as he sat there pallid in black tights, with his ribs sticking out so prominently, not even on a seat but down among straw on the ground, sometimes giving a courteous nod, answering questions with a constrained smile, or perhaps stretching an arm through the bars so that one might feel how thin it was, and then again withdrawing deep into himself, paying no attention to anyone or anything, not even to the all-important striking of the clock that was the only piece of furniture in his cage, but merely staring into vacancy with half-shut eyes, now and then taking a sip from a tiny glass of water to moisten his lips.

Besides casual onlookers there were also relays of permanent watchers selected by the public, usually butchers, strangely enough, and it was their task to watch the hunger artist day and night, three of them at a time, in case he should have some secret recourse to nourishment. This was nothing but a formality, instituted to reassure the masses, for the initiates knew well enough that during his fast the artist would never in any circumstances, not even under forcible compulsion, swallow the smallest morsel of food; the honour of his profession forbade it. Not every watcher, of course, was capable of understanding this, there were often groups of night watchers who were very lax in carrying out their duties and deliberately huddled together in a retired corner to play cards with great absorption, obviously intending to give the hunger artist the chance of a little refreshment, which they supposed he could draw from some private hoard. Nothing annoyed the artist more than such watchers; they made him miserable; they made his fast seem unendurable; sometimes he mastered his feebleness sufficiently to sing during their watch for as long as he could keep going, to show them how unjust their suspicions were. But that was of little use; they only wondered at his cleverness in being able to fill his mouth even while singing. Much more to his taste were the watchers who sat close up to the bars, who were not content with the dim night lighting of the hall but focused him in the full glare of the electric pocket torch given them by the impresario. The harsh light did not trouble him at all, in any case he could never sleep properly, and he could always drowse a little, whatever the light, at any hour, even when the hall was thronged with noisy onlookers. He was quite happy at the prospect of spending a sleepless night with such watchers; he was ready to exchange jokes with them, to tell them stories out of his nomadic life, anything at all to keep them awake and demonstrate to them again that he had no eatables in his cage and that he was fasting as not one of them could fast. But his happiest moment was when the morning came and an enormous breakfast was brought them, at his expense, on which they flung themselves with the keen appetite of healthy men after a weary night of wakefulness. Of course there were people who argued that this breakfast was an unfair attempt to bribe the watchers, but that was going rather too far, and when they were invited to take on a night's vigil without a breakfast, merely for the sake of the cause, they made themselves scarce, although they stuck stubbornly to their suspicions.

Such suspicions, anyhow, were a necessary accompaniment to the profession of fasting. No one could possibly watch the hunger artist continuously, day and night, and so no one could produce first-hand evidence that the fast had really been rigorous and continuous; only the artist himself could know that, he was therefore bound to be the sole completely satisfied spectator of his own fast. Yet for other reasons he was never satisfied; it was not perhaps mere fasting that had brought him to such skeleton thinness that many people had regretfully to keep away from his exhibitions, because the sight of him was too much for them, perhaps it was dissatisfaction with himself that had worn him down. For he alone knew, what no other initiate knew, how easy it was to fast. It was the easiest thing in the world. He made no secret of this, yet people did not believe him, at the best they set him down as modest, most of them, however, thought he was out for publicity or else was some kind of cheat who found it easy to fast because he had discovered a way of making it easy, and then had the impudence to admit the fact, more or less. He had to put up with all that, and in the course of time had got used to it, but his inner dissatisfaction always rankled, and never yet, after any term of fasting – this must be granted to his credit – had he left the cage of his own free will. The longest period of fasting was fixed by his impresario at forty days, beyond that term he was not allowed to go, not even in great cities, and there was good reason for it, too. Experience had proved that for about forty days the interest of the public could be stimulated by a steadily increasing pressure of advertisement, but after that the town began to lose interest, sympathetic support began notably to fall off; there were of course local variations as between one town and another or one country and another, but as a general rule forty days marked the limit. So on the fortieth day the flower-bedecked cage was opened, enthusiastic spectators filled the hall, a military band played, two doctors entered the cage to measure the results of the fast, which were announced through a megaphone, and finally two young ladies appeared, blissful at having been selected for the honour, to help the hunger artist down the few steps leading to a small table on which was spread a carefully chosen invalid repast. And at this very moment the artist always turned stubborn. True, he would entrust his bony arms to the outstretched helping hands of the ladies bending over him, but stand up he would not. Why stop fasting at this particular moment, after forty days of it? He had held out for a long time, an illimitably long time; why stop now, when he was in his best fasting form, or rather, not yet quite in his best fasting form? Why should he be cheated of the fame he would get for fasting longer, for being not only the record hunger artist of all time, which presumably he was already, but for beating his own record by a performance beyond human imagination, since he felt that there were no limits to his capacity for fasting? His public pretended to admire him so much, why should it have so little patience with him; if he could endure fasting longer, why shouldn't the public endure it? Besides, he was tired, he was comfortable sitting in the straw, and now he was supposed to lift himself to his full height and go down to a meal the very thought of which gave him a nausea that only the presence of the ladies kept him from betraying, and even that with an effort. And he looked up into the eyes of the ladies who were apparently so friendly and in reality so cruel, and shook his head, which felt too heavy on its strengthless neck. But then there happened yet again what always happened. The impresario came forward, without a word – for the band made speech impossible – lifted his arms in the air above the artist, as if inviting Heaven to look down upon its creature here in the straw, this suffering martyr, which indeed he was, although in quite another sense; grasped him around the emaciated waist, with exaggerated caution, so that the frail condition he was in might be appreciated; and committed him to the care of the blenching ladies, not without secretly giving him a shaking so that his legs and body tottered and swayed. The artist now submitted completely; his head lolled on his breast as if it had landed there by chance; his body was hollowed out; his legs in a spasm of self-preservation clung close to each other at the knees, yet scraped on the ground as if it were not really solid ground, as if they were only trying to find solid ground; and the whole weight of his body, a featherweight after all, relapsed onto one of the ladies, who, looking around for help and panting a little – this post of honour was not at all what she had expected it to be – first stretched her neck as far as she could to keep her face at least free from contact with the artist, then finding this impossible, and her more fortunate companion not coming to her aid but merely holding extended in her own trembling hand the little bunch of knucklebones that was the artist's, to the great delight of the spectators burst into tears and had to be replaced by an attendant who had long been stationed in readiness. Then came the food, a little of which the impresario managed to get between the artist's lips, while he sat in a kind of half-fainting trance, to the accompaniment of cheerful patter designed to distract the public's attention from the artist's condition; after that, a toast was drunk to the public, supposedly prompted by a whisper from the artist in the impresario's ear; the band confirmed it with a mighty flourish, the spectators melted away, and no one had any cause to be dissatisfied with the proceedings, no one except the hunger artist himself, he only, as always.

So he lived for many years, with small regular intervals of recuperation, in visible glory, honoured by the world, yet in spite of that troubled in spirit, and all the more troubled because no one would take his trouble seriously. What comfort could he possibly need? What more could he possibly wish for? And if some good-natured person, feeling sorry for him, tried to console him by pointing out that his melancholy was probably caused by fasting, it could happen, especially when he had been fasting for some time, that he reacted with an outburst of fury and to the general alarm began to shake the bars of his cage like a wild animal. Yet the impresario had a way of punishing these outbreaks which he rather enjoyed putting into operation. He would apologize publicly for the artist's behaviour, which was only to be excused, he admitted, because of the irritability caused by fasting; a condition hardly to be understood by well-fed people; then by natural transition he went on to mention the artist's equally incomprehensible boast that he could fast for much longer than he was doing; he praised the high ambition, the good will, the great self-denial undoubtedly implicit in such a statement; and then quite simply countered it by bringing out photographs, which were also on sale to the public, showing the artist on the fortieth day of a fast lying in bed almost dead from exhaustion. This perversion of the truth, familiar to the artist though it was, always unnerved him afresh and proved too much for him. What was a consequence of the premature ending of his fast was here presented as the cause of it! To fight against this lack of understanding, against a whole world of non-understanding, was impossible. Time and again in good faith he stood by the bars listening to the impresario, but as soon as the photographs appeared he always let go and sank with a groan back onto his straw, and the reassured public could once more come close and gaze at him.

A few years later when the witnesses of such scenes called them to mind, they often failed to understand themselves at all. For meanwhile the aforementioned change in public interest had set in; it seemed to happen almost overnight; there may have been profound causes for it, but who was going to bother about that; at any rate the pampered hunger artist suddenly found himself deserted one fine day by the amusement-seekers, who went streaming past him to other more-favoured attractions. For the last time the impresario hurried him over half Europe to discover whether the old interest might still survive here and there; all in vain; everywhere, as if by secret agreement, a positive revulsion from professional fasting was in evidence. Of course it could not really have sprung up so suddenly as all that, and many premonitory symptoms which had not been sufficiently remarked or suppressed during the rush and glitter of success now came retrospectively to mind, but it was now too late to take any countermeasures. Fasting would surely come into fashion again at some future date, yet that was no comfort for those living in the present. What, then, was the hunger artist to do? He had been applauded by thousands in his time and could hardly come down to showing himself in a street booth at village fairs, and as for adopting another profession, he was not only too old for that but too fanatically devoted to fasting. So he took leave of the impresario, his partner in an unparalleled career, and hired himself to a large circus; in order to spare his own feelings he avoided reading the conditions of his contract.

A large circus with its enormous traffic in replacing and recruiting men, animals, and apparatus can always find a use for people at any time, even for a hunger artist, provided of course that he does not ask too much, and in this particular case anyhow it was not only the artist who was taken on but his famous and long-known name as well, indeed considering the peculiar nature of his performance, which was not impaired by advancing age, it could not be objected that here was an artist past his prime, no longer at the height of his professional skill, seeking a refuge in some quiet corner of a circus; on the contrary, the hunger artist averred that he could fast as well as ever, which was entirely credible, he even alleged that if he were allowed to fast as he liked, and this was at once promised him without more ado, he could astound the world by establishing a record never yet achieved, a statement that certainly provoked a smile among the other professionals, since it left out of account the change in public opinion, which the hunger artist in his zeal conveniently forgot.

He had not, however, actually lost his sense of the real situation and took it as a matter of course that he and his cage should be stationed, not in the middle of the ring as a main attraction, but outside, near the animal cages, on a site that was after all easily accessible. Large and gaily painted placards made a frame for the cage and announced what was to be seen inside it. When the public came thronging out in the intervals to see the animals, they could hardly avoid passing the hunger artist's cage and stopping there for a moment, perhaps they might even have stayed longer had not those pressing behind them in the narrow gangway, who did not understand why they should be held up on their way toward the excitements of the menagerie, made it impossible for anyone to stand gazing quietly for any length of time. And that was the reason why the hunger artist, who had of course been looking forward to these visiting hours as the main achievement of his life, began instead to shrink from them. At first he could hardly wait for the intervals; it was exhilarating to watch the crowds come streaming his way, until only too soon – not even the most obstinate self-deception, clung to almost consciously, could hold out against the fact – the conviction was borne in upon him that these people, most of them, to judge from their actions, again and again, without exception, were all on their way to the menagerie. And the first sight of them from the distance remained the best. For when they reached his cage he was at once deafened by the storm of shouting and abuse that arose from the two contending factions, which renewed themselves continuously, of those who wanted to stop and stare at him – he soon began to dislike them more than the others – not out of real interest but only out of obstinate self-assertiveness, and those who wanted to go straight on to the animals. When the first great rush was past, the stragglers came along, and these, whom nothing could have prevented from stopping to look at him as long as they had breath, raced past with long strides, hardly even glancing at him, in their haste to get to the menagerie in time. And all too rarely did it happen that he had a stroke of luck, when some father of a family fetched up before him with his children, pointed a finger at the hunger artist, and explained at length what the phenomenon meant, telling stories of earlier years when he himself had watched similar but much more thrilling performances, and the children, still rather uncomprehending, since neither inside nor outside school had they been sufficiently prepared for this lesson – what did they care about fasting? – yet showed by the brightness of their intent eyes that new and better times might be coming. Perhaps, said the hunger artist to himself many a time, things would be a little better if his cage were set not quite so near the menagerie. That made it too easy for people to make their choice, to say nothing of what he suffered from the stench of the menagerie, the animals' restlessness by night, the carrying past of raw lumps of flesh for the beasts of prey, the roaring at feeding times, which depressed him continually. But he did not dare to lodge a complaint with the management; after all, he had the animals to thank for the troops of people who passed his cage, among whom there might always be one here and there to take an interest in him, and who could tell where they might seclude him if he called attention to his existence and thereby to the fact that, strictly speaking, he was only an impediment on the way to the menagerie.

A small impediment, to be sure, one that grew steadily less. People grew familiar with the strange idea that they could be expected, in times like these, to take an interest in a hunger artist, and with this familiarity the verdict went out against him. He might fast as much as he could, and he did so; but nothing could save him now, people passed him by. Just try to explain to anyone the art of fasting! Anyone who has no feeling for it cannot be made to understand it. The fine placards grew dirty and illegible, they were torn down; the little notice board telling the number of fast days achieved, which at first was changed carefully every day, had long stayed at the same figure, for after the first few weeks even this small task seemed pointless to the staff; and so the artist simply fasted on and on, as he had once dreamed of doing, and it was no trouble to him, just as he had always foretold, but no one counted the days, no one, not even the artist himself, knew what records he was already breaking, and his heart grew heavy. And when once in a while some lei-surely passer-by stopped, made merry over the old figure on the board, and spoke of swindling, that was in its way the stupidest lie ever invented by indifference and inborn malice, since it was not the hunger artist who was cheating, he was working honestly, but the world was cheating him of his reward.

Many more days went by, however, and that too came to an end. An overseer's eye fell on the cage one day and he asked the attendants why this perfectly good cage should be left standing there unused with dirty straw inside it; nobody knew, until one man, helped out by the notice board, remembered about the hunger artist. They poked into the straw with sticks and found him in it. 'Are you still fasting?' asked the overseer, 'when on earth do you mean to stop?' 'Forgive me, everybody,' whispered the hunger artist; only the overseer, who had his ear to the bars, understood him. 'Of course,' said the overseer, and tapped his forehead with a finger to let the attendants know what state the man was in, 'we forgive you.' 'I always wanted you to admire my fasting,' said the hunger artist. 'We do admire it,' said the overseer, affably. 'But you shouldn't admire it,' said the hunger artist. 'Well then we don't admire it,' said the overseer, 'but why shouldn't we admire it?' 'Because I have to fast, I can't help it,' said the hunger artist. 'What a fellow you are,' said the overseer, 'and why can't you help it?' 'Because,' said the hunger artist, lifting his head a little and speaking, with his lips pursed, as if for a kiss, right into the overseer's ear, so that no syllable might be lost, 'because I couldn't find the food I liked. If I had found it, believe me, I should have made no fuss and stuffed myself like you or anyone else.' These were his last words, but in his dimming eyes remained the firm though no longer proud persuasion that he was still continuing to fast.

'Well, clear this out now!' said the overseer, and they buried the hunger artist, straw and all. Into the cage they put a young panther. Even the most insensitive felt it refreshing to see this wild creature leaping around the cage that had so long been dreary. The panther was all right. The food he liked was brought him without hesitation by the attendants; he seemed not even to miss his freedom; his noble body, furnished almost to the bursting point with all that it needed, seemed to carry freedom around with it too; somewhere in his jaws it seemed to lurk; and the joy of life streamed with such ardent passion from his throat that for the onlookers it was not easy to stand the shock of it. But they braced themselves, crowded around the cage, and did not want ever to move away.

In the Penal Colony

'It's a remarkable piece of apparatus,' said the officer to the explorer and surveyed with a certain air of admiration the apparatus which was after all quite familiar to him. The explorer seemed to have accepted merely out of politeness the Commandant's invitation to witness the execution of a soldier condemned to death for disobedience and insulting behaviour to a superior. Nor did the colony itself betray much interest in this execution. At least, in the small sandy valley, a deep hollow surrounded on all sides by naked crags, there was no one present save the officer, the explorer, the condemned man, who was a stupid-looking, wide-mouthed creature with bewildered hair and face, and the soldier who held the heavy chain controlling the small chains locked on the prisoner's ankles, wrists, and neck, chains that were themselves attached to each other by communicating links. In any case, the condemned man looked so like a submissive dog that one might have thought he could be left to run free on the surrounding hills and would only need to be whistled for when the execution was due to begin.

The explorer did not much care about the apparatus and walked up and down behind the prisoner with almost visible indifference while the officer made the last adjustments, now creeping beneath the structure, which was bedded deep in the earth, now climbing a ladder to inspect its upper parts. These were tasks that might well have been left to a mechanic, but the officer performed them with great zeal, whether because he was a devoted admirer of the apparatus or because of other reasons the work could be entrusted to no one else. 'Ready now!' he called at last and climbed down from the ladder. He looked uncommonly limp, breathed with his mouth wide open, and had tucked two fine ladies' handkerchiefs under the collar of his uniform. 'These uniforms are too heavy for the tropics, surely,' said the explorer, instead of making some inquiry about the apparatus, as the officer had expected. 'Of course,' said the officer, washing his oily and greasy hands in a bucket of water that stood ready, 'but they mean home to us; we don't want to forget about home. Now just have a look at this machine,' he added at once, simultaneously drying his hands on a towel and indicating the apparatus. 'Up till now a few things still had to be set by hand, but from this moment it works all by itself.' The explorer nodded and followed him. The officer, anxious to secure himself against all contingencies, said: 'Things sometimes go wrong, of course; I hope that nothing goes wrong today, but we have to allow for the possibility. The machinery should go on working continuously for twelve hours. But if anything does go wrong it will only be some small matter that can be set right at once.'

'Won't you take a seat?' he asked finally, drawing a cane chair out from among a heap of them and offering it to the explorer, who could not refuse it. He was now sitting at the edge of a pit, into which he glanced for a fleeting moment. It was not very deep. On one side of the pit the excavated soil had been piled up in a rampart, on the other side of it stood the apparatus. 'I don't know,' said the officer, 'if the Commandant has already explained this apparatus to you.' The explorer waved one hand vaguely; the officer asked for nothing better, since now he could explain the apparatus himself. 'This apparatus,' he said, taking hold of a crank handle and leaning against it, 'was invented by our former Commandant. I assisted at the very earliest experiments and had a share in all the work until its completion. But the credit of inventing it belongs to him alone. Have you ever heard of our former Commandant? No? Well, it isn't saying too much if I tell you that the organization of the whole penal colony is his work. We who were his friends knew even before he died that the organization of the colony was so perfect that his successor, even with a thousand new schemes in his head, would find it impossible to alter anything, at least for many years to come. And our prophecy has come true; the new Commandant has had to acknowledge its truth. A pity you never met the old Commandant! – But,' the officer interrupted himself, 'I am rambling on, and here stands his apparatus before us. It consists, as you see, of three parts. In the course of time each of these parts has acquired a kind of popular nickname. The lower one is called the "Bed", the upper one the "Designer",' and this one here in the middle that moves up and down is called the "Harrow".' 'The Harrow?' asked the explorer. He had not been listening very attentively, the glare of the sun in the shadeless valley was altogether too strong, it was difficult to collect one's thoughts. All the more did he admire the officer, who in spite of his tight-fitting full-dress uniform coat, amply befrogged and weighed down by epaulettes, was pursuing his subject with such enthusiasm and, besides talking, was still tightening a screw here and there with a spanner. As for the soldier, he seemed to be in much the same condition as the explorer. He had wound the prisoner's chain around both his wrists, propped himself on his rifle, let his head hang, and was paying no attention to anything. That did not surprise the explorer, for the officer was speaking French, and certainly neither the soldier nor the prisoner understood a word of French. It was all the more remarkable, therefore, that the prisoner was nonetheless making an effort to follow the officer's explanations. With a kind of drowsy persistence he directed his gaze wherever the officer pointed a finger, and at the interruption of the explorer's question he, too, as well as the officer, looked around.

'Yes, the Harrow,' said the officer, 'a good name for it. The needles are set in like the teeth of a harrow and the whole thing works something like a harrow, although its action is limited to one place and contrived with much more artistic skill. Anyhow, you'll soon understand it. On the Bed here the condemned man is laid – I'm going to describe the apparatus first before I set it in motion. Then you'll be able to follow the proceedings better. Besides, one of the cogwheels in the Designer is badly worn; it creaks a lot when it's working; you can hardly hear yourself speak; spare parts, unfortunately, are difficult to get here. – Well, here is the Bed, as I told you. It is completely covered with a layer of cotton wool; you'll find out why later. On this cotton wool the condemned man is laid, face down, quite naked, of course; here are straps for the hands, here for the feet, and here for the neck, to bind him fast. Here at the head of the Bed, where the man, as I said, first lays down his face, is this little gag of felt, which can be easily regulated to go straight into his mouth. It is meant to keep him from screaming and biting his tongue. Of course the man is forced to take the felt into his mouth, for otherwise his neck would be broken by the strap.' 'Is that cotton wool?' asked the explorer, bending forward. 'Yes, certainly,' said the officer, with a smile, 'feel it for yourself.' He took the explorer's hand and guided it over the Bed. 'It's specially prepared cotton wool, that's why it looks so different; I'll tell you presently what it's for.' The explorer already felt a dawning interest in the apparatus; he sheltered his eyes from the sun with one hand and gazed up at the structure. It was a huge affair. The Bed and the Designer were of the same size and looked like two dark wooden chests. The Designer hung about two metres above the Bed; each of them was bound at the corners with four rods of brass that almost flashed out rays in the sunlight. Between the chests shuttled the Harrow on a ribbon of steel.

The officer had scarcely noticed the explorer's previous indifference, but he was now well aware of his dawning interest; so he stopped explaining in order to leave a space of time for quiet observation. The condemned man imitated the explorer; since he could not use a hand to shelter his eyes he gazed upwards without shade.

'Well, the man lies down,' said the explorer, leaning back in his chair and crossing his legs.

'Yes,' said the officer, pushing his cap back a little and passing one hand over his heated face, 'now listen! Both the Bed and the Designer have an electric battery each; the Bed needs one for itself, the Designer for the Harrow. As soon as the man is strapped down, the Bed is set in motion. It quivers in minute, very rapid vibrations, both from side to side and up and down. You will have seen similar apparatus in hospitals; but in our Bed the movements are all precisely calculated; you see, they have to correspond very exactly to the movements of the Harrow. And the Harrow is the instrument for the actual execution of the sentence.'

'And how does the sentence run?' asked the explorer.

'You don't know that either?' said the officer in amazement, and bit his lips. 'Forgive me if my explanations seem rather incoherent. I do beg your pardon. You see, the Commandant always used to do the explaining; but the new Commandant shirks this duty; yet that such an important visitor' – the explorer tried to deprecate the honour with both hands, the officer, however, insisted – 'that such an important visitor should not even be told about the kind of sentence we pass is a new development, which –' He was just on the point of using strong language but checked himself and said only: 'I was not informed, it is not my fault. In any case, I am certainly the best person to explain our procedure, since I have here' – he patted his breast pocket – 'the relevant drawings made by our former Commandant.'

'The Commandant's own drawings?' asked the explorer. 'Did he combine everything in himself, then? Was he soldier, judge, mechanic, chemist, and draughtsman?'

'Indeed he was,' said the officer, nodding assent, with a remote, glassy look. Then he inspected his hands critically; they did not seem clean enough to him for touching the drawings; so he went over to the bucket and washed them again. Then he drew out a small leather wallet and said: 'Our sentence does not sound severe. Whatever commandment the prisoner has disobeyed is written upon his body by the Harrow. This prisoner, for instance' – the officer indicated the man – 'will have written on his body: HONOUR THY SUPERIORS!'

The explorer glanced at the man; he stood, as the officer pointed him out, with bent head, apparently listening with all his ears in an effort to catch what was being said. Yet the movement of his blubber lips, closely pressed together, showed clearly that he could not understand a word. Many questions were troubling the explorer, but at the sight of the prisoner he asked only: 'Does he know his sentence?' 'No,' said the officer, eager to go on with his exposition, but the explorer interrupted him: 'He doesn't know the sentence that has been passed on him?' 'No,' said the officer again, pausing a moment as if to let the explorer elaborate his question, and then said: 'There would be no point in telling him. He'll learn it on his body.' The explorer intended to make no answer, but he felt the prisoner's gaze turned on him; it seemed to ask if he approved such goings-on. So he bent forward again, having already leaned back in his chair, and put another question: 'But surely he knows that he has been sentenced?' 'Nor that either,' said the officer, smiling at the explorer as if expecting him to make further surprising remarks. 'No,' said the explorer, wiping his forehead, 'then he can't know either whether his defence was effective?' 'He has had no chance of putting up a defence,' said the officer, turning his eyes away as if speaking to himself and so sparing the explorer the shame of hearing self-evident matters explained. 'But he must have had some chance of defending himself,' said the explorer, and rose from his seat.

The officer realized that he was in danger of having his exposition of the apparatus held up for a long time; so he went up to the explorer, took him by the arm, waved a hand toward the condemned man, who was standing very straight now that he had so obviously become the centre of attention – the soldier had also given the chain a jerk – and said: 'This is how the matter stands. I have been appointed judge in this penal colony. Despite my youth. For I was the former Commandant's assistant in all penal matters and know more about the apparatus than anyone. My guiding principle is this: Guilt is never to be doubted. Other courts cannot follow that principle, for they consist of several opinions and have higher courts to scrutinize them. That is not the case here, or at least, it was not the case in the former Commandant's time. The new man has certainly shown some inclination to interfere with my judgments, but so far I have succeeded in fending him off and will go on succeeding. You wanted to have the case explained; it is quite simple, like all of them. A captain reported to me this morning that this man, who had been assigned to him as a servant and sleeps before his door, had been asleep on duty. It is his duty, you see, to get up every time the hour strikes and salute the captain's door. Not an exacting duty, and very necessary, since he has to be a sentry as well as a servant, and must be alert in both functions. Last night the captain wanted to see if the man was doing his duty. He opened the door as the clock struck two and there was his man curled up asleep.

He took his riding whip and lashed him across the face. Instead of getting up and begging pardon, the man caught hold of his master's legs, shook him, and cried: "Throw that whip away or I'll eat you alive." – That's the evidence. The captain came to me an hour ago, I wrote down his statement and appended the sentence to it. Then I had the man put in chains. That was all quite simple. If I had first called the man before me and interrogated him, things would have got into a confused tangle. He would have told lies, and had I exposed these lies he would have backed them up with more lies, and so on and so forth. As it is, I've got him and I won't let him go. – Is that quite clear now? But we're wasting time, the execution should be beginning and I haven't finished explaining the apparatus yet.' He pressed the explorer back into his chair, went up again to the apparatus, and began: 'As you see, the shape of the Harrow corresponds to the human form; here is the harrow for the torso, here are the harrows for the legs. For the head there is only this one small spike. Is that quite clear?' He bent amiably forward toward the explorer, eager to provide the most comprehensive explanations.

The explorer considered the Harrow with a frown. The explanation of the judicial procedure had not satisfied him. He had to remind himself that this was in any case a penal colony where extraordinary measures were needed and that military discipline must be enforced to the last. He also felt that some hope might be set on the new Commandant, who was apparently of a mind to bring in, although gradually, a new kind of procedure which the officer's narrow mind was incapable of understanding. This train of thought prompted his next question: 'Will the Commandant attend the execution?' 'It is not certain,' said the officer, wincing at the direct question, and his friendly expression darkened. 'That is just why we have to lose no time. Much as I dislike it, I shall have to cut my explanations short. But of course tomorrow, when the apparatus has been cleaned – its one drawback is that it gets so messy – I can recapitulate all the details. For the present, then, only the essentials. – When the man lies down on the Bed and it begins to vibrate, the Harrow is lowered onto his body. It regulates itself automatically so that the needles barely touch his skin; once contact is made the steel ribbon stiffens immediately into a rigid band. And then the performance begins. An ignorant onlooker would see no difference between one punishment and another. The Harrow appears to do its work with uniform regularity. As it quivers, its points pierce the skin of the body which is itself quivering from the vibration of the Bed. So that the actual progress of the sentence can be watched, the Harrow is made of glass. Getting the needles fixed in the glass was a technical problem, but after many experiments we overcame the difficulty. No trouble was too great for us to take, you see. And now anyone can look through the glass and watch the inscription taking form on the body. Wouldn't you care to come a little nearer and have a look at the needles?'

The explorer got up slowly, walked across, and bent over the Harrow. 'You see,' said the officer, 'there are two kinds of needles arranged in multiple patterns. Each long needle has a short one beside it. The long needle does the writing, and the short needle sprays a jet of water to wash away the blood and keep the inscription clear. Blood and water together are then conducted here through small runnels into this main runnel and down a waste pipe into the pit.' With his finger the officer traced the exact course taken by the blood and water. To make the picture as vivid as possible he held both hands below the outlet of the waste pipe as if to catch the outflow, and when he did this the explorer drew back his head and feeling behind him with one hand sought to return to his chair. To his horror he found that the condemned man too had obeyed the officer's invitation to examine the Harrow at close quarters and had followed him. He had pulled forward the sleepy soldier with the chain and was bending over the glass. One could see that his uncertain eyes were trying to perceive what the two gentlemen had been looking at, but since he had not understood the explanation he could not make head or tail of it. He was peering this way and that way. He kept running his eyes along the glass. The explorer wanted to drive him away, since what he was doing was probably culpable. But the officer firmly restrained the explorer with one hand and with the other took a clod of earth from the rampart and threw it at the soldier. He opened his eyes with a jerk, saw what the condemned man had dared to do, let his rifle fall, dug his heels into the ground, dragged his prisoner back so that he stumbled and fell immediately, and then stood looking down at him, watching him struggling and rattling in his chains. 'Set him on his feet!' yelled the officer, for he noticed that the explorer's attention was being too much distracted by the prisoner. In fact he was even leaning right across the Harrow, without taking any notice of it, intent only on finding out what was happening to the prisoner. 'Be careful with him!' cried the officer again. He ran around the apparatus, himself caught the condemned man under the shoulders, and with the soldier's help got him up on his feet, which kept slithering from under him.

'Now I know all about it,' said the explorer as the officer came back to him. 'All except the most important thing,' he answered, seizing the explorer's arm and pointing upwards: 'In the Designer are all the cogwheels that control the movements of the Harrow, and this machinery is regulated according to the inscription demanded by the sentence. I am still using the guiding plans drawn by the former Commandant. Here they are' – he extracted some sheets from the leather wallet – 'but I'm sorry I can't let you handle them, they are my most precious possessions. Just take a seat and I'll hold them in front of you like this, then you'll be able to see everything quite well.' He spread out the first sheet of paper. The explorer would have liked to say something appreciative, but all he could see was a labyrinth of lines crossing and recrossing each other, which covered the paper so thickly that it was difficult to discern the blank spaces between them. 'Read it,' said the officer. 'I can't,' said the explorer. 'Yet it's clear enough,' said the officer. 'It's very ingenious,' said the explorer evasively, 'but I can't make it out.' 'Yes,' said the officer with a laugh, putting the paper away again, 'it's no calligraphy for school children. It needs to be studied closely. I'm quite sure that in the end you would understand it too. Of course the script can't be a simple one; it's not supposed to kill a man straight off, but only after an interval of, on an average, twelve hours; the turning point is reckoned to come at the sixth hour. So there have to be lots and lots of flourishes around the actual script; the script itself runs around the body only in a narrow girdle; the rest of the body is reserved for the embellishments. Can you appreciate now the work accomplished by the Harrow and the whole apparatus? – Just watch it!' He ran up the ladder, turned a wheel, called down: 'Look out, keep to one side!' and everything started working. If the wheel had not creaked, it would have been marvellous. The officer, as if surprised by the noise of the wheel, shook his fist at it, then spread out his arms in excuse to the explorer, and climbed down rapidly to peer at the working of the machine from below. Something perceptible to no one save himself was still not in order; he clambered up again, did something with both hands in the interior of the Designer, then slid down one of the rods, instead of using the ladder, so as to get down quicker, and with the full force of his lungs, to make himself heard at all in the noise, yelled in the explorer's ear: 'Can you follow it? The Harrow is beginning to write; when it finishes the first draft of the inscription on the man's back, the layer of cotton wool begins to roll and slowly turns the body over, to give the Harrow fresh space for writing. Meanwhile the raw part that has been written on lies on the cotton wool, which is specially prepared to staunch the bleeding and so makes all ready for a new deepening of the script. Then these teeth at the edge of the Harrow, as the body turns further around, tear the cotton wool away from the wounds, throw it into the pit, and there is more work for the Harrow. So it keeps on writing deeper and deeper for the whole twelve hours. The first six hours the condemned man stays alive almost as before, he suffers only pain. After two hours the felt gag is taken away, for he has no longer strength to scream. Here, into this electrically heated basin at the head of the Bed, some warm rice pap is poured, from which the man, if he feels like it, can take as much as his tongue can lap. Not one of them ever misses the chance. I can remember none, and my experience is extensive. Only about the sixth hour does the man lose all desire to eat. I usually kneel down here at that moment and observe what happens. The man rarely swallows his last mouthful, he only rolls it around his mouth and spits it out into the pit. I have to duck just then or he would spit it in my face. But how quiet he grows at just about the sixth hour! Enlightenment comes to the most dull-witted. It begins around the eyes. From there it radiates. A moment that might tempt one to get under the Harrow oneself. Nothing more happens than that the man begins to understand the inscription, he purses his mouth as if he were listening. You have seen how difficult it is to decipher the script with one's eyes; but our man deciphers it with his wounds. To be sure, that is a hard task; he needs six hours to accomplish it. By that time the Harrow has pierced him quite through and casts him into the pit, where he pitches down upon the blood and water and the cotton wool. Then the judgment has been fulfilled, and we, the soldier and I, bury him.'

The explorer had inclined his ear to the officer and with his hands in his jacket pockets watched the machine at work. The condemned man watched it too, but uncomprehendingly. He bent forward a little and was intent on the moving needles when the soldier, at a sign from the officer, slashed through his shirt and trousers from behind with a knife, so that they fell off; he tried to catch at his falling clothes to cover his nakedness, but the soldier lifted him into the air and shook the last remnants from him. The officer stopped the machine, and in the sudden silence the condemned man was laid under the Harrow. The chains were loosened and the straps fastened on instead; in the first moment that seemed almost a relief to the prisoner. And now the Harrow was adjusted a little lower, since he was a thin man. When the needle points touched him a shudder ran over his skin; while the soldier was busy strapping his right hand, he flung out his left hand blindly; but it happened to be in the direction toward where the explorer was standing. The officer kept watching the explorer sideways, as if seeking to read from his face the impression made on him by the execution, which had been at least cursorily explained to him.

The wrist strap broke; probably the soldier had drawn it too tight. The officer had to intervene, the soldier held up the broken piece of strap to show him. So the officer went over to him and said, his face still turned toward the explorer: 'This is a very complex machine, it can't be helped that things are breaking or giving way here and there; but one must not thereby allow oneself to be diverted in one's general judgment. In any case, this strap is easily made good; I shall simply use a chain; the delicacy of the vibrations for the right arm will of course be a little impaired.' And while he fastened the chains, he added: 'The resources for maintaining the machine are now very much reduced. Under the former Commandant I had free access to a sum of money set aside entirely for this purpose. There was a store, too, in which spare parts were kept for repairs of all kinds. I confess I have been almost prodigal with them, I mean in the past, not now as the new Commandant pretends, always looking for an excuse to attack our old way of doing things. Now he has taken charge of the machine money himself, and if I send for a new strap they ask for the broken old strap as evidence, and the new strap takes ten days to appear and then is of shoddy material and not much good. But how I am supposed to work the machine without a strap, that's something nobody bothers about.'

The explorer thought to himself: It's always a ticklish matter to intervene decisively in other people's affairs. He was neither a member of the penal colony nor a citizen of the state to which it belonged. Were he to denounce this execution or actually try to stop it, they could say to him: You are a foreigner, mind your own business. He could make no answer to that, unless he were to add that he was amazed at himself in this connection, for he travelled only as an observer, with no intention at all of altering other people's methods of administering justice. Yet here he found himself strongly tempted. The injustice of the procedure and the inhumanity of the execution were undeniable. No one could suppose that he had any selfish interest in the matter, for the condemned man was a complete stranger, not a fellow countryman or even at all sympathetic to him. The explorer himself had recommendations from high quarters, had been received here with great courtesy, and the very fact that he had been invited to attend the execution seemed to suggest that his views would be welcome. And this was all the more likely since the Commandant, as he had heard only too plainly, was no upholder of the procedure and maintained an attitude almost of hostility to the officer.

At that moment the explorer heard the officer cry out in rage.

He had just, with considerable difficulty, forced the felt gag into the condemned man's mouth when the man in an irresistible access of nausea shut his eyes and vomited. Hastily the officer snatched him away from the gag and tried to hold his head over the pit; but it was too late, the vomit was running all over the machine. 'It's all the fault of that Commandant!' cried the officer, senselessly shaking the brass rods in front, 'the machine is befouled like a pigsty.' With trembling hands he indicated to the explorer what had happened. 'Have I not tried for hours at a time to get the Commandant to understand that the prisoner must fast for a whole day before the execution. But our new, mild doctrine thinks otherwise. The Commandant's ladies stuff the man with sugar candy before he's led off. He has lived on stinking fish his whole life long and now he has to eat sugar candy! But it could still be possible, I should have nothing to say against it, but why won't they get me a new felt gag, which I have been begging for the last three months. How should a man not feel sick when he takes a felt gag into his mouth which more than a hundred men have already slobbered and gnawed in their dying moments?'

The condemned man had laid his head down and looked peaceful, the soldier was busy trying to clean the machine with the prisoner's shirt. The officer advanced toward the explorer who in some vague presentiment fell back a pace, but the officer seized him by the hand, and drew him to one side. 'I should like to exchange a few words with you in confidence,' he said, 'may I?' 'Of course,' said the explorer, and listened with downcast eyes.

'This procedure and method of execution, which you are now having the opportunity to admire, has at the moment no longer any open adherents in our colony. I am its sole advocate, and at the same time the sole advocate of the old Commandant's tradition. I can no longer reckon on any further extension of the method, it takes all my energy to maintain it as it is. During the old Commandant's lifetime the colony was full of his adherents; his strength of conviction I still have in some measure, but not an atom of his power; consequently the adherents have skulked out of sight, there are still many of them but none of them will admit it. If you were to go into the teahouse today, on execution day, and listen to what is being said, you would perhaps hear only ambiguous remarks. These would all be made by adherents, but under the present Commandant and his present doctrines they are of no use to me. And now I ask you: because of this Commandant and the women who influence him, is such a piece of work, the work of a lifetime' – he pointed to the machine – 'to perish? Ought one to let that happen? Even if one has only come as a stranger to our island for a few days? But there's no time to lose, an attack of some kind is impending on my function as judge; conferences are already being held in the Commandant's office from which I am excluded; even your coming here today seems to me a significant move; they are cowards and use you as a screen, you, a stranger. – How different an execution was in the old days! A whole day before the ceremony the valley was packed with people; they all came only to look on; early in the morning the Commandant appeared with his ladies; fanfares roused the whole camp; I reported that everything was in readiness; the assembled company – no high official dared to absent himself – arranged itself around the machine; this pile of cane chairs is a miserable survival from that epoch. The machine was freshly cleaned and glittering, I got new spare parts for almost every execution. Before hundreds of spectators – all of them standing on tiptoe as far as the heights there – the condemned man was laid under the Harrow by the Commandant himself. What is left today for a common soldier to do was then my task, the task of the presiding judge, and was an honour for me. And then the execution began! No discordant noise spoiled the working of the machine. Many did not care to watch it but lay with closed eyes in the sand; they all knew: Now Justice is being done. In the silence one heard nothing but the condemned man's sighs, half muffled by the felt gag. Nowadays the machine can no longer wring from anyone a sigh louder than the felt gag can stifle; but in those days the writing needles let drop an acid fluid, which we're no longer permitted to use. Well, and then came the sixth hour! It was impossible to grant all the requests to be allowed to watch it from nearby. The Commandant in his wisdom ordained that the children should have the preference;

I, of course, because of my office had the privilege of always being at hand; often enough I would be squatting there with a small child in either arm. How we all absorbed the look of transfiguration on the face of the sufferer, how we bathed our cheeks in the radiance of that justice, achieved at last and fading so quickly! What times these were, my comrade!' The officer had obviously forgotten whom he was addressing; he had embraced the explorer and laid his head on his shoulder. The explorer was deeply embarrassed, impatiently he stared over the officer's head. The soldier had finished his cleaning job and was now pouring rice pap from a pot into the basin. As soon as the condemned man, who seemed to have recovered entirely, noticed this action he began to reach for the rice with his tongue. The soldier kept pushing him away, since the rice pap was certainly meant for a later hour, yet it was just as unfitting that the soldier himself should thrust his dirty hands into the basin and eat out of it before the other's avid face.

The officer quickly pulled himself together. 'I didn't want to upset you,' he said, 'I know it is impossible to make those days credible now. Anyhow, the machine is still working and it is still effective in itself. It is effective in itself even though it stands alone in this valley. And the corpse still falls at the last into the pit with an incomprehensibly gentle wafting motion, even though there are no hundreds of people swarming around like flies as formerly. In those days we had to put a strong fence around the pit, it has long since been torn down.'

The explorer wanted to withdraw his face from the officer and looked around him at random. The officer thought he was surveying the valley's desolation; so he seized him by the hands, turned him around to meet his eyes, and asked: 'Do you realize the shame of it?'

But the explorer said nothing. The officer left him alone for a little; with legs apart, hands on hips, he stood very still, gazing at the ground. Then he smiled encouragingly at the explorer and said: 'I was quite near you yesterday when the Commandant gave you the invitation. I heard him giving it. I know the Commandant. I divined at once what he was after. Although he is powerful enough to take measures against me, he doesn't dare to do it yet, but he certainly means to use your verdict against me, the verdict of an illustrious foreigner. He has calculated it carefully: this is your second day on the island, you did not know the old Commandant and his ways, you are conditioned by European ways of thought, perhaps you object on principle to capital punishment in general and to such mechanical instruments of death in particular, besides you will see that the execution has no support from the public, a shabby ceremony – carried out with a machine already somewhat old and worn-now, taking all that into consideration, would it not be likely (so thinks the Commandant) that you might disapprove of my methods? And if you disapprove, you wouldn't conceal the fact (I'm still speaking from the Commandant's point of view), for you are a man to feel confidence in your own well-tried conclusions. True, you have seen and learned to appreciate the peculiarities of many peoples, and so you would not be likely to take a strong line against our proceedings, as you might do in your own country. But the Commandant has no need of that. A casual, even an unguarded remark will be enough. It doesn't even need to represent what you really think, so long as it can be used speciously to serve his purpose. He will try to prompt you with sly questions, of that I am certain. And his ladies will sit around you and prick up their ears; you might be saying something like this: "In our country we have a different criminal procedure," or "In our country the prisoner is interrogated before he is sentenced," or "We haven't used torture since the Middle Ages." All these statements are as true as they seem natural to you, harmless remarks that pass no judgment on my methods. But how would the Commandant react to them? I can see him, our good Commandant, pushing his chair away immediately and rushing onto the balcony, I can see his ladies streaming out after him, I can hear his voice – the ladies call it a voice of thunder – well, and this is what he says: "A famous Western investigator, sent out to study criminal procedure in all the countries of the world, has just said that our old tradition of administering justice is inhumane. Such a verdict from such a personality makes it impossible for me to countenance these methods any longer. Therefore from this very day I ordain . . ." and so on. You may want to interpose that you never said any such thing, that you never called my methods inhumane, on the

246

contrary your profound experience leads you to believe they are most humane and most in consonance with human dignity, and you admire the machine greatly – but it will be too late; you won't even get onto the balcony, crowded as it will be with ladies; you may try to draw attention to yourself; you may want to scream out; but a lady's hand will close your lips – and I and the work of the old Commandant will be done for.'

The explorer had to suppress a smile; so easy, then, was the task he had felt to be so difficult. He said evasively: 'You overestimate my influence; the Commandant has read my letters of recommendation, he knows that I am no expert in criminal procedure. If I were to give an opinion, it would be as a private individual, an opinion no more influential than that of any ordinary person, and in any case much less influential than that of the Commandant, who, I am given to understand, has very extensive powers in this penal colony. If his attitude to your procedure is as definitely hostile as you believe, then I fear the end of your tradition is at hand, even without any humble assistance from me.'

Had it dawned on the officer at last? No, he still did not understand. He shook his head emphatically, glanced briefly around at the condemned man and the soldier, who both flinched away from the rice, came close up to the explorer, and without looking at his face but fixing his eye on some spot on his coat said in a lower voice than before: 'You don't know the Commandant; you feel yourself – forgive the expression – a kind of outsider so far as all of us are concerned; yet, believe me, your influence cannot be rated too highly. I was simply delighted when I heard that you were to attend the execution all by yourself. The Commandant arranged it to aim a blow at me, but I shall turn it to my advantage. Without being distracted by lying whispers and contemptuous glances – which could not have been avoided had a crowd of people attended the execution – you have heard my explanations, seen the machine, and are now in course of watching the execution. You have doubtless already formed your own judgment; if you still have some small uncertainties the sight of the execution will resolve them. And now I make this request to you: help me against the Commandant!'

The explorer would not let him go on. 'How could I do that,' he cried, 'it's quite impossible. I can neither help nor hinder you.'

'Yes, you can,' the officer said. The explorer saw with a certain apprehension that the officer had clenched his fists. 'Yes, you can,' repeated the officer, still more insistently. 'I have a plan that is bound to succeed. You believe your influence is insufficient. I know that it is sufficient. But even granted that you are right, is it not necessary, for the sake of preserving this tradition, to try even what might prove insufficient? Listen to my plan, then. The first thing necessary for you to carry it out is to be as reticent as possible today regarding your verdict on these proceedings. Unless you are asked a direct question you must say nothing at all; but what you do say must be brief and general; let it be remarked that you would prefer not to discuss the matter, that you are out of patience with it, that if you are to let yourself go you would use strong language. I don't ask you to tell any lies; by no means; you should only give curt answers, such as: "Yes, I saw the execution," or "Yes, I had it explained to me." Just that, nothing more. There are grounds enough for any impatience you betray, although not such as will occur to the Commandant. Of course, he will mistake your meaning and interpret it to please himself. That's what my plan depends on. Tomorrow in the Commandant's office there is to be a large conference of all the high administrative officials, the Commandant presiding. Of course the Commandant is the kind of man to have turned these conferences into public spectacles. He has had a gallery built that is always packed with spectators. I am compelled to take part in the conferences, but they make me sick with disgust. Now, whatever happens, you will certainly be invited to this conference; if you behave today as I suggest, the invitation will become an urgent request. But if for some mysterious reason you're not invited, you'll have to ask for an invitation; there's no doubt of your getting it then. So tomorrow you're sitting in the Commandant's box with the ladies. He keeps looking up to make sure you're there. After various trivial and ridiculous matters, brought in merely to impress the audience – mostly harbour works, nothing but harbour works! – our judicial procedure comes up for discussion too. If the Commandant doesn't introduce it, or not soon enough, I'll see that it's mentioned. I'll stand up and report that today's execution has taken place. Quite briefly, only a statement. Such a statement is not usual, but I shall make it. The Commandant thanks me, as always, with an amiable smile, and then he can't restrain himself, he seizes the excellent opportunity. "It has just been reported," he will say, or words to that effect, "that an execution has taken place. I should like merely to add that this execution was witnessed by the famous explorer who has, as you all know, honoured our colony so greatly by his visit to us. His presence at today's session of our conference also contributes to the importance of this occasion. Should we not now ask the famous explorer to give us his verdict on our traditional mode of execution and the procedure that leads up to it?" Of course there is loud applause, general agreement, I am more insistent than anyone. The Commandant bows to you and says: "Then in the name of the assembled company, I put the question to you." And now you advance to the front of the box. Lay your hands where everyone can see them, or the ladies will catch them and press your fingers. – And then at last you can speak out. I don't know how I'm going to endure the tension of waiting for that moment. Don't put any restraint on yourself when you make your speech, publish the truth aloud, lean over the front of the box, shout, yes indeed, shout your verdict, your unshakable conviction, at the Commandant. Yet perhaps you wouldn't care to do that, it's not in keeping with your character, in your country perhaps people do these things differently, well, that's all right too, that will be quite as effective, don't even stand up, just say a few words, even in a whisper, so that only the officials beneath you will hear them, that will be quite enough, you don't even need to mention the lack of public support for the execution, the creaking wheel, the broken strap, the filthy gag of felt, no, I'll take all that upon me, and, believe me, if my indictment doesn't drive him out of the conference hall, it will force him to his knees to make the acknowledgment: Old Commandant, I humble myself before you. – That is my plan; will you help me to carry it out? But of course you are willing, what is more, you must.' And the officer seized the explorer by both arms and gazed, breathing heavily, into his face. He had shouted the last sentence so loudly that even the soldier and the condemned man were startled into attending; they had not understood a word but they stopped eating and looked over at the explorer, chewing their previous mouthfuls.

From the very beginning the explorer had no doubt about what answer he must give; in his lifetime he had experienced too much to have any uncertainty here; he was fundamentally honourable and unafraid. And yet now, facing the soldier and the condemned man, he did hesitate, for as long as it took to draw one breath. At last, however, he said, as he had to: 'No.' The officer blinked several times but did not turn his eyes away. 'Would you like me to explain?' asked the explorer. The officer nodded wordlessly. 'I do not approve of your procedure,' said the explorer then, 'even before you took me into your confidence – of course I shall never in any circumstances betray your confidence – I was already wondering whether it would be my duty to intervene and whether my intervention would have the slightest chance of success. I realized to whom I ought to turn: to the Commandant, of course. You have made that fact even clearer, but without having strengthened my resolution, on the contrary, your sincere conviction has touched me, even though it cannot influence my judgment.'

The officer remained mute, turned to the machine, caught hold of a brass rod, and then, leaning back a little, gazed at the Designer as if to assure himself that all was in order. The soldier and the condemned man seemed to have come to some understanding; the condemned man was making signs to the soldier, difficult though his movements were because of the tight straps; the soldier was bending down to him; the condemned man whispered something and the soldier nodded.

The explorer followed the officer and said: 'You don't know yet what I mean to do. I shall tell the Commandant what I think of the procedure, certainly, but not at a public conference, only in private; nor shall I stay here long enough to attend any conference; I am going away early tomorrow morning, or at least embarking on my ship.'

It did not look as if the officer had been listening. 'So you did not find the procedure convincing,' he said to himself and smiled, as an old man smiles at childish nonsense and yet pursues his own meditations behind the smile.

'Then the time has come,' he said at last, and suddenly looked at the explorer with bright eyes that held some challenge, some appeal for cooperation. 'The time for what?' asked the explorer uneasily, but got no answer.

'You are free,' said the officer to the condemned man in the native tongue. The man did not believe it at first. 'Yes, you are set free,' said the officer. For the first time the condemned man's face woke to real animation. Was it true? Was it only a caprice of the officer's, that might change again? Had the foreign explorer begged him off? What was it? One could read these questions on his face. But not for long. Whatever it might be, he wanted to be really free if he might, and he began to struggle so far as the Harrow permitted him.

'You'll burst my straps,' cried the officer, 'lie still! We'll soon loosen them.' And signing the soldier to help him, he set about doing so. The condemned man laughed wordlessly to himself, now he turned his face left toward the officer, now right toward the soldier, nor did he forget the explorer.

'Draw him out,' ordered the officer. Because of the Harrow this had to be done with some care. The condemned man had already torn himself a little in the back through his impatience.

From now on, however, the officer paid hardly any attention to him. He went up to the explorer, pulled out the small leather wallet again, turned over the papers in it, found the one he wanted, and showed it to the explorer. 'Read it,' he said. 'I can't,' said the explorer, 'I told you before that I can't make out these scripts.' 'Try taking a close look at it,' said the officer and came quite near to the explorer so that they might read it together. But when even that proved useless, he outlined the script with his little finger, holding it high above the paper as if the surface dared not be sullied by touch, in order to help the explorer to follow the script in that way. The explorer did make an effort, meaning to please the officer in this respect at least, but he was quite unable to follow. Now the officer began to spell it, letter by letter, and then read out the words. '"BE JUST!" is what is written there,' he said, 'surely you can read it now.' The explorer bent so close to the paper that the officer feared he might touch it and drew it farther away; the explorer made no remark, yet it was clear that he still could not decipher it. '"BE JUST!" is what is written there,' said the officer once more. 'Maybe,' said the explorer, 'I am prepared to believe you.' 'Well, then,' said the officer, at least partly satisfied, and climbed up the ladder with the paper; very carefully he laid it inside the Designer and seemed to be changing the disposition of all the cogwheels; it was a troublesome piece of work and must have involved wheels that were extremely small, for sometimes the officer's head vanished altogether from sight inside the Designer, so precisely did he have to regulate the machinery.

The explorer, down below, watched the labour uninterruptedly, his neck grew stiff and his eyes smarted from the glare of sunshine over the sky. The soldier and the condemned man were now busy together. The man's shirt and trousers, which were already lying in the pit, were fished out by the point of the soldier's bayonet. The shirt was abominably dirty and its owner washed it in the bucket of water. When he put on the shirt and trousers both he and the soldier could not help guffawing, for the garments were of course slit up behind. Perhaps the condemned man felt it incumbent on him to amuse the soldier, he turned around and around in his slashed garments before the soldier, who squatted on the ground beating his knees with mirth. All the same, they presently controlled their mirth out of respect for the gentlemen.

When the officer had at length finished his task aloft, he surveyed the machinery in all its details once more, with a smile, but this time shut the lid of the Designer, which had stayed open till now, climbed down, looked into the pit and then at the condemned man, noting with satisfaction that the clothing had been taken out, then went over to wash his hands in the water bucket, perceived too late that it was disgustingly dirty, was unhappy because he could not wash his hands, in the end thrust them into the sand – this alternative did not please him, but he had to put up with it – then stood upright and began to unbutton his uniform jacket. As he did this, the two ladies' handkerchiefs he had tucked under his collar fell into his hands. 'Here are your handkerchiefs,' he said, and threw them to the condemned man. And to the explorer he said in explanation: 'A gift from the ladies.'

In spite of the obvious haste with which he was discarding first his uniform jacket and then all his clothing, he handled each garment with loving care, he even ran his fingers caressingly over the silver lace on the jacket and shook a tassel into place. This loving care was certainly out of keeping with the fact that as soon as he had a garment off he flung it at once with a kind of unwilling jerk into the pit. The last thing left to him was his short sword with the sword belt. He drew it out of the scabbard, broke it, then gathered all together, the bits of the sword, the scabbard, and the belt, and flung them so violently down that they clattered into the pit.

Now he stood naked there. The explorer bit his lips and said nothing. He knew very well what was going to happen, but he had no right to obstruct the officer in anything. If the judicial procedure which the officer cherished were really so near its end – possibly as a result of his own intervention, as to which he felt himself pledged – then the officer was doing the right thing; in his place the explorer would not have acted otherwise.

The soldier and the condemned man did not understand at first what was happening, at first they were not even looking on. The condemned man was gleeful at having got the handkerchiefs back, but he was not allowed to enjoy them for long, since the soldier snatched them with a sudden, unexpected grab. Now the condemned man in turn was trying to twitch them from under the belt where the soldier had tucked them, but the soldier was on his guard. So they were wrestling, half in jest. Only when the officer stood quite naked was their attention caught. The condemned man especially seemed struck with the notion that some great change was impending. What had happened to him was now going to happen to the officer. Perhaps even to the very end. Apparently the foreign explorer had given the order for it. So this was revenge. Although he himself had not suffered to the end, he was to be revenged to the end. A broad, silent grin now appeared on his face and stayed there all the rest of the time.

The officer, however, had turned to the machine. It had been clear enough previously that he understood the machine well, but now it was almost staggering to see how he managed it and how it obeyed him. His hand had only to approach the Harrow for it to rise and sink several times till it was adjusted to the right position for receiving him; he touched only the edge of the Bed and already it was vibrating; the felt gag came to meet his mouth, one could see that the officer was really reluctant to take it but he shrank from it only a moment, soon he submitted and received it. Everything was ready, only the straps hung down at the sides, yet they were obviously unnecessary, the officer did not need to be fastened down. Then the condemned man noticed the loose straps, in his opinion the execution was incomplete unless the straps were buckled, he gestured eagerly to the soldier and they ran together to strap the officer down. The latter had already stretched out one foot to push the lever that started the Designer; he saw the two men coming up; so he drew his foot back and let himself be buckled in. But now he could not reach the lever; neither the soldier nor the condemned man would be able to find it, and the explorer was determined not to lift a finger.

It was not necessary; as soon as the straps were fastened the machine began to work; the Bed vibrated, the needles flickered above the skin, the Harrow rose and fell. The explorer had been staring at it quite a while before he remembered that a wheel in the Designer should have been creaking; but everything was quiet, not even the slightest hum could be heard.

Because it was working so silently the machine simply escaped one's attention. The explorer observed the soldier and the condemned man. The latter was the more animated of the two, everything in the machine interested him, now he was bending down and now stretching up on tiptoe, his forefinger was extended all the time pointing out details to the soldier. This annoyed the explorer. He was resolved to stay till the end, but he could not bear the sight of these two. 'Go back home,' he said. The soldier would have been willing enough, but the condemned man took the order as a punishment. With clasped hands he implored to be allowed to stay, and when the explorer shook his head and would not relent, he even went down on his knees. The explorer saw that it was no use merely giving orders, he was on the point of going over and driving them away. At that moment he heard a noise above him in the Designer. He looked up. Was that cogwheel going to make trouble after all? But it was something quite different. Slowly the lid of the Designer rose up and then clicked wide open. The teeth of a cogwheel showed themselves and rose higher, soon the whole wheel was visible, it was as if some enormous force were squeezing the

Designer so that there was no longer room for the wheel, the wheel moved up till it came to the very edge of the Designer, fell down, rolled along the sand a little on its rim, and then lay flat. But a second wheel was already rising after it, followed by many others, large and small and indistinguishably minute, the same thing happened to all of them, at every moment one imagined the Designer must now really be empty, but another complex of numerous wheels was already rising into sight, falling down, trundling along the sand, and lying flat. This phenomenon made the condemned man completely forget the explorer's command, the cogwheels fascinated him, he was always trying to catch one and at the same time urging the soldier to help, but always drew back his hand in alarm, for another wheel always came hopping along which, at least on its first advance, scared him off.

The explorer, on the other hand, felt greatly troubled; the machine was obviously going to pieces; its silent working was a delusion; he had a feeling that he must now stand by the officer, since the officer was no longer able to look after himself. But while the tumbling cogwheels absorbed his whole attention he had forgotten to keep an eye on the rest of the machine; now that the last cogwheel had left the Designer, however, he bent over the Harrow and had a new and still more unpleasant surprise. The Harrow was not writing, it was only jabbing, and the Bed was not turning the body over but only bringing it up quivering against the needles. The explorer wanted to do something, if possible, to bring the whole machine to a standstill, for this was no exquisite torture such as the officer desired, this was plain murder. He stretched out his hands. But at that moment the Harrow rose with the body spitted on it and moved to the side, as it usually did only when the twelfth hour had come. Blood was flowing in a hundred streams, not mingled with water, the water jets too had failed to function. And now the last action failed to fulfil itself, the body did not drop off the long needles, streaming with blood it went on hanging over the pit without falling into it. The Harrow tried to move back to its old position, but as if it had itself noticed that it had not yet got rid of its burden it stuck after all where it was, over the pit. 'Come and help!' cried the explorer to the other two, and himself seized the officer's feet. He wanted to push against the feet while the others seized the head from the opposite side and so the officer might be slowly eased off the needles. But the other two could not make up their minds to come; the condemned man actually turned away; the explorer had to go over to them and force them into position at the officer's head. And here, almost against his will, he had to look at the face of the corpse. It was as it had been in life; no sign was visible of the promised redemption; what the others had found in the machine the officer had not found; the lips were firmly pressed together, the eyes were open, with the same expression as in life, the look was calm and convinced, through the forehead went the point of the great iron spike.

*

As the explorer, with the soldier and the condemned man behind him, reached the first houses of the colony, the soldier pointed to one of them and said: 'There is the teahouse.'

In the ground floor of the house was a deep, low, cavernous space, its walls and ceiling blackened with smoke. It was open to the road all along its length. Although this teahouse was very little different from the other houses of the colony, which were all very dilapidated, even up to the Commandant's palatial headquarters, it made on the explorer the impression of a historic tradition of some kind, and he felt the power of past days. He went near to it, followed by his companions, right up between the empty tables that stood in the street before it, and breathed the cool, heavy air that came from the interior. 'The old man's buried here,' said the soldier, 'the priest wouldn't let him lie in the churchyard. Nobody knew where to bury him for a while, but in the end they buried him here. The officer never told you about that, for sure, because of course that's what he was most ashamed of. He even tried several times to dig the old man up by night, but he was always chased away.' 'Where is the grave?' asked the explorer, who found it impossible to believe the soldier. At once both of them, the soldier and the condemned man, ran before him pointing with outstretched hands in the direction where the grave should be. They led the explorer right up to the back wall, where guests were sitting at a few tables. They were apparently dock labourers, strong men with short, glistening, full black beards. None had a jacket, their shirts were torn, they were poor, humble creatures. As the explorer drew near, some of them got up, pressed close to the wall, and stared at him. 'It's a foreigner,' ran the whisper around him, 'he wants to see the grave.' They pushed one of the tables aside, and under it there was really a gravestone. It was a simple stone, low enough to be covered by a table. There was an inscription on it in very small letters, the explorer had to kneel down to read it. This was what it said: 'Here rests the old Commandant. His adherents, who now must be nameless, have dug this grave and set up this stone. There is a prophecy that after a certain number of years the Commandant will rise again and lead his adherents from this house to recover the colony. Have faith and wait!' When the explorer had read this and risen to his feet he saw all the bystanders around him smiling, as if they too had read the inscription, had found it ridiculous, and were expecting him to agree with them. The explorer ignored this, distributed a few coins among them, waiting till the table was pushed over the grave again, quitted the teahouse, and made for the harbour.

The soldier and the condemned man had found some acquaintances in the teahouse, who detained them. But they must have soon shaken them off, for the explorer was only halfway down the long flight of steps leading to the boats when they came rushing after him. Probably they wanted to force him at the last minute to take them with him. While he was bargaining below with a ferryman to row him to the steamer, the two of them came headlong down the steps, in silence, for they did not dare to shout. But by the time they reached the foot of the steps the explorer was already in the boat, and the ferryman was just casting off from the shore. They could have jumped into the boat, but the explorer lifted a heavy knotted rope from the floor boards, threatened them with it, and so kept them from attempting the leap.

The Vulture

A vulture was hacking at my feet. It had already torn my boots and stockings to shreds, now it was hacking at the feet themselves. Again and again it struck at them, then circled several times restlessly around me, then returned to continue its work. A gentleman passed by, looked on for a while, then asked me why I suffered the vulture. 'I'm helpless,' I said. 'When it came and began to attack me, I of course tried to drive it away, even to strangle it, but these animals are very strong, it was about to spring at my face, but I preferred to sacrifice my feet. Now they are almost torn to bits.' 'Fancy letting yourself be tortured like this!' said the gentleman. 'One shot and that's the end of the vulture.' 'Really?' I said, 'and would you do that?' 'With pleasure,' said the gentleman, 'I've only got to go home and get my gun. Could you wait another half-hour?' 'I'm not sure about that,' said I, and stood for a moment rigid with pain. Then I said: 'Do try it in any case, please.' 'Very well,' said the gentleman, 'I'll be as quick as I can.' During this conversation the vulture had been calmly listening, letting its eye rove between me and the gentleman. Now I realized that it had understood everything; it took wing, leaned far back to gain impetus, and then, like a javelin thrower, thrust its beak through my mouth, deep into me. Falling back, with a sense of release, I could feel him drowning irretrievably in my blood, which was filling every depth, flooding every shore.

The Truth About Sancho Panza

Without making any boast of it Sancho Panza succeeded in the
course of years, by feeding him a great number of romances of
chivalry and adventure in the evening and night hours, in so
diverting from himself his demon, whom he later called Don
Quixote, that this demon thereupon set out, uninhibited, on the
maddest exploits, which, however, for the lack of a preordained
object, which should have been Sancho Panza himself, harmed
nobody. A free man, Sancho Panza philosophically followed Don
Quixote on his crusades, perhaps out of a sense of responsibility,
and had of them a great and edifying entertainment to the end
of his days.

Robinson Crusoe

Had Robinson Crusoe never left the highest, or more correctly the most visible point of his island, from desire for comfort, or timidity, or fear, or ignorance, or longing, he would soon have perished; but since without paying any attention to passing ships and their feeble telescopes he started to explore the whole island and take pleasure in it, he managed to keep himself alive and finally was found after all, by a chain of causality that was, of course, logically inevitable.

The Sirens

These are the seductive voices of the night; the Sirens, too, sang that way. It would be doing them an injustice to think that they wanted to seduce; they knew they had claws and sterile wombs, and they lamented this aloud. They could not help it if their laments sounded so beautiful.

The Silence of the Sirens

Proof that inadequate, even childish measures may serve to rescue one from peril:

To protect himself from the Sirens Ulysses stopped his ears with wax and had himself bound to the mast of his ship. Naturally any and every traveller before him could have done the same, except those whom the Sirens allured even from a great distance; but it was known to all the world that such things were of no help whatever. The song of the Sirens could pierce through everything, and the longing of those they seduced would have broken far stronger bonds than chains and masts. But Ulysses did not think of that, although he had probably heard of it. He trusted absolutely to his handful of wax and his fathom of chain, and in innocent elation over his little stratagem sailed out to meet the Sirens.

Now the Sirens have a still more fatal weapon than their song, namely their silence. And though admittedly such a thing has never happened, still it is conceivable that someone might possibly have escaped from their singing; but from their silence certainly never. Against the feeling of having triumphed over them by one's own strength, and the consequent exaltation that bears down everything before it, no earthly powers can resist.

And when Ulysses approached them the potent songstresses actually did not sing, whether because they thought that this enemy could be vanquished only by their silence, or because the look of bliss on the face of Ulysses, who was thinking of nothing but his wax and his chains, made them forget their singing.

But Ulysses, if one may so express it, did not hear their silence; he thought they were singing and that he alone did not hear them. For a fleeting moment he saw their throats rising and falling, their breasts lifting, their eyes filled with tears, their lips half parted, but believed that these were accompaniments to the airs which died unheard around him. Soon, however, all this faded from his sight as he fixed his gaze on the distance, the Sirens literally vanished before his resolution, and at the very moment when they were nearest to him he knew of them no longer.

But they — lovelier than ever — stretched their necks and turned, let their awesome hair flutter free in the wind, and freely stretched their claws on the rocks. They no longer had any desire to allure; all that they wanted was to hold as long as they could the radiance that fell from Ulysses' great eyes.

If the Sirens had possessed consciousness they would have

been annihilated at that moment. But they remained as they had been; all that had happened was that Ulysses had escaped them.

A codicil to the foregoing has also been handed down. Ulysses, it is said, was so full of guile, was such a fox, that not even the goddess of fate could pierce his armour. Perhaps he had really noticed, although here the human understanding is beyond its depths, that the Sirens were silent, and held up to them and to the gods the aforementioned pretence merely as a sort of shield.

Prometheus

There are four legends concerning Prometheus:

According to the first he was clamped to a rock in the Caucasus for betraying the secrets of the gods to men, and the gods sent eagles to feed on his liver, which was perpetually renewed.

According to the second Prometheus, goaded by the pain of the tearing beaks, pressed himself deeper and deeper into the rock until he became one with it.

According to the third his treachery was forgotten in the course of thousands of years, forgotten by the gods, the eagles, forgotten by himself.

According to the fourth everyone grew weary of the meaningless affair. The gods grew weary, the eagles grew weary, the wound closed wearily.

There remained the inexplicable mass of rock. The legend tried to explain the inexplicable. As it came out of a substratum of truth it had in turn to end in the inexplicable.

Poseidon

Poseidon sat at his desk, going over the accounts. The administration of all the waters gave him endless work. He could have had as many assistants as he wanted, and indeed he had quite a number, but since he took his job very seriously he insisted on going through all the accounts again himself, and so his assistants were of little help to him. It cannot be said that he enjoyed the work; he carried it out simply because it was assigned to him; indeed he had frequently applied for what he called more cheerful work, but whenever various suggestions were put to him it turned out that nothing suited him so well as his present employment. Needless to say, it was very difficult to find him another job. After all, he could not possibly be put in charge of one particular ocean. Quite apart from the fact that in this case the work involved would not be less, only more petty, the great Poseidon could hold only a superior position. And when he was offered a post unrelated to the waters, the very idea made him feel sick, his divine breath came short and his brazen chest began to heave. As a matter of fact, no one took his troubles very seriously; when a mighty man complains one must pretend to make concessions, even if the case is hopeless. No one ever really considered relieving Poseidon of his position; he had been destined to be God of the Seas since time immemorial, and that was how it had to remain.

What annoyed him most – and this was the chief cause of discontent with his job – was to learn of the rumours that were circulating about him; for instance, that he was constantly cruising through the waves with his trident. Instead of which here he was sitting in the depths of the world's ocean endlessly going over the accounts, an occasional journey to Jupiter being the only interruption of the monotony, a journey moreover from which he invariably returned in a furious temper. As a result he had hardly seen the oceans, save fleetingly during his hasty ascent to Olympus, and had never really sailed upon them. He used to say that he was postponing this until the end of the world, for then there might come a quiet moment when, just before the end and having gone through the last account, he could still make a quick little tour.

The City Coat of Arms

At first all the arrangements for building the Tower of Babel were characterized by fairly good order; indeed the order was perhaps too perfect, too much thought was given to guides, interpreters, accommodations for the workmen, and roads of communication, as if there were centuries before one to do the work in. In fact, the general opinion at that time was that one simply could not build too slowly; a very little insistence on this would have sufficed to make one hesitate to lay the foundations at all. People argued in this way: The essential thing in the whole business is the idea of building a tower that will reach to heaven. In comparison with that idea everything else is secondary. The idea, once seized in its magnitude, can never vanish again; so long as there are men on the earth there will be also the irresistible desire to complete the building. That being so, however, one need have no anxiety about the future; on the contrary, human knowledge is increasing, the art of building has made progress and will make further progress, a piece of work which takes us a year may perhaps be done in half the time in another hundred years, and better done, too, more enduringly. So why exert oneself to the extreme limit of one's present powers? There would be some sense in doing that only if it were likely that the tower could be completed in one generation. But that is beyond all hope. It is far more likely that the next generation with their perfected knowledge will find the work of their predecessors bad, and tear down what has been built so as to begin anew. Such thoughts paralysed people's powers, and so they troubled less about the tower than the construction of a city for the workmen. Every nationality wanted the finest quarter for itself, and this gave rise to disputes, which developed into bloody conflicts. These conflicts never came to an end; to the leaders they were a new proof that, in the absence of the necessary unity, the building of the tower must be done very slowly, or indeed preferably postponed until universal peace was declared. But the time was spent not only in conflict; the town was embellished in the intervals, and this unfortunately enough evoked fresh envy and fresh conflict. In this fashion the age of the first generation went past, but none of the succeeding ones showed any difference; except that technical skill increased and with it occasion for conflict. To this must be added that the second or third generation had already recognized the senselessness of building a heaven-reaching tower; but by that time everybody was too deeply involved to leave the city.

All the legends and songs that came to birth in that city are filled with longing for a prophesied day when the city would be destroyed by five successive blows from a gigantic fist. It is for that reason too that the city has a closed fist on its coat of arms.

The Problem of Our Laws

Our laws, unfortunately, are not generally known; they are kept secret by the small group of nobles who rule us. We are convinced that these ancient laws are scrupulously administered; nevertheless it is an extremely painful thing to be ruled by laws that one does not know. I am not thinking of possible discrepancies that may arise in the interpretation of the laws, or of the disadvantages involved when only a few and not the whole people are allowed to have a say in their interpretation. These disadvantages are perhaps of no great importance. For the laws are very ancient; their interpretation has been the work of centuries, and has itself doubtless acquired the status of law; and though there is still a possible freedom of interpretation left, it has now become very restricted. Moreover the nobles have obviously no cause to let their personal interest interpret the laws to our disadvantage, since these laws were made to the advantage of the nobles from the very beginning;

they themselves stand above the law, and that seems to be why the laws were entrusted exclusively into their hands. Of course, there is wisdom in that – who doubts the wisdom of the ancient laws? – but also hardship for us; probably that is unavoidable.

Moreover these apparent laws are really no more than a matter of conjecture. There is a tradition that they exist and that they are a mystery confided to the nobility, but it is not and cannot be more than a mere tradition sanctioned by age, since the nature of such laws requires that their existence be kept secret. If some among the people have attentively scrutinized the doings of the nobility since the earliest times and possess records made by our forefathers – records which we have conscientiously continued – and if we claim to recognize amid the countless number of facts certain main tendencies which permit of this or that historical formulation, and if in accordance with these scrupulously tested and logical conclusions we then seek to put order into our lives for the present or future – well, all that is in the highest degree uncertain, and perhaps a mere intellectual game, for it may be that these laws we are trying to unravel do not exist at all. There is a small party who are actually of this opinion and who try to show that, if any law exists, it can only be this: The Law is whatever the nobles do. This party see everywhere only the arbitrary acts of the nobility, and reject the popular tradition, which according to them possesses only certain trifling and incidental advantages that do not offset its heavy drawbacks, for it gives the people a false, deceptive, and overconfident security in confronting coming events. This cannot be gainsaid, but the overwhelming majority of our people account for it by the fact that the tradition is far from complete and must be much more fully investigated, that the material available, prodigious as it looks, is still too meagre, and that several centuries will have to pass before it becomes really adequate. This view, so comfortless as far as the present is concerned, is lightened only by the belief that a time will eventually come when the tradition and our research into it will jointly reach their conclusion, as it were with a sigh of relief, when everything will have become clear, the law will belong to the people, and the nobility will vanish. This is not maintained in any spirit of hatred against the nobility; not at all, and by no one; rather do we hate ourselves, because we have not yet shown ourselves worthy of being entrusted with the laws. And that is the real reason why the party who believe that there is no law have remained so few – although their doctrine is in certain ways so attractive, for it unequivocally recognizes the nobility and its right to go on existing. Actually one can express the problem only in a sort of paradox: Any party that would repudiate not only all belief in the laws, but the nobility as well, would have the whole people behind it; yet no such party can come into existence, for nobody would dare to repudiate the nobility. We live on this razor's edge. A writer once summed the matter up in this way: The sole visible and indubitable law that is imposed upon us is the nobility, and must we ourselves deprive ourselves of that one law?

On Parables

Many complain that the words of the wise are always merely parables and of no use in daily life, which is the only life we have. When the sage says: 'Go over,' he does not mean that we should cross to some actual place, which we could do anyhow if the labour were worth it; he means some fabulous yonder, something unknown to us, something that he cannot designate more precisely either, and therefore cannot help us here in the very least. All these parables really set out to say merely that the incomprehensible is incomprehensible, and we know that already. But the cares we have to struggle with every day: that is a different matter.

Concerning this a man once said: Why such reluctance? If you only followed the parables you yourselves would become parables and with that rid of all your daily cares.

Another said: I bet that is also a parable.

The first said: You have won.

The second said: But unfortunately only in parable.

The first said: No, in reality: in parable you have lost.

Before the Law

Before the law stands a doorkeeper. To this doorkeeper there comes a man from the country and prays for admittance to the Law. But the doorkeeper says that he cannot grant admittance at the moment. The man thinks it over and then asks if he will be allowed in later. 'It is possible,' says the doorkeeper, 'but not at the moment.' Since the gate stands open, as usual, and the doorkeeper steps to one side, the man stoops to peer through the gateway into the interior. Observing that, the doorkeeper laughs and says: 'If you are so drawn to it, just try to go in despite my veto. But take note: I am powerful. And I am only the least of the doorkeepers. From hall to hall there is one doorkeeper after another, each more powerful than the last. The third doorkeeper is already so terrible that even I cannot bear to look at him.' These are difficulties the man from the country has not expected; the Law, he thinks, should surely be accessible at all times and to everyone, but as he now takes a closer look at the doorkeeper in his fur coat, with his big sharp nose and long, thin, black

Tartar beard, he decides that it is better to wait until he gets permission to enter. The doorkeeper gives him a stool and lets him sit down at one side of the door. There he sits for days and years. He makes many attempts to be admitted, and wearies the doorkeeper by his importunity. The doorkeeper frequently has little interviews with him, asking him questions about his home and many other things, but the questions are put indifferently, as great lords put them, and always finish with the statement that he cannot be let in yet. The man, who has furnished himself with many things for his journey, sacrifices all he has, however valuable, to bribe the doorkeeper. The doorkeeper accepts everything, but always with the remark: 'I am only taking it to keep you from thinking you have omitted anything.' During these many years the man fixes his attention almost continuously on the doorkeeper. He forgets the other doorkeepers, and this first one seems to him the sole obstacle preventing access to the Law. He curses his bad luck, in his early years boldly and loudly; later, as he grows old, he only grumbles to himself. He becomes childish, and since in his year-long contemplation of the doorkeeper he has come to know even the fleas in his fur collar, he begs the fleas as well to help him and to change the doorkeeper's mind. At length his eyesight begins to fail, and he does not know whether the world is really darker or whether his eyes are only deceiving him. Yet in his darkness he is now aware of a radiance that streams inextinguishably from the gateway of the Law. Now he has not very long to live. Before he dies, all his experiences in these long years gather themselves in his head to one point, a question he has not yet asked the doorkeeper. He waves him nearer, since he can no longer raise his stiffening body. The doorkeeper has to bend low toward him, for the difference in height between them has altered much to the man's disadvantage. 'What do you want to know now?' asks the doorkeeper; 'you are insatiable.' 'Everyone strives to reach the Law,' says the man, 'so how does it happen that for all these many years no one but myself has ever begged for admittance?' The doorkeeper recognizes that the man has reached his end, and, to let his failing senses catch the words, roars in his ear: 'No one else could ever be admitted here, since this gate was made only for you. I am now going to shut it.'

Posterity

The reason why posterity's judgment of individuals is juster than the contemporary one lies in their being dead. One develops in one's own way only after death, only when one is alone. Death is to the individual as Saturday evening to the chimney sweep; it washes the dirt from his body. Then it can be seen whether his contemporaries harmed him more, or whether he did the more harm to his contemporaries; in the latter case he was a great man.

He

He has two antagonists: the first pushes him from behind, from his birth, the second blocks the road in front of him. He struggles with both. Actually the first supports him in his struggle with the second, for the first wants to push him forward; and in the same way the second supports him in his struggle with the first; for the second of course is trying to force him back. But it is only theoretically so. For it is not only the two protagonists that are present, but he himself as well, and who really knows his intentions? However that may be, he has a dream that some time in an unguarded moment – it would require too, one must admit, a night darker than any night there has ever been – he will spring out of the fighting line and be promoted, on account of his experiences of such warfare, as judge over his struggling antagonists.

List of Translators

'Paradise'   Eithne Wilkins and Ernst Kaiser

'The Tower of Babel'   Eithne Wilkins and Ernst Kaiser

'The Pit of Babel'   Eithne Wilkins and Ernst Kaiser

'The Bush'   Eithne Wilkins and Ernst Kaiser

'The Building of the Temple'   Eithne Wilkins and Ernst Kaiser

'The Holy of Holies'   Eithne Wilkins and Ernst Kaiser

'The Coming of the Messiah'   Clement Greenberg

'The Great Wall of China'   Willa and Edwin Muir

'Leopards in the Temple'   Eithne Wilkins and Ernst Kaiser

'Jackals and Arabs'   Willa and Edwin Muir

'A Report to an Academy'   Willa and Edwin Muir

'A Report to an Academy: Two Fragments'   Tania and James Stern

'The Negro'   Eithne Wilkins and Ernst Kaiser

'A Crossbreed'   Willa and Edwin Muir

'The Cares of a Family Man'   Willa and Edwin Muir

'A Life'   Eithne Wilkins and Ernst Kaiser

'At Night'   Tania and James Stern

'Morning'   Joseph Kresh

'The Helmsman'   Tania and James Stern

'The Bridge'   Willa and Edwin Muir

'The Next Village'   Willa and Edwin Muir

'The Knock at the Manor Gate'   Willa and Edwin Muir

'A Country Doctor'   Willa and Edwin Muir

'An Old Manuscript'   Willa and Edwin Muir

'The Refusal'   Tania and James Stern

'The Test'   Tania and James Stern

'The Village Schoolmaster'   Willa and Edwin Muir

'The Burrow'   Willa and Edwin Muir

'Josephine the Singer'   Willa and Edwin Muir

'A Little Fable'   Willa and Edwin Muir

'The True Path'   Eithne Wilkins and Ernst Kaiser

'The Noose'   Joseph Kresh

'First Sorrow'   Willa and Edwin Muir

'Up in the Gallery'   Willa and Edwin Muir

'The Whip'   Eithne Wilkins and Ernst Kaiser

'The Snake Charmer'   Eithne Wilkins and Ernst Kaiser

'The Snake'   Joseph Kresh

'Joys'   Eithne Wilkins and Ernst Kaiser

'The Top'   Tania and James Stern

'A Chinese Puzzle'   Eithne Wilkins and Ernst Kaiser?

'A Hunger Artist'   Willa and Edwin Muir

'In the Penal Colony'   Willa and Edwin Muir

'The Vulture'   Tania and James Stern

'The Truth About Sancho Panza'   Willa and Edwin Muir

'Robinson Crusoe'   Willa and Edwin Muir

'The Sirens'   Clement Greenberg

'The Silence of the Sirens'   Willa and Edwin Muir

'Prometheus'   Willa and Edwin Muir

'Poseidon'   Tania and James Stern

'The City Coat of Arms'   Willa and Edwin Muir

'The Problem of Our Laws'   Willa and Edwin Muir

'On Parables'   Willa and Edwin Muir

'Before the Law'   Willa and Edwin Muir

'Posterity'   Willa and Edwin Muir

'He'   Willa and Edwin Muir

Permissions Acknowledgments